The Midnight Daughter

The Dark Moon Series
Book One

Andrea Wilson

Possum Prints Publishing Pty Ltd
Melbourne Australia

Copyright © 2022 All rights reserved.

POSSUM PRINTS
Publishing

For Dylan and Harry

Contents

Map of Elatonia

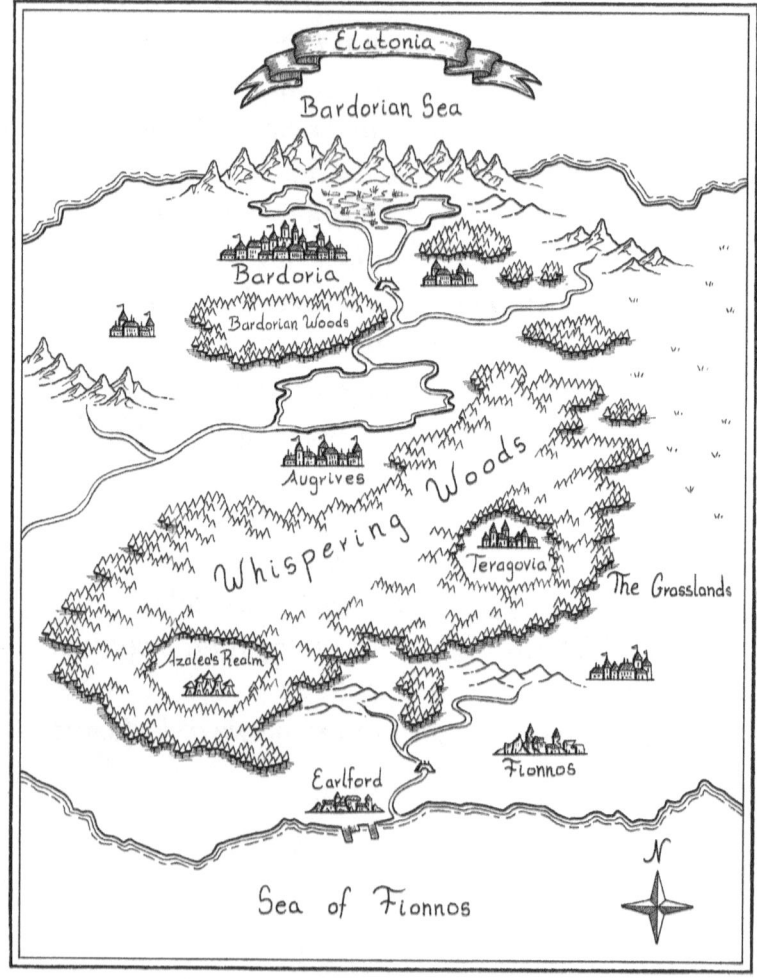

Elatonia

Bardorian Sea

Bardoria

Bardorian Woods

Augrives

Whispering Woods

Teraqovia

The Grasslands

Azalea's Realm

Fionnos

Earlford

Sea of Fionnos

N

Chapter One

The tower

If Eliza had known that this would be her last day in the tower, she might have done things differently. She might have placed one foot in front of the other and counted the steps between her wooden cot and splintered table. She might have savoured the thick trickle of gruel as it chugged down the expanse of her throat. She might have leaned out of the single window, pushed her face between the rusty iron bars, and let the cold wind burn the tip of her nose into a crimson point so that she could take in the view that had been her entire world for eleven years.

She did none of these things. Instead, she sat with her back against the wall; a parchment flattened on the stone floor in front of her. She had a piece of charcoal in her left hand. She ignored the dull throb of her headache and focused on the task. She moved the charcoal across the crisp yellowed surface in small strokes, stopping only to make a smudging motion with her right thumb. When she was satisfied with what was on the page, she held it up. The bleak autumn light fell from the window in a fading shaft and brightened up the parchment just enough to reveal a caricature of a majestic horse. It had a large mane that billowed into small wave-like crests on account of invisible wind. It had eyes and teeth like a human's and a long tail that looked like her own hair when she tied it with a strip of cloth. Eliza had only ever seen horses from up above. Sometimes a fleet of warhorses was made to run along the coast. The sound of their hooves always brought her to the window. They appeared to her the way they might to a bird of prey - oblong, dark, and restless creatures, confined to the flat plane of the earth. She had never seen them up close. And yet, she kept dreaming of their faces, the softness of their fur when her hands would stroke their heaving bellies, the way their eyelashes would flutter in the breeze.

These weren't the only dreams Eliza had. Everything she could see from the window would return to her in the night, especially when the moon bulged from behind the clouds as a full rotund disc. In her dreams, the angry white seagulls that squawked in front of her would turn into flocks of regal grey birds with wingspans larger than the length of her chamber and swoop in and out from the distant mountain peaks of Casilly. She would dream of tall trees with moss clinging to their trunks, all of them speaking to each other in a tongue she could not understand. She would dream of the sea, the one she could see in the distance when the mist parted for long enough to expose the thin stretch of brackish grey on the other side of the steep cliffs. She dreamed of a sheer blue glaze that hinted at an eternal summer, an impossible dream for summer passed in what felt like minutes each year.

Eliza had thought little of her dreams until last winter. She had asked Hugo once whether there were creatures in the land with fanged teeth and beady eyes, creatures that frothed at the snout before plunging their claws into other beasts. Hugo had looked startled and asked her in his deep rumble of a voice if she was describing wolves. Eliza had shrugged; the name meant nothing to her, for she had never seen nor heard of such a beast. Ever since then, Hugo brought a spare parchment whenever he could get his hands on one and left her with a piece of charcoal. She was to sketch out all of her dreams. Hugo would peer at each drawing through his rounded glasses and mutter, 'marvelous! Simply marvelous!' Eliza didn't know what he did with her drawings, but he took them away each time. She pictured a stack of them as high as her hip sitting next to the table in his chamber, wherever it was.

Hugo didn't deem it important enough to tell Eliza what he did with her drawings or what he did outside the hours he tutored her. He was a wizened old man with a plump belly and a snowy beard that always had breadcrumbs in it. He wore glasses and thick navy coats and never seemed to be in a rush to get to the end of his sentences. He had been her only companion for the entirety of her life, and this was all she knew about him. He was more interested in correcting her Latin pronunciations than answering her endless litany of questions. It wasn't her fault that her mind bubbled over with curiosity. She wanted to know how long birds could fly before they needed a rest, she wanted to know the true colour of the sea, she wanted to know who lived in the other towers along the coast, and a hundred other such matters that Hugo dismissed with a flick of his wrist.

Every now and then, if he happened to be in a good mood, his eyes would twinkle, and he'd take a moment to humour her. 'The sea is the colour of your mood, little one,' he'd say. 'When you've been tormenting old Hugo with your befuddling questions, the sea turns grey. On the rare occasion that you are quiet and good, the sun comes out, and the sea is blue, and the land rejoices.'

To which she'd say, 'who else is in this land? What do people do when they rejoice?'

He usually shook his head in exasperation and changed the topic, but sometimes, his breath smelled acrid, and his eyes became unfocused, and he launched into a tirade that went something like - 'oh this mighty land, little one, how I wish I could take you on a journey around it! The great kingdom of Bardoria stretches far and wide, from the peaks of Casilly to the Whispering Woods. Ever since the mighty King Grandalford defeated the auld King Leon, we have flourished. We have the biggest machines and the warmest homes and weapons so far advanced that no one else in the entire realm of Elatonia dares challenge us. Now is the age of man, little one, now that Bardoria has cast a bright glow on the land.'

'Take me, Hugo, take me to see Bardoria!' she would plead, her small hands clasping his large ones.

His face would grow solemn, and he'd turn away. 'Aye, I would if I could. This chamber's no place for a youngin like yourself. You'd be best served in a home with a hearth and a hot meal. My missus asks after ya every day. We never did have a daughter, only sons. They're good boys, the lot of them, but not much compares to a sweetling in the home, baking bread with her Ma and hustling her poor old Pa for a coin to go buy some sweets. '

'Let's go, Hugo! Take me with you today!'

'Aye, I hope too. Someday. Perhaps when you come of age, and we find out that these dreams of yours are nothing but a child's imagination. It's a pity that humans and whisperers are completely different breeds, but they look the same. The same noses and mouths and ears. The same hands and feet. The same tongue, even. And yet the likes of them whisper under their breath and call out curses from the Auld World. Now, if only the whisperers' fledglings were born with a marking, a flash of green on their toe, or something like that. We'd know, we'd know right away. Ah, but what is there to do but wait?'

But now, the waiting was done. She was at the brink of the fourteenth winter of her life, the time when her bloodline would show itself. The commencement of her moon cycle would make her a woman. Either a whisperer or human. Eliza knew that being a human meant freedom. It meant getting out of the dreary old chamber and entering a new one in Hugo's home. It meant brothers and a Ma and a Pa. It meant horses and warm bread and machines. Eliza wanted it desperately, so desperately that she was willing to lie to Hugo if that was what it took.

Eliza got up, placed the parchment on the table, and walked to the window. Her eyes flitted over the usual landmarks. The tall dark hills, the grey sea, and the cliffs jutted out like daggers into the coast. The last of the warmth had faded from the air. Icy fingers of cold were brought in by the wind. Heaps of once orange and red leaves had turned into brown mulch across the grounds. The trees looked bare and naked, like they had been stripped to the bone. Although Eliza was used to the receding of nature in the cold months, the sight brought tears to her eyes.

'Things shift in a woman once she comes of age,' Hugo had warned her. 'You'll find yourself feeling and saying and doing all types of things you could never have imagined.'

Eliza hadn't paid him much mind. What did a middle-aged father of only sons know about womanhood? She had no women in her midst to run his claims past, so she had left them in a state of suspended judgment. Until recently, when the inevitable had happened.

A week ago, Eliza had woken up to find bright red drops of blood on her thighs. Her dreams had peaked into delirium. The horses began to spring from the roiling grey sea, the birds began to drop dead from the sky without warning, and the voices of the trees got mixed together into a screeching cacophony. She woke up most mornings with a splitting headache. It was as though a little hidden man stood inside her skull, pelting the inner walls with sharpened rocks. Hugo had been observing her keenly, but she said nothing. There was no whisperer blood in her; coming of age had changed nothing. Soon he would be convinced of her humanness, and then she would be free from this lonely chamber forever.

So she had drawn yet another horse. It was an ordinary horse from her earlier dreams, nothing magical or strange about it. She had no desire to reveal the changing nature of her dreams to Hugo, to trace the charcoal across the sheet and render the carcasses of cats and wolves and other beasts next to mounds of fallen trees. There was something sinister about what her mind cooked up while she was asleep. It frightened her and made her feel like she was communing with evil beings. Only whisperers could commune, and she was no whisperer. She was a human, a brave, gentle human, and everyone knew that humans were known for only one thing: their spirit. They didn't whisper spells or commune with evil beings. They used only their spirit to propel them forward. Hugo said this with unmistakable pride when he came to her chamber with particularly foul breath. The spirit of innovation, the spirit of novelty, the spirit of discovery - that was what the human spirit was about. And Eliza was determined that she possessed this spirit. After all, who could be more curious than her? Who but a human would want human things as intensely as she did?

So you can imagine her surprise when several pairs of feet plodded down the corridor outside her chamber. There were muffled screams and shouts—the sound of a scuffle and then a heaving thud. The heavy wooden door burst open, hanging onto the frame by a single hinge. In front of her stood four women of different ages. They were dressed in dirty brown tunics, armed from head to toe in weapons Eliza could not recognise. One of them rushed towards her. She had a mop of short silver hair, several studded rings on her fingers and a look of devilish arrogance in her eyes.

A small scream escaped Eliza's lips. She found herself calling for Hugo.

'Be quiet, winter daughter. We mean you no harm,' said the silver-haired woman.

'Who are you? And why have you broken into my chamber? Does Hugo know you're here?'

One of the other girls tut-tutted. She looked younger, barely older than Eliza. 'Seems like we've got a reluctant escapee on our hands, sisters,' she said to the others. Turning to Eliza, she said matter of factly, 'we are the freedom fighters of Teragovia. And we're here to free you!'

Chapter Two

The price of freedom

Eliza took a step back and arched an eyebrow. She opened her mouth, but no words would come out. She looked at the door longingly, wishing Hugo would enter through it and explain all of this. Two of the women stood as sentries by the door, and the other two stepped closer to her.

'Come on; we don't have much time. There are always guards patrolling these bleedin' towers,' said the silver-haired woman. 'We need to go!'

'Go where? I'm not going anywhere with you!' Eliza said, crossing her arms over her chest. 'I've never heard of the freedom fighters of Teragovia!'

'Of course you haven't. The people that imprisoned you wouldn't want you knowing the names of your rescuers, would they now?'

'Imprisoned? I haven't been imprisoned!'

'Then why have you spent your entire life in a cell in a high tower from which you cannot leave?'

Eliza was stumped. She had known she wasn't free, but she had never equated that to be the same as imprisonment. The difference between the two seemed negligible now.

'Where do you want to take me?'

'We'll tell you everything once we get out of this tower. Bardorian city air clogs my chest, and I'd like to get back to the woods without further ado.'

'Watch what you say about Bardoria! We have the biggest machines and the warmest homes and weapons so far advanced that no one else in the entire realm of Elatonia dares challenge us.'

The women laughed in unison. Eliza's face flushed, and she looked away, out of the window, into the world that she had never set foot into.

'My goodness, she's been well and truly brainwashed, hasn't she? She has no idea who she is!'

'I know who I am,' said Eliza, locking her eyes with the silver-haired woman.

'And who would that be?'

'I'm Eliza, an ordinary human girl who will be moved into the home of Hugo and his missus as soon as it is evident to all that I'm no whisperer. I'll have my freedom and a home and a family soon. Oh, and I'll live in Bardoria till the end of my days!'

The women exchanged glances. The younger one put her hand on the silver-haired woman's shoulder and said, 'allow me, Tierza.'

She walked over to Eliza and held her hand out. 'My name is Lillian. I'm a freedom fighter from the city of Azra. I've pledged my life to Elatonia. All I've done in my adult life is scout winter daughters in imprisonment such as yourself and set them free. I can only imagine what a shock our sudden appearance must be to you. But you're going to have to trust us. We are not enemies. We are possibly the only people in the world that mean you no harm. You have to come with us. It's not safe to linger here!'

Eliza's stomach was coiling into a leaden mass. She shook her head. 'I don't understand any of this. I have no reason to trust you! I won't be going anywhere without Hugo!'

The tension in the chamber was palpable. For a few heated seconds, Eliza thought the two women would take her by force. Before her intuition could be proved right or wrong, the sentries hissed, 'footsteps in the stairwell. It must be the guards approaching!'

They all pulled blades out from holsters that were buckled to their belts. The blades were long and glassy with carved wooden hilts. They had matching emblems set in the middle of the hilts. Eliza couldn't make out what the symbol was. Her heart raced, and her brow was laden with sweat. She had never seen a drawn sword so close before. The women stood in position, ready to attack anyone that made the mistake of turning into the corridor. The footsteps got closer. Acting on impulse alone, a shriek escaped Eliza's lips.

'HELPPPPP!' she cried out.

Tierza flashed her a savage look and placed her palm tightly over her open mouth. With her other hand, she held onto Eliza's waist so she couldn't escape. Eliza squirmed and tried to bite her way out of Tierza's iron grip but to no avail. Tierza barely flinched. The footsteps had picked up their pace.

The sentries pussyfooted out of Eliza's line of sight. There was the sound of something heavy being dropped, probably the bowl of gruel that would have been Eliza's supper, and a few low groans punctuated the silence.

'Got him,' one of the sentries called out. 'Not a guard, though.'

They marched Hugo in with his arms behind his back. The sentries held him tightly. He looked aghast. 'What's the meaning of this?' he cried out. 'Why've you got Eliza muzzled in this fashion? I demand that you set her free right this minute!'

'Bit rich coming from you, don't you think? You who have aided the imprisonment of this whisperling and dozens of others across the towers,' said Tierza in a steely voice. But she relented and dropped her palm from Eliza's mouth.

'Why do they keep saying that, Hugo? Why do they keep calling me a prisoner?'

Hugo gave her a long and weary look and then turned away, his gaze focused on the clawed foot of her table.

'Please, Hugo! Now is not the time to leave my questions unanswered.'

'Go on,' Tierza snarled. 'Tell her. The poor thing believes that you'll take her in if she turns out to be a human child. Does she know you've already sent word to your king about her being a moonblood? Does she know the fate you have in store for her?'

And still, Hugo said nothing. A lump began to form in Eliza's throat. 'Hugo. Please just tell me they're lying, and I'll believe you.'

'He's not going to say anything now. This man is not your family, Eliza. He is a traitor to you. He knows you are a whisperling and has already set your enslavement in motion. If you were to stay here, you would be marched into a camp full of whisperers whose magic is forcibly used against them within days. How do you think the Barodorian mines are powered? Or the Bardorian machines? Or even the hearths in Bardorian homes? Enslaved whisperers. Moonblood's like yourself. You've been groomed for refined slavery, nothing more. Don't ever think that the human commitment to total dominion has room for compassion. Not for us, especially not for us.'

Eliza opened and closed her mouth. She had the simultaneous urge to scream and melt into the ground. She looked at Tierza's feral face and Hugo's dismal one. Why wouldn't he look her in the eye!

'Were you ever going to take me home to your missus? Was any of it true?'

Hugo looked at her at last. 'Aye, I wanted to. If you were a human child, I would've fought tooth and nail for your freedom. But you're a whisperling. I've always known it, but I didn't want to believe it. But the guards know. You've been screaming in your sleep. Dead trees and dead people and dead animals. That's not the type of thing the human mind wanders to. I've done my best with you, little one, but old Hugo can only do so much.'

'So you were going to send me to these camps?'

Hugo looked crestfallen. He shook his head slowly. 'I'm ashamed to say it. I've not confirmed a thing to the King yet. But even if I said you were a human child, the guards would know. And they'd sell us both for half a coin; we all know they would. And then the King would have me butchered for sedition, and where would that leave my missus and my boys?'

Eliza felt the energy evaporate from her body. Something cold seemed to slither underneath her skin. Her teeth began to chatter involuntarily.

'You're a good girl, Eliza. There's nothing I like about any of this. If Eliza turns out to be a human child, I told myself, I'll turn in my badge and go home for good. I'll take her with me. I can't be doing this job any longer. You'd have to have a slab of iron for a heart to do it with a clean conscience, you would.'

'You lied to me, Hugo. All my life. Every single day.' Eliza experienced the sound of her voice as something external and unlike her own.

'It wasn't easy for me, little one. D'ya think I liked it? D'ya think I slept well at night?'

Tierza poked him in the belly with the flashy tip of her sword. 'Don't be professing an account of your hardship to guilt the girl, traitor. She has suffered enough. There's no need for her to suffer for you as well.'

The sentries poked their heads back in. They both had shining black eyes and short hair cropped close to their heads. 'More footsteps in the stairwell. Scores of them. Most definitely guards this time!'

'We need to go. Now!' Tierza muttered.

'We'll have to fight the guards if we leave from the stairwell. There's about a dozen of them,' one of the sentries said.

'Is there another route, traitor?' Tierza asked, poking Hugo in the belly again, harder this time.

Hugo looked at the furrowed brows of the women around him and gulped. 'You're asking me to betray my sworn oath to Bardoria.'

Tierza dug the blade deeper into his distended belly. Hugo sucked in a deep breath. The footsteps grew louder.

'If you help us escape, consider our score settled. The freedom fighters of Teragovia will not harm you.'

Hugo looked up at Eliza's trembling lip, the wetness around her blackpool eyes, and swore loudly. 'I have kept much from you, little one. But I did love you as a daughter, even when I knew what you were. That was not a lie. You must run with these wildlings and promise never to return to Bardoria. They'll be searching for you from the peaks of Casilly to the Whispering Woods.'

On Eliza's last day in the tower, she did not have a moment to take in the view or count the steps from her cot to the table. Nor did she have a moment to feast on one last bowl of gruel. In those final minutes, all she could do was take in every inch of Hugo's face. His thick, worm-like brows, the flour-dusted breadcrumbs on his beard, the patched navy coat that his missus had to darn at the start of each winter, the round brown eyes; were sadder than she'd ever seen them.

Things happened in a flash. Hugo led them down a corridor, then another one, and then up another flight of stairs and down another. Tierza held Eliza by the hand, and the party scurried across the route as quickly as possible. Every few paces, Eliza would see another wooden door that led to chambers unknown. She wondered how many young girls there were, just like herself, trapped for eternity and fed lies. How many prisoners thought they were on the verge of having a family. How many horrors had been witnessed by these walls?

Hugo tugged at an old patterned rug. A cloud of dust emerged from it. Eliza coughed and flapped her hand to clear the air before her face. When the dust settled, she saw a trap door where the rug used to be. Tierza and Lillian were already bent over it. It opened with a low creak.

'Quick, get in there, Eliza,' Lillian called.

Eliza took one last look at Hugo. 'Why don't you escape with us?' she asked him. 'We can be outlaws together.'

He shook his head. 'I'm a Bardorian man. There's no life for me outside this realm.'

'Will you be in trouble?' Eliza asked.

'Aye, that's no business of yours. Run along, little one; you need all the advantage you can get. Be good, Eliza, don't ask too many questions. I'll know if you do. All I have to do is look at the sea, and I'll know if you've been good. Old Hugo will know. Run along now, go on, go on.'

Eliza disappeared down the trapdoor after Lillian, and the others followed. Hugo closed the door over them. It became pitch black. Eliza's heart was caught in her throat. She swallowed back bile. Who would have thought that this would be what freedom tasted like?

Chapter Three

The end of darkness

Tierza relieved them from darkness by opening her palm to reveal a small yellow glowing orb. Eliza's eyes widened. 'What is that?' she asked, reaching out to touch it. Her fingers went right through the glow, barely registering any warmth.

'This is an Igneous Orb. It's a little piece of moonlight in my pocket. Every whisperer has the ability to wield the moonlight.'

'What about me? Am I a whisperer? Can I do this too?'

'You'll be taught soon, whisperling.'

Eliza kept her eyes fixed on the orb as they trudged along the cavernous passageway. The path rose and fell without warning. The walls around them were cold and stony. Occasionally they heard the calls of bats in the distance. One of them swooped past Eliza's shoulder, tickling her neck with its wing. A train of goosebumps erupted from her neck and traveled down to her toes.

The sentries kept silent. Eliza asked them their names, and they responded solemnly.

'Kiani.'

'Riani.'

They left Eliza's questions to Tierza and Lillian and walked to the front, their swords perpetually drawn.

'You never know what you might find in underground tunnels,' Lillian explained.

The passage widened to the size of her chamber at one point. The light of the orb revealed scat splattered across the floor. Eliza stooped low to get a better look at it.

'We are in the lair of wolves, Eliza. You'd be better off without the scent of their scat on your robes.'

Eliza jerked back and fell into step with the others. The passage often thinned to a crack, and they would have to squeeze themselves in bit by bit. Their limbs tumbled out haphazardly from the meagre holes between rock faces as they made their way through. The air was thick and musty and cold. Eliza was startled at how anyone could find a home in such conditions, yet they walked past the webs of spiders, the lairs of wolves, and low ceilinged caves with bats hanging upside down from the roof.

'Where are we going?' Eliza asked, her feet weary from the walk.

'We'll see where the tunnel ends. And from there, we will make our way back to the camp. Who knows how long it will take?'

A few minutes later, Eliza asked, 'Are you sure I'm a whisperer?'

'As sure as anything. Moonblood's have abilities that humans can't fathom. We can always sniff out the magic that runs in the veins of our own.'

'If humans have no special abilities, then how come they imprisoned so many whisperers and kept them in camps?'

'Humans are cunning. No depth is too low to stoop to if it serves the end of dominion. They capture whisperlings before their moon cycles when their powers have barely formed. They separate families and build their great cities on the backs of our broken homes.'

Eliza fell silent. She had spent a lifetime listening to tales about the greatness of Bardoria. Her body still bristled when Tierza spoke of it callously. Part of her waited with bated breath to chance upon information of a more redeeming quality. But such news did not come to pass.

Eliza's stomach rumbled. She thought of the fallen gruel somewhere outside her chamber. Her heart quaked at the thought of her chamber, and she resolved not to think of it again. She was marching towards the only thing she had ever wanted - freedom. Granted, she might not have expected to find quite as much wolf scat on the way to it, but she was in no mood to be picky.

After what felt like hours, a pinprick of light appeared at the end of the tunnel. The collective pace of their steps quickened. Eliza found herself walking slower than the others. The pinprick soon became the size of her window, which was the most she had ever seen of the outside world. Except it continued to grow bigger and bigger as they walked closer to it. She could see a thin sheet of clouds partially obscuring the yolk-yellow winter sun. The tops of trees swayed in the breeze. A few of them still had leaves on their branches. Moss-covered rocks, still damp from recent rain, glistened at the mouth of the cave. From the corner of her eye, Eliza saw movement at the back. Miniature versions of the wolves in her dreams stretched lazily in the shade of a boulder. She smiled at them and bent low with her hands outstretched as the others clambered over the rocks to climb out of the cave. One of the wolves scuttled over to her and buried its fuzzy snout into her fingers. She scratched its head and ran her hands along the length of its chubby body.

'Come on now, Eliza, step into the real world for the first time!' Lillian's voice felt far away even though she was only on the other side of the opening.

Eliza bid the wolf cubs goodbye and took one shaky step onto the rocks. She crouched down onto fours as she had seen the others do and slowly scaled the pile of rocks until she was within reach of the opening. Shrubs of purple flowers ringed the entrance in front of her. The floor was covered with overgrown brambled grass. Eliza felt the enormity of the moment as her entire body grew warm and light. She planted a step onto wet earth for the first time, then another, until she stood tall with the grass grazing her knees. She looked around her and saw the grass turn into a thicket of trees, all of whom seemed to be wearing welcoming smiles within the lines on their barks. The seagulls squawked overhead, and it sounded like a melody to Eliza. She grabbed fistfuls of grass and crouched low to stick her fingers in the squishy texture of the mud. Before she could cry out or exclaim with glee, a sudden headache seized her, a pain so sharp that it was blinding. With a razor-like bolt, Eliza's head was pierced over and over again, and a high-pitched shriek replaced the sound of the wind. Within a fraction of a second, Eliza collapsed onto the mildewed grass in a dead faint.

Chapter Four
The winter daughters

When Eliza opened her eyes, she found herself looking up at either Kiani or Riani's face. She was being carried like a child through a thicket of trees. Her eyes were bleary, and although the worst of her headache was gone, there was still a dull throb that persisted somewhere behind her eyes.

'Put me down!' Eliza cried out. 'I'm not an infant!' Her request was obliged.

'Morning sunshine!' Lillian said with a smile on her face. She handed her a waterskin. 'Here, drink from this.

'I don't know what happened! One moment I was ecstatic, and the next, my head started to hurt, and I saw only blackness.'

'It's been a taxing day. It's no wonder your body gave out. Nothing to be ashamed of.' Lillian then mumbled something about moon cycles bringing forth all manners of responses within the body, and Eliza was reminded of Hugo. She pushed him out of her mind. She had no reason to think of him ever again. He would have sacrificed her to the Bardorian cause if not for these strange women and their rescue mission.

'How long was I out for?'

'Not too long. Less than an hour. We splashed water on your face, but you wouldn't budge. Your absence in the tower will be noticed, and a search party will be gaining on us soon. We deemed it crucial to continue the journey.' Tierza pointed to the sky, now covered in a thick white sheet of clouds. 'We have only a few hours before the sun sets. If we keep this pace up, we should make it back to the camp by nightfall.'

'And then where do we go?' Eliza asked, trying to match Tierza's long strides.

'Back home. Back to Teragovia,' she said, the first glimmer of a smile returning to her face.

'Where's that?'

'Oh, that's impossible to say. No one really knows.'

'How will we find it then?'

'The mythstones will lead the way.'

Without offering any further explanation, Tierza caught up with Riani and Kiani and began to discuss the route back to the camp.

Eliza trudged along a few paces behind the group for the rest of the afternoon. Every now and then, Riani and Kiani would turn back to make sure she was with the party, but aside from that, Eliza was invisible. This suited her well because, for once in her life, Eliza did not care to ask questions. Wide-eyed and open-mouthed, she found herself almost intoxicated by this new breathless world around her. She relished the sinking feeling of her feet walking through mud, the crispness of the cold that gnawed at her ears and nose, and the various shades of brown that took over the landscape as winter brought a rush of decay with it. Fallen leaves, strips of bark, bare branches, wet mud - each bleak hue felt magical to Eliza, who had seen little but the grey of the clouds from her window high in the tower.

Sometimes, she would see creatures stirring. One time, a rabbit bolted from its burrow right next to her, and she squealed at the sight of its floppy ears and slight body. Large fluffy squirrels scurried across skinny branches. They seemed to look at Eliza with an equal amount of interest, their gaze following her path as their cheeks bulged with nuts and seeds.

As the day began to dull and the evening beckoned, she saw starlings dance in peculiar patterns across the sky. Their formations shape-shifted, each bird aware of the next move in the choreography of its journey despite the shared silence between its comrades. Eliza longed to know how they knew but the questions dried up in her mouth. She walked in a trance, greeting every beetle and every bee with the gift of her senses as she joined the dots within the bottomless well of creation that had eluded her for her whole life.

The sun disappeared behind the hills of Casilly, and soon, darkness took hold once again. Cold gusts of wind blew in from the nearby sea somewhere out yonder, on the other side of the woods. Eliza began to wonder if the journey would ever end. The creatures of the night came out. Crickets chirped in the bushes, owls hooted from the trees, and bats flew out of caves and threaded their way through the gaps in the canopy.

'Longer strides, Eliza,' Tierza called out. 'Or we'll lose you to the night, and the day's efforts will have been for naught.'

'Nearly there,' came Lillian's reassuring voice.

'How come you don't have the Igneous Orb out now?' Eliza asked, falling in line with Lillian.

'Whisperers can navigate by moonlight as long as we're out in the open. In the tunnel, we needed the Orb because layers of thick rock blocked the moon channel. Out in the forest, we are guided by the moon herself.'

Eliza had never been told that the moon was female, and she accepted this fact right away, just as she knew she would have to accept thousands of others. 'I'm not sure I'm very good at it,' she said.

'Oh, but you will be. Once your eyes have learned to see. If you don't know what you're looking for, how will you know when you find it?'

Eliza nodded, although she was still perplexed. They walked through the brambles and mud until she thought her feet would fall off. In a moment of weakness, she considered fainting again, just so Kiani or Riani could lug her for the rest of the way. Through gritted teeth, she continued nevertheless, determined to make it back to the camp, even if it was only to delay her collapse by a few more paces.

The party approached a ring of trees. Nobody said anything, but Eliza knew they were there. Tierza unsheathed her sword from its holster and pressed the emblem into the heart of a large oak tree. It left a glimmering impression even after she removed it. Soft whispers, undecipherable to Eliza, emanated from Tierza's lips. The oak tree seemed to understand, and when Tierza was done, it groaned loudly and lifted one of its branches so they could pass through the ring and enter the clearing.

Eliza shivered and walked into the ring. A small fire crackled merrily on the other side, and a group of young girls like herself gathered around it. A pot was mounted on a wooden pole above the fire. Something aromatic bubbled in it.

'About time! We nearly ate the stew without you lot. And it's the last of the fey spice we have, mind you, so tomorrow's stew won't be half as good.' A tall girl with golden hair got up and came to greet them.

'How good of you to wait for us patiently while we risked our lives and broke another winter daughter out from a cold tower!' said Tierza, winking at her. 'Apologies that our missions don't always align with supper time.'

'Consider it forgotten. Now, who do we have here?'

'That'll be Eliza. The last of them.'

'Does this mean that we march home tomorrow?'

'It does.'

There were about eight other girls sitting by the fire. Slowly, all of them got up and came over to Eliza. Their faces glistened in the soft glow of the moonlight. Fair-haired, dark-haired, red-haired, pointy-nosed, button-nosed, light-skinned, dark-skinned, short, tall, skinny, plump - each girl was a complex medley of different features. Eliza had never seen so many kinds of faces in front of her.

'Girls, this is Eliza. Eliza, these are the other winter daughters.'

'Amelie,' the golden-haired girl said, extending a hand to Eliza.

They all followed suit.

'Aoife'

'Seena'

'Zuha'

'Maud'

'Elena'

'Flora'

'Nala'

'Esther'

Eliza stood in front of them, crossing and uncrossing her arms. She opened her mouth to say something, but she didn't know what to say. She had never met anyone of her own age. Though they had done nothing to scare her, their very existence was unfathomable to Eliza.

'Let's eat, girls, I don't know about the lot of you, but I'm absolutely famished!' Lillian led everyone back to the fire. Eliza sat next to her while the others began to pass bowls and spoons around in a known order. When handed a bowl, Eliza immediately began to spoon the brothy mixture of vegetables and herbs into her mouth like an animal. Unlike the cloudy mush of the gruel, the stew consisted of various textures and flavours. Her teeth crunched on softened carrots and beets. The dried sprinkling of thyme and rosemary swirled around her mouth, introducing her to the notion of food being an enjoyable experience.

While Eliza ate, the fire crackled and sputtered in front of them. All the girls talked, laughed, and shared the day's sightings with Tierza and Lillian. The one named Amelie seemed to be the most raucous.

'We heard footsteps around dusk. We drew our swords and bows and arrows and ringed the camp like you taught us. I even called out to the trees and birds and bees. The soldiers could sense us; we knew they could, but the enchantment held, and we were able to carry on undisturbed.'

'Well done,' Tierza said. 'We knew the daughters would be safe with you.'

Although Eliza's body was weary, her mind was racing. The glow of the fire lit up the youthful faces around her, sculpting them in shadows and light. Eliza's bowl was empty long before the others, who paused to chat to one another in between mouthfuls. They talked about other woods they had journeyed through, distant lands, and brighter seasons. Each of them had seen more of the world than Eliza, and she felt herself shrinking on the inside as she searched for things to say to the others.

'Time for rest, winter daughters,' Tierza declared after each bowl had been licked clean. 'We'll be setting off before dawn tomorrow. Back to Teragovia!'

'Back to Teragovia!' the others repeated, their fists pumping in the air.

'Eliza, you can share your bedding with Amelie,' Lillian said, pointing to a spot in the trees. Eliza couldn't make out a chamber or any sort of silhouette in the inky darkness.

'Oh, but I've never had to share my bedding before!' Amelie cried out sullenly.

'All the daughters sleep in pairs. We let you have your own space until we could. Now that there are ten daughters, you must oblige.'

Amelie said nothing but stalked off in the direction that Lillian had pointed to. She seemed to have no trouble seeing in the dark. Eliza scampered after her, trying to keep up without tripping over the thick roots of the trees that curved along the ground in undulating lines. Amelie stopped abruptly outside a thick hollow tree. It opened wide enough to create a chamber fit to sleep two small bodies. The floor had been covered with heather. A cloak of myrtle green was flung on top. Eliza waited outside the hole while Amelie seemed to deliberate which side she preferred to sleep on. The blackness stretched out ominously in all directions, but Eliza felt safe in the night. She looked up. The branches of taller trees crisscrossed to form a canopy overhead, but she could make out an expanse of twinkling stars through the gaps. Her breathing slowed. Through her window, the stars had often felt like her only friends. Right in her line of sight, they kept her afloat in a bed of dreams. She often had the feeling that she could reach out and grab these mighty glowing rocks if she tried. Now, with her feet firmly planted in the ground, it was strange to see the net of stars cast so far away from her, out of reach, barely in sight.

Amelie poked her head out and said, 'you can have the right side. There's termites there, so don't be surprised if you wake up with powder all over your face. It's only wood.'

Eliza nodded gratefully, without fully understanding what Amelie meant. She crawled into the hole and sat on her knees, running her fingers over the soft grass that had been patted down to make her bed. She took off her own cloak, a patched-up shaggy thing sent over by Hugo's missus and spread it over her side of the bed.

'Amelie,' she said softly.

'What?'

'Are you a whisperer?'

Amelie's nose emitted a loud snort. 'Yes, Eliza, I am a whisperer. Just like you and all of the other winter daughters.'

'Oh. We're all whisperers? There's no humans in our party?'

'God, no. As if we could trust humans with our secrets. They're known to foil our plans and augment our hardships; they'd be an absolute liability on this mission.'

'Are they all bad? These humans?'

'Have you known any good ones?'

Eliza was about to launch into a story of Hugo, the time he'd sneaked in sugary Yule treats for her so she could get a taste of the shortest night of the year. But then she remembered that he had been on the verge of turning her in, sending her to a life of imprisonment in Bardorian camps. She shook her head imperceptibly.

'That's what I thought.'

'Amelie, why do Tierza and Lillian refer to us as the winter daughters?'

'Oh dear. Have they not told you a thing?'

Eliza stayed silent.

'The prophecy? Our mission? Any of it?'

Amelie propped herself up on her elbows and said dramatically, 'as always, they leave the hardest tasks to me! Listen hard, Eliza, for your fate is about to change!'

Goosebumps began to snake their way up Eliza's shins. She gestured for Amelie to continue.

'The ten of us born at the brink of winter are part of a great prophecy. It is known that a darkness threatens to devour the land. All of Elatonia breathes in peril. One of the ten daughters born at the brink of winter is the Midnight Daughter. She will single-handedly save the realm and all of its people.'

'Do we know who the Midnight Daughter is?'

'Well, formally, we do not. It could be any of us. It could even be you!'

'Me? the Midnight Daughter?'

'Aye, there's a wee chance.'

Eliza's vision clouded, and her bones grew heavy. She nodded meekly and fell into bed, her mind resistant to any more knowledge that might put an end to her sanity. She was not only most definitely not a human; she was a whisperer; she might even be the Midnight Daughter. The day felt like a joke, something that her wicked mind had conjured in her sleep. As the day's events roiled fiercely in the choppy sea of her head, Eliza longed to wake up and discover that it had all been a dream. She wished to be a girl in the tower, the one who had never known betrayal, whose life still contained the promise of a home and family. She shook her head and pushed all the errant thoughts out of her mind. She let it drift, let her body fall slack into the warm heather. That night, for the first time in her life, Eliza slept long and deep, without a single dream playing on her mind.

Chapter Five

A debt is made

The next morning, Amelie had to shake Eliza out of her fatigued stupor. Eliza lay still like a log on the forest floor. It was still dark outside when Amelie roused her, but a faint murmur could be heard in the thicket. The calls of birds trilled through the silence, signaling that daybreak was near. Eliza sat up bleary-eyed and tried to make sense of her bearings. At the same time, Amelie fastened her cloak to her shoulders, gathered her sparse belongings into a knapsack, and scattered the neatly patted down heather all over the place.

'Why are you doing that?' Eliza asked, her eyes threatening to shut again if she didn't find a way to awaken her mind.

'To hide our tracks. Once we leave, the enchantment will be lifted, and the Bardorian soldiers will be able to enter this thicket. We can't be leaving breadcrumbs for them to follow all the way to Teragovia, can we now?'

The new facts of her life stacked up on top of each other as she began to follow Amelie's lead. She fastened the cloak back on her back and messed up the heather so it looked more like a wild animal's nest than a whisperer's bedding.

Just yesterday, Eliza had woken up without a care except for drawing ordinary horses so she could prove her humanness to Hugo, and today, she was allegedly a whisperer, and the Bardorian's were her enemies. She was about to march to somewhere known as Teragovia, a place whose location was unknown, and yet, they were confident that they'd find it. They, as in, the new legion of fresh-faced women that she had been initiated into. Oh, and there was the whole matter about the Midnight Daughter, but Eliza actively pushed it further away into some anterior chamber of her mind. The things she knew were tumultuous enough without the added stress of conjecture about what the unknown might bring.

She walked behind Amelie through the last dregs of darkness. The black of the sky was turning a purplish-blue with streaks of orange erupting beyond the hills of Casilly. It was the first sunrise of her little life, and Eliza was bewildered that no one else seemed to care. The others spooned porridge into their mouths or washed and packed up the cooking implements.

'Can I help?' she asked.

'Ah, we're nearly finished,' said Lillian, crouching over the firepit. 'Just empty out your porridge bowl and pack it into your knapsack. We won't be eating until supper, so you'd best make it count.'

Eliza sat in the same spot as the night before and busied herself with the sweet clumpy paste in her bowl. There was no sign of the remains of a fire in front of her.

The ash had been covered with a bramble bush, and the embers tossed into the dirt, unmistakable from the rocks. Lillian's words harked back to her. Eliza could see the sleight of the whisperers' hands because she knew what she was looking for. Satisfied with her discovery and a belly full of porridge, she gazed at the sky and watched it change colour again. The purple had succumbed to a dim lick of blue, growing lighter and lighter by the second. Behind her, in the direction of Bardoria, dark clouds had taken over. They inched closer and closer to the splash of colour above her.

'I remember my first sunrise,' one of the girls said, standing next to her. 'I wasn't sure if the sky was going mental or I was.'

Eliza remembered her as Aoife. She was a skinny red-haired girl, shorter than Eliza, light on her toes, and graceful in her movements. 'Have you seen many of them?'

'I've seen one every morning since I was freed.'

'Have you been free for very long?'

'I've counted it to eight moons now.'

'These sunrises must get old then.'

'They do, for some. But never for me. Even when they're not this spectacular, they do something to me.' She paused for a moment to gather her thoughts. Her voice was sweet and low. 'I suppose they remind me that I've risen another day, alive and free.'

Eliza felt a tremor in her chest. She wolfed down the remnants of the porridge and rinsed it in a pool of water that had gathered in the rain. A pile of stones stopped the water from penetrating into the ground. By

42

the time they set off, the sun had fully emerged from beyond the hills of Casilly. The air was crisp and cold, and it lurched Eliza into wakefulness. Tierza and Lillian inspected the campsite, deemed it safe to leave it as it was, and walked over to the same old oak tree that had lifted its branches to grant them passage into the clearing. They put their palms flat on its trunk and whispered under their breath. Eliza tilted her head and tried to decipher what they were saying, but their incantations sounded more like a rustle in the bushes than actual words.

'Do you know what they're saying?' Eliza asked no one in particular.

This time it was the dark-skinned Nala who answered her. Her hair fell in ringlets around an angular face. She was tall and looked much stronger than Eliza.

'They're giving thanks to the forest for protecting us and lifting the enchantment.'

'Must they lift the enchantment? If they left this thicket hidden, the soldiers could never follow our tracks.'

'Ah, the Bardorian in her has spoken!' remarked the one named Esther. 'Their instinct is always to exploit, never to exchange.'

Nala ignored the remark and continued to speak. 'An enchantment is no small task, Eliza. We take much from the trees when we conscript their services. If they were to hide this thicket for eternity, the trees would be putting out more energy than they were taking in. They'd die centuries before the end of their natural life! We must hide our tracks and give our thanks to the trees for what they have granted us.'

43

Eliza nodded, but her face burned with shame. Did some part of Bardoria live inside of her? Was she wired to see the world as hers for the taking? She had knowingly been a whisperer only for a day, but she had been reared as a human under Hugo's tutelage for her entire life. Would she ever be able to shake that off? And most importantly: did she even want to?

The party set off once the enchantment had been lifted. The girls burst into occasional babble with one another but mostly, they walked in silence to conserve their strength for the journey. They walked deeper and deeper into the thicket so that the gap between the trees narrowed, and they had to fall into a single line. The branches hung low at certain points, and they had to stoop or even crawl through patches on all fours.

'I wish we'd take the central path!' Amelie grumbled loudly enough to be heard by Tierza. 'It'd just be a week's march into the Whispering Woods. This way will take us three times as long!'

'And walk right into the maw of the Bardorian search party? How very kind that would be to the human cause.'

'We're strong enough to defend ourselves against their fickle armies. Humans are always fighting amongst one another; they haven't got the mettle to best us.'

'I admire your confidence, but I fear for your life,' Tierza said curtly, parting a sheet of vines from the path in front of her.

Eliza did her best to stifle her shrieks whenever she got cut by a thorny bush. She had little experience in the wilderness and did not always look before grasping a thick vine for support. Often, her boot would disappear into a hole in the ground, just barely covered by leaves. She learned the hard way that the understory was dominated by various furry creatures that dug burrows deep inside the earth and that they cared little for the discomfort of whisperlings. By the time they made their first stop for rest, her boots were covered in mud all the way up to her shins, and her neck and hands were dotted with a thousand tiny cuts. Eliza knew it couldn't be real but she felt as though she heard mocking laughter emerge from the hollows in the trees every time she slipped or cut herself.

Everyone slumped against the trunk of a tree and fell to the floor. Lillian passed a waterskin around. The girls drank thirstily. The dark reach of the clouds had already taken over, and the sun's insipid glow was obscured. It was hard to tell how much time had passed since they had left the campsite, but it felt like days to Eliza. The trees towered up high, and their branches intersected to hide much of the sky from the ground. Several of them had retained their leaves, a dark emerald green. Others had needle-like accoutrements that Eliza never saw falling, and yet the ground was covered in them. She grabbed a fistful of fallen leaves and used them to scrape the mud from her boots. No one else had wrecked their boots as she had. No one else had fresh cuts either.

After a few minutes of relief, they were on their way again. Eliza ended up in the line behind Amelie, whose long, lithe frame tread lightly. Eliza tried to emulate her movements, the way she lightly tapped a branch to check for thorns before grabbing it, the way she kept her gaze on the path in front of her rather than pointed upwards in the direction of the irksome sky, so she didn't fall into holes in the ground. She reached out into spiky bushes now and then and twisted small red berries from the twine. Eliza, already famished, kept an eye out for the next bush. She stuck her hand straight into it through the spiky needles, and bit back the pain as her fingers searched for berries.

Without looking back, Amelie called out in a haughty voice, 'most berries are poisonous, I'll have you know. I wouldn't put any odd thing from the woods into my mouth if I were you!'

Sheepishly, Eliza withdrew her bloodied hand and kept her head down the rest of the way. She ignored the rumble of her belly and tried to hone her senses into seeing, really seeing all that was around her. Soon, the murky forest opened up by a foggy hill. Upon walking closer to its edge, they saw that it was a large rock face, smooth and bald, with little by way of footholds. It was surrounded by opaque gluey marsh on either side. The consensus was that they would have to go over the rocky hill rather than around it.

'Be careful now,' Lillian said. 'The grooves are slick, so your fingers won't hold for very long. It might seem contrary to common logic, but it's wiser to move faster rather than slower.'

Nervously, Eliza fell to the back of the queue while the others made a quick ascent. She followed their movements with her eyes and prepared herself to do just the same. Amelie swiftly hopped from one groove to another and made her way up like a spider moving across a wall. When it was Eliza's turn, she used a tree branch to hoist herself onto the main face of the rock, its slick surface glistening in front of her. This was the easy part. She reached out with her left hand and tucked her right foot firmly onto the furthest edge of the branch. When she was sure her weight would be supported, she lifted herself off the branch and dug her boot into one of the footholds. Each limb was now attached to the rock face.

'Don't look down,' came Amelie's voice from up above.

Eliza swallowed. She searched for another groove for her hands. Right hand, left foot, left hand, right foot. She was doing well, despite herself. Her body seemed to possess a rhythmic movement unbeknownst to her waking mind. Perhaps she wasn't such a lost cause; perhaps she was moonblooded as they said, maybe she was deserving of her freedom from the ghastly tower and its sole window.

'Nearly there,' she said to herself. She could see Amelie's bored face peering over the edge, waiting for her to make her way to the top.

And then Eliza's foot skidded on a particularly smooth hold, and she screamed as solid ground disappeared from underneath her. She did the one thing she had been told not to do and looked down. She was dangling from two grooves with only her hands holding on for dear life. Her feet quivered like jelly when she saw what lay below. The ground was further away than she could have imagined. She could make out boulders the shape of fangs hemming the rock face dangerously. She felt her fingers slipping, the cold, wet edges of the groove resisting her grip.

'Oh no, oh no, oh NOOOOO!'

Before she could see what was happening, Amelie had glided down the rock face and was holding her hand out.

'Here, take my hand,' she said. One of Amelie's arms held onto the top of the cliff's edge, using a firmly wedged stone to stay tethered. The other arm was extended to Eliza.

'I can't reach it! I don't know how!'

'Lift yourself from the arms, use the force from your stomach and grab my arm. Go on, quick!'

For a second, Eliza did nothing. And then she tightened her belly, launched herself up, and caught hold of Amelie's hand.

'Now find a groove for each of your feet,' she said.

Eliza did as she was told.

'And keep climbing as you were. Go on, go on.'

Eliza gingerly made her way over the last stretch of the rock face. She hauled herself to the top and fell to her knees. She gulped lungfuls of clean air and exhaled it back out like a chimney, plumes of foggy breath disappearing into the mist. She lifted her hands to her face and found that they were trembling from the shock of having narrowly escaped a brutal fall.

Amelie leaped up from behind her, as poised and unfazed as ever. She walked ahead without casting another glance at her. Eliza scrambled to her feet and followed, her face flushed. The others waited for them at a point where the mist had cleared. Eliza gasped when she saw what lay ahead. The sea, a rich cerulean hue, glowed in the distance, beyond vast patches of leafy-headed trees. It shimmered in the pale yellow sun, which had escaped the shackles of the clouds for long enough to grant the sea its majesty, if only for a few moments.

'What took you so long?' Tierza said, an eyebrow arched.

Eliza, suddenly embarrassed to have held up the party, opened her mouth to apologise but Amelie cut her off.

'We were only picking some berries for the lot of you,' she said, reaching deep into her pockets and holding out the berries that Eliza knew she had spent all day picking for herself. The others crowded around her, popping the juicy red fruit into their mouths.

Before they set off again, Amelie shot Eliza a look, her eyebrows slightly furrowed and her mouth flattened into a thin line. Now Eliza hadn't been around people long enough to recognise what each facial expression meant, but even she knew what was being communicated to her. It was a look that clearly said: you owe me.

Chapter Six

The crossing

The next few days surged past in a mechanical hum. After they descended the other side of the rock face, they reentered the woods on the other side, which were every bit as grim as the ones they had just left behind. Tierza plotted gruelling routes every day because they had to reach the sea before the night of the full moon passed them by. Eliza had been sure that they would reach the sea in no time, but she had clearly underestimated the density of the forest and how much time it took to cross it. Much of their plan hinged on reaching the crossing point by the full moon, which meant that they often had to cut through bogs instead of walking around them. Eliza hated the days when they waded through the murky water, its floor sinking from underneath, threatening to suck her right into the abyss. The vegetation looked hauntingly monotonous all around her, with the occasional sheet of mist draping itself through the vines and twines. She longed for the openness of the sky above but was shrouded by the icy breath of the mist instead.

The unexpected side effect of Amelie saving Eliza from certain death was that Amelie now saw herself as somewhat responsible for her. Amelie taught her how to tell the poisonous berries apart from the tasty ones and said, 'so you don't die from eating the wrong ones.' She showed her how to fill her waterskin from the fresh dew collected on the leaves' broad planes each morning and said, 'so you don't fall into a faint while we're wading through marshland.' Maybe all it meant was that Amelie didn't want to keep an eye out for Eliza's pitiful survival skills to fail her, but this was the closest Eliza had come to having a friend since Hugo, and she was grateful for it.

'Humans passed through here not long ago,' Amelie told Eliza one day, picking up a piece of branch from the forest floor. 'You see this? It's been severed by a machete. You can never tell if a whisperer has been in the forest because we deem it vital to leave it the way we found it. We'll crawl and climb and expend ourselves fully to make sure of this. A human will do the opposite. They'll bludgeon their way through the path and hack away anything that dares to come in the way rather than bending their backs for a sole moment.'

This added yet another thing to Eliza's repository of things she could see because she knew what to look for. An arm's length above her head, she could see the sharp open faces of fractured branches.

Although they didn't have to, they camped together as they had on Eliza's first night. They collected heather at the end of the day and patted it into place together. Eliza wasn't sure what had changed, but Amelie had gone from total disinterest to genuine camaraderie.

Something was growing between them, and even if Amelie had only taken her under her wing to make sure she didn't almost die again, Eliza was grateful for the lukewarm attention.

Another bonus was that Amelie answered Eliza's questions with far more readiness than Hugo ever had. She told her about the other winter daughters. The first one to be freed was Nala, and the others had followed close behind. They had all been imprisoned in towers across the Bardorian land. Aoife had spent her entire life trapped in the cellar without so much as a speck of daylight. Esther, the one who had accused Eliza of being intrinsically Bardorian, had suffered the most at the hands of the humans. The freedom fighters of Teragovia had been almost too late to save her, and she had done a full year in the camps before they were able to break her out. Amelie said that Esther was bound to the cause by bitterness, and if she turned out to be the Midnight Daughter, she would likely annihilate the human race. Eliza's stomach churned at the thought of Esther's rage wiping out Hugo and his missus and his boys, and she hoped with all her heart that Esther, like herself, was just another winter daughter who would soon be proved to be an ordinary whisperling.

'I thought you were the first one to be freed,' Eliza said to Amelie as they lay in bed, on the brink of sleep.

'Freed? I was never captured, Eliza. I was raised in Teragovia alongside the freedom fighters. I have no kin besides them. The woods are my home. This life is all I've ever known.'

It made sense why Amelie was treated differently to the other winter daughters. She was, in fact, different from them. She was more a part of the Daughter of Elatonia, the rescuers, than the winter daughters who were the ones that needed rescuing. Eliza envied her. How wonderful it must have been to grow up in the woods, have a sisterhood that looked after you, and be groomed for your destiny from the very beginning.

Eliza noticed that Amelie didn't chat much with the rest of the winter daughters. She was serene and silent, her face often caught in the look of suffering perpetual tedium. She bantered effortlessly with Tierza and Lillian, and it was evident that she and Tierza were particularly close. But she seemed to care little for the other daughters and placed herself above them as though they were not worthy of her time. And yet, she willingly showed Eliza how to hide the traces of their evening fires, how to arrange the rocks into a basin that would collect rainwater, and how to fold the leaves into cones so that the berries wouldn't sully the insides of their pockets when squished together. Her insides glowed warmly every time Amelie turned around to make sure that Eliza was still there, like a candle had been lit after a long and dark night.

After the fire had been put out, Eliza would often stare at the evening sky, searching for stars. Even if the gaps in the canopy gave way to snatches of sky, the clouds presented themselves as an insurmountable barrier. She found herself wondering less and less if Hugo and his missus and his boys were looking up at the same night sky. She slept easier in the woods than she had in the tower, somehow comforted by the embrace of the tufts of heather that she sank into. With each day that passed, her muscles grew stronger and her bones felt lighter. She found herself keeping up with the rest of the party more easily than before. Having cones full of berries tucked into her pockets, she was less likely to succumb to hunger before they camped out in the night and cooked a stew.

Sometimes, the party would come across patches of baldness in the middle of the dense overgrowth. Empty circles full of scores of tree stumps littered the ground, their surfaces ringed with aged wrinkles, their growth brought to an abrupt halt by Bardorian blades. Each time the whisperlings came to a rough-hewn clearing like this, Tierza and Lillian instructed them to run their hands over the wounded stumps and whisper their thanks to the trees. The first time Eliza brushed her hands along the grainy ridges, she felt a song of sadness well up inside her, ricocheting between her bones and organs, swelling her entire body in a deep gloom. She gave her thanks and bit back tears.

'And that is why Bardorian homes are the warmest. They don't break branches like the rest of us; they take the whole trees,' Amelie told her, the disgust evident in her voice.

According to Amelie, they had been walking on foot for about ten days who knew what the capricious moon looked like even when she was hidden by the flare of the sun. Just when Eliza began to enjoy the unabashed murkiness of the forest, they finally reached the sea. Eliza found herself mesmerised by the relentless expanse in front of her. They stood at the edge of a pebbled beach, where the soft blue-grey water licked the coast ever so gently. They were at the mouth of a small crescent-shaped bay, part of which was obscured by the cloudy mist.

'We need to go through that to get to the other side,' Tierza said. The sun had begun its slow descent over the woods. They had barely an hour of light left. Eliza traced the water's surface with her fingertips and drew her hand back instantly. So, so cold. How did they intend to cross the frosty waters? They'd die from the chill if they stayed in the water longer than a few moments.

'We're in luck. We've made it over here on the full moon,' Tierza said to them. 'Our powers might be at their peak; however, the Bardorian search party is still at large. We don't know if they've picked up our trail and intend to ambush us in the mist.'

'Can't we ask the fey of these woods if they have seen anything?' Amelie piped up.

'I have tried, and I have failed. The few fey that still live in the Bardorian woods trusts no beings other than their own kind. The Bardorian's have laid waste to many a medicine garden and sacred grove that belonged to fey families for hundreds of years. And now, because we have the same build and faces as the humans, we too must suffer for their sins. We have no friends in these parts, winter daughters. We only have the moon.'

Tierza instructed them to go into the forest and search for sturdy pieces of wood so that they could fashion a raft out of them. Eliza bounded up beside Amelie and spent a quarter of an hour learning what type of wood was unsuitable for raft-making. Everything Eliza picked up was too small, too big, or too damp. Amelie stacked up mostly dry, mid-sized logs that had fallen only a day or two ago. As they searched and selected the best logs to take back to the pebbled beach, Amelie filled Eliza in on the plan.

'The safest night for whisperers to undertake a dangerous passage is the night of the full moon. The sea accepts the moon as her liege and churns large waves whenever the full moon is visible to her, making the sea hard to navigate. But the powers of whisperers are at their peak on such nights, so we make it past the currents and the chop with ease. Humans dare not enter the frigid waters when they roil, especially not on a full moon.'

'And what happens when the moon wanes into nothingness?'

'The dark moon dilutes our powers. On nights like that, we must confine ourselves to our homes and hearths rather than head into the open and tempt fate.'

Back at the pebbled beach, the pieces of wood had been gathered. Tierza, along with Riani and Kiani, was tying the logs into a platform large enough to carry all of them. The three women worked rapidly without speaking, each knowing the next step in their joint task. They reminded Eliza of the dancing starlings who seemed to dance in perfect unison without anyone to tell them what to do. Next to them, Seena and Lillian carved large flat paddles out of slabs of wood. Seena, from what Amelie said, possessed an innate knowledge of woodwork and would have assembled a whole ship by herself if they had the time. Her hair was long and tangled and hung to her waist, her eyes a honey brown that was only a few shades darker than her skin. Her gaze was fixed on the assembly of the raft, her hands moving to their own tune, unafraid of the blade that moved rapidly back and forth over the edges of the paddle. A simple structure had been put together. Logs of wood were tied together and bound by the spells that the three women uttered under their breath. It looked like a precarious old platform that could never have held the weight of so many without magic aiding their quest.

Kiani and Riani pushed the raft into the water just as the sun began to set. Eliza gasped when they jumped on top of it, but it stayed afloat. Signaling to the others to join them, they dug the oars into the sand to stop the vessel from drifting. A log of wood was laid out, connecting the beach to the raft so they could get onto it without wading through the water. The girls made their way over the log one by one, some crouching, some teetering. Amelie sauntered across it, fully erect, as though it was a wide road and not a thin line. Eliza followed her, crawling along the length of the log, the soft waves hissing under her belly. She paused at the end to look at a starfish, all of its five arms splayed on a pebble underwater, and almost lost her balance. Amelie caught her, and Eliza made it safely on board.

'It's like having a child, Eliza,' Amelie muttered, rolling her eyes, but her features were soft, and Eliza knew that Amelie never truly minded helping her.

Once all of them were aboard, Kiani and Riani lifted the oars out of the water and thrust them back in with greater force. Eliza watched their smooth motions, the clean lines that the oars drew on the water's inky surface.

'Get one last look at Bardoria,' Lillian said. 'If you are fortunate, you will never have to see this land again.'

Eliza turned around and watched the marshy forest with its vines and spiky bushes move further and further away. The woods were so dense that they appeared as a thick mass of brown and muddied green. She couldn't tell where one tree ended and another one began. Despite herself, she felt hot tears fall from her eyes. This was the land she had been brought up to believe was the greatest. The land with the biggest machines, warmest homes, and weapons so far advanced that no one else in the entire realm of Elatonia dared challenge them. Except Eliza was now part of a party that sought nothing but to challenge Bardorian greatness, even make a mockery of it. The land that had once contained the promise of home and family had been revealed to be the place that had seized both from her.

Riani and Kiani rowed methodically, the pair of them perfectly in sync. The sound of the oars was soothing; the gentle clip-clop reminded her of the horses' hooves when they ran across the grounds to the coastal road. Eliza wondered if they would be visible from her window in the tower, a blurry speck drifting at sea.

And then suddenly, they were blanketed by the mist. The sea relinquished its steady motion and began to whir around them as though shaking from a fevered dream. The last of Bardoria was drowned by the fog, and Eliza's heart raced. The white cloud around her was so thick that she could not even see her own hands. She flung her arms out and held onto someone's cloak. Her breath caught in her throat as she tried her best to stay steady despite the raucous chop of the sea. Although she couldn't see the waves, Eliza could sense that they were growing larger and larger from the way they bashed against the edges of the platform. Each wave felt like a roar from the belly of an enraged beast. Icy saltwater spray slashed her face like spiky thorn bushes. She feared that the magic that held the logs together would fail, and they would break free from their bonds and plummet the whisperlings and their rescuers into the deep, dark, frigid sea.

And then a sound penetrated the roars, something low and sweet. Incantations that were being whispered and yet were loud enough to ring through the cry of the waves. A golden-white pinprick began to emerge from the centre of the raft. It grew bigger and bigger until its glow lit up the raft like a fire would. Tierza and Lillian stood at the centre with their eyes closed and palms pressed against one another's. Their lips moved, but their voices seemed to emanate from the outside, reverberating around the dome of light that now enclosed them. The raft steadied as the dome continued to grow. Once the entire platform was held within it, the glow stopped growing and simply increased in its brightness.

Eliza could see the face of each one of them illuminated in the ethereal light. It flickered like a flame but left no shadows, reaching the back of their heads as well as their foreheads. It was as though it had no single source or centre but emanated individually from everything encased within the dome, as though a billion invisible fireflies had joined forces to offer light on their journey.

Down below, Eliza could once again see the oars carving through the water. Outside the dome, the sea continued to froth and snarl. But within the dome, there was a peacefulness to the waters, as though it had never occurred to them to be rough or inelegant in any way. Up ahead, where Kiani and Riani rowed and steered, a few paces were lit up so they could avoid the towering rocks that jutted out from the seafloor.

Eliza looked up and saw the bulging white shield of the moon smiling down at them. Eliza gasped. This was the first large display of the whisperers' famed magic that she had been able to witness. It was this power that had been captured to fuel Bardorian mines and machines and hearths. It was this power that she would be taught to wield soon. The sadness of leaving Bardoria behind started to melt in the warmth of the dome, and something new took its place. Something that felt like hope, like excitement for the first time. A lightness that made her feet feel springy, her shoulders relaxed and she realised that she no longer had to fight who she was. She was no human - if exploitation was what they were about, then she would never be a good one. But maybe, just maybe, she could be a half-decent whisperer. There was only one way to find out!

Chapter Seven

The storm from nowhere

Just when Eliza had sworn to embrace who she really was, fate played a cruel trick on her. The raft, encased in its peculiar golden glow, made it safely through the mist and the rocks and pushed into the wet grainy sand on the other side. By then, the night had draped everything in a cloak of darkness, and there didn't seem to be anyone else on the beach. Once everyone had disembarked, Tierza and Lillian joined their palms together again and whispered an incantation to lift the spell. The glow softly faded, shrinking in mass and gathering close together until it was a column of dim light. And then it shifted upwards, in the direction of the moon, unwavering in the bite of the breeze, traveling up and away until Eliza couldn't see it anymore. The two women continued to chant and the magic that held the logs together was lifted too. Instantly, the wear and tear of the sea was evident. The logs broke apart and appeared to have aged dramatically in the course of the journey. The waves had splintered and softened the edges, soaking the whole contraption in so much water that it would not have stayed buoyant without the magic. Now, scattered on the faint yellow beach, the logs looked like driftwood that the bitter sea had thrown up.

'The worst of our journey is done,' Tierza said, sitting down on the sand, looking exhausted for the first time. She rubbed her eyes and then ran her fingers through her smooth silver hair. 'We are no longer in Bardorian territory, but we are still in human land. This means that we will have to pretend to be humans if asked. One small whisper, one accidental remark, and we'll be strung out to dry if they learn our true identity. Winter daughters, heed my warnings and commit yourself to a human role until we are safe in the Whispering Woods.'

Eliza stared at her blankly. Moments ago, she had pledged to wear her whisperer skin proudly, and now she was being asked to take a few steps back and pretend once again!

'We'll set up camp in the nearby woods tonight; it's less than an hour's march from here. Half a day's march tomorrow and we'll be in the Whispering Woods, where we have many friends and just as many foes.'

By the time they arrived at the new campsite, Eliza's head had begun to throb. They selected a small clearing as their lodging for the night and patted heather into place in the boughs of tall trees. The air smelled sweeter in the forest than it did in Bardoria, as though night blossoms were hanging off distant bushes. Eliza glanced at the gossamer moon, thinly veiled and yet so vibrant behind the sheen of clouds. Something inside of that capricious being controlled the mighty ocean as well as her own powers. How could something so far away have such a vast effect on the matters of mere mortals?

Eliza was asleep before her head even hit her bed of dried grass. She fell into a slumber so deep that it seemed to transport her into another world. The dreams of the last few weeks surged with doubled vigour, threatening to cleave her skull into two from their ferocity. A reel of fallen trees crumbling into dust in an unending winter gripped her from the inside. A high-pitched wail sounded like a gong echoing through the sparse forest. Wolves howled and snapped their bloodied jaws as they feasted on the remains of bodies; she couldn't tell if they were humans or whisperers. The chorus of a lament was hummed by invisible creatures as everything that was green and alive began to dull into a muted icy grey.

Eliza was shaken out of her nightmare by Amelie. 'Eliza! Wake up! You're talking in your sleep. Loudly, might I add!'

With her face flushed, and her body covered in a cold sweat, Eliza sat up and touched her fingers to her temples massaging them slowly in the hopes of easing the throbbing. She looked over to Amelie to say something about her dream before it slipped away from her memory, but the cloak was already pulled over Amelie's soft blonde hair, and her breaths were slow and deep. Eliza felt seasick, as though giant waves were crashing on the inside wall of her head and she was marooned somewhere in between them, fighting for her life in a riptide that did not cease. She gulped in the fresh night air and lay back down, unable to sleep. By the time morning rolled around, Eliza was even more fatigued than before.

They began their march towards the Whispering Woods. The sky was overcast with thick grey slabs of rain clouds, giving the appearance of late evening, rather than first light. Amelie was gay at the prospect of reentering her beloved woods and wouldn't stop sharing garbled advice about them to Eliza. Advice seemed to be Amelie's primary form of showing affection and Eliza, for whom each day brought about a new set of challenges and things she was yet to learn, didn't mind one bit.

'Remember that every butterfly was once a caterpillar, so mind your heavy-footed treading and be gentle to the forest floor.'

'Stay away from the fey, Eliza; they're not to be trusted.'

'If you spot a four-leafed clover, pick it up. They're awfully lucky!'

Eliza took in the nuggets of information without teasing it apart with questions as she normally would have. Although the headache had receded, her head still felt inflamed.

At their first rest stop, Tierza gathered them close and said, 'we are only a few paces from the human kingdom of Augrives. It is the last human settlement before the woods begin. Now, we'll be taking the long way into the woods by going around the town instead of through it. We don't know the level of alarm that the Bardorian search parties have raised, so we'd better not risk it. If anybody asks, we're humans from the town of

Otterdale. The Otterdaleans are known to train their girls in fields and forests so no one will question your garb.'

They kept walking through the forest, crunching on freshly fallen leaves underfoot. Reds and oranges littered the floor, clearly visible through the twigs and needles. They had barely walked a quarter of an hour when they met a middle-aged man on a brown horse, a stiff hat on his head and a waxy coat with insignia, fluttering in the breeze behind him. A pipe was stuck to his mouth, emitting plumes of wispy fragrant smoke. Eliza looked at the horse with her mouth agape. It looked so different from up close, its body taut and muscled, its fur glowing despite the lack of light. It neighed at her, putting all of its teeth on display. Its sad brown eyes looked directly into Eliza's, and she nodded knowingly at it, wishing she could rub its nose.

'A very good morning to you,' the man said. 'Forgive me for not bowing to a gaggle of womenfolk, but you must understand it's no easy feat for an old man such as myself to jump on and off a horse. If I break a hip over a failed politeness to such a delightful party, my wife will be incensed and will most definitely take it up with you!'

Tierza laughed in an exaggerated manner. 'Don't bother yourself with such formalities, good sir. We're only school mistresses foraging with our girls. The fey has ravaged the mushrooms over in our woods so we've wandered some yards to find some around these parts. I hope you'll take no offence at that!'

'Of course not; there's plenty to forage in our woods,' said the old man, flicking his wrist to display how trifling a matter this was to him. 'Augrives might not be

65

the most powerful kingdom in the human terrain, but we're known to provide plenty for our brethren all over the land. Might I ask, where do you hail from?'

'Otterdale, Sir. I thank you for your kindness.'

'Why, my sister was married to a gentleman in Otterdale. The merchant of spice, they still call him. Between you and me, it's all fey spice bought cheap and sold for twice the coin. The auld Lord Cannaby, beloved to all.'

Tierza nodded. 'But of course! Now that's sensitive information, that right there. I'll be sure to haggle for a lower price the next time I make my purchase. We'll be on our way now. We're meant to bring the girls back to their fathers with fat bags of mushrooms by nightfall. Farewell!'

The old man raised his hat again and trotted off on his horse. The smell of tobacco from his pipe hung heavy in the air. Eliza was surprised at how easy it was to pretend to be someone else. No one would question you if you had the right type of story.

They passed by several humans along the way. At first, they stopped to chat about the pumpkin harvest or complain about the fey who were allegedly stealing small portions of the yield, small enough that the farmers couldn't quite tell if they'd miscounted or the theft was real. As the clouds grew denser and darker, whips of lightning began to strike the sky. Rumbling thunder made Eliza's heart pace faster. The humans they met thereafter all seemed to be in a hurry to return to their homes and barely paused to tip their hat to the party.

Torrential rain began to pelt down from the sky. Eliza had never experienced anything like this. The drops were fat, cold, and heavy. They felt like daggers descending from the sky. She wrapped her cloak as tightly as she could around her.

'We'll walk deep into the woods and cast an enchantment on a thick canopy so that it protects us from the rain. Come on girls, let's go!'

They walked as fast as they could, but the wind had turned into a vicious force that pushed back against them. Eliza strained to move forward. Up above, the trees swung wildly in the shower, branches snapping off like twigs and dropping to the ground in dull thuds that were drowned by the wind. Eliza was soaked to the bone, shivering, and on the verge of tears. The sky was almost black, raging on the brittle earth, and showed no signs of letting up. They arrived at a cluster of trees whose branches were straining against the gale. Tierza lifted her hands to the sky and whispered under her breath. Eliza could see her mouth moving, but the sound barely made a dent in the wind. Tierza looked up, her expression bewildered, and shook her head. She closed her eyes and lifted her palms again. When she opened them, she appeared frustrated. Lillian joined her palms with Tierza's, and the two women combined their powers to cast the enchantment.

Eliza's teeth chattered, and she wrapped her arms around herself to steady her shaking body. She sensed some movement up above and looked up just in time to see a tall fir tree shudder in the gale, crack in the middle, and tumble to the ground.

For a second, Eliza was frozen, staring at the leafy head of the tree as it fell straight towards her. And then her body sent out commands without her notice, and her feet took a few backward steps and gave the falling giant a wide berth. The tree looked utterly defeated, planted facedown in the mud, its branches splayed haphazardly around it. The lament from her dream the night before came back to her loudly despite the roar of the rain. Eliza looked around to see if anyone else could hear it, but they gave no signs to suggest so. The rain came down in curtains, and the other firs and pines quaked with the wind.

'Oh my word!' Lillian exclaimed. After ensuring that Eliza was unscathed, she muttered with a quiver in her voice, 'there is something unnatural about this storm. Even the trees appear to be puzzled by it. They gave us no warning before such a devastating crash.'

'And now the enchantment refuses to take hold.' Tierza cried. 'It is not wise to head into the forest any longer. If mighty trees are falling, we might not find safe passage through there. No, we must do the unthinkable. We must seek shelter in Augrives until the storm passes!'

Chapter Eight

The human town

The girls sped back the way they had come. Because of the pushback from the wind, they had barely covered any ground into the forest and were able to be at the entrance to the town in no time. Even in the rain, the town looked incredible to Eliza. A muddied path stretched out in front of them, with houses on each side. Each wooden cottage had a large garden, a porch, and some bushes growing around the edges. Curious faces came to the windows to check who was entering the town in the middle of such a dangerous gale. They walked past the red and blue doors of the quaint homes and made their way to the centre of the town. The houses grew more elegant here, taller in their build, with grand staircases leading up to their doors.

A large tavern stood smack in the middle of the town square, an old barn that had found a new life when one of the more enterprising young men had decided to take over. They opened the heavy wooden doors and shuttled in. A wooden bar counter stood by the back wall. A wrinkled gentleman with a mop of curly hair served bubbly beers to the other men. A fire crackled merrily in the fireplace in the corner. There were no women in the tavern, only a dozen men, their hands hard and browned from tilling the land and their eyes red and unfocused from the drink. Every pair of eyes was now pointed to them. Eliza felt her stomach collapse onto itself. What good could come from such potent scrutiny?

'Please good sirs, we apologise for our sudden intrusion into your establishment,' said Lillian, whose pleasant manner lent itself more naturally to the role of a schoolmistress. 'We're over from Otterdale and were picking mushrooms when this ghastly storm blew in. The girls are cold and tired, and we'd like to seek shelter here until the sky clears, if you'd be so kind.'

'If you were picking mushrooms, where are yer bags of mushrooms then?' asked one of the men, his eyes darting from one pair of empty hands to another.

'Leave them alone, Wald; they must have dropped them in the rain. A fat lot of good wet mushrooms will do to you! Barkeep, what do you say?' spoke another man, his bushy beard trembling with every word he uttered.

'Anyone with a coin to spend is welcome in my establishment. Rain or shine, man or woman, that's me only rule,' said the barkeep, wiping empty glasses with a rag that looked dirtier than whatever was in the glasses.

Lillian ordered pots of tea, fluffy bread, and hard cheese for the party. The gentlemen by the fire cleared the area for them so that the young girls could dry their soaked clothing in the warmth. With her palms cupped around a tumbler of hot milky tea, Eliza was seconds away from falling asleep.

There was one large window on the other side of the tavern. Through it, a rectangular patch of the landscape was revealed, caught in the fury of the downpour. Eliza could make out a row of shops around a town square, all locked and bolted due to the rain. She could see pastures in the distance, dotted by little white sheep and cows. So this was what a human town looked like. She wondered if it had a castle with a surrounding moat, a garden full of flowering bushes and bumble bees, a bakery where the townspeople queued up and quarrelled so they could get their hands on the freshest loaf. Hugo had told her this much about human towns. She could picture him in a place like this, especially now that she recognised that acrid scent on his breath to be that of beer. What would he say if she told him that she had set foot in a tavern!

When the bread and cheese were placed in front of them, she had to apply great strength to stop herself from tearing at them like a wolf. Lillian and Tierza kept up a contrived conversation between themselves and the girls, referring to matters such as the harvest, the declining state of Otterdale's gentry, and the dresses they planned to wear to the Yule dance. None of these things were comprehensible to Eliza, but she nodded along, oohing and aahing whenever Aoife or Nala would. Amelie sat next to her, picking at her long golden braid until it was open. Her hair fell free like a curtain of sunshine around her, and Eliza had the strangest urge to touch it. From the way some of the farmers had begun to stare, Eliza wasn't the only one taken by Amelie's beauty. Either oblivious or unfazed, Amelie ran her fingers through her hair to tease out the tangles. When she was satisfied, she twisted the length of her hair to squeeze out the water that still clung to it and then fasted it into a braid again. Eliza touched her own dark hair, matted and damp and stuck to the sides of her face. She munched on the cheese absent-mindedly, wondering if she had what it took to produce such a rare effect on others.

She excused herself from the table and asked the barkeep where she could go to relieve herself. He pointed to a short back door and said to walk down the passage and then enter the door on the right. Eliza pushed the door back with a slight grunt, it was heavier than it looked! She had to duck to enter the cavity and walk along the stone corridor uneasily. Being in a dark and narrow place reminded her of the tunnel she had walked through to take her first step into freedom. Walking through yet another one gave her the feeling of returning to the tower, marching back into the arms of incarceration. So dizzy she was when she arrived at the end of the short passage that she entered the door on the right instead of the left!

The door opened into a sitting room with a set of armchairs and a plushy couch pointed in the direction of the fireplace. There was no one there, but a bowl of apples stood unattended on the low table in the middle. Paintings of birds with red crests and blue throats and vibrant plumages hung from the walls. There was even a charcoal sketch of a little boy sitting on a horse. Eliza's fingers itched to get her hands on charcoal so she could sketch her dreams again. She took a few tentative steps into the sitting room, searching for someone who could point her in the direction of the toilet. She walked to the other side of the room, where a huge window displayed a lush field where four horses stood, their manes and tails flying like flags in the wind. They dipped their heads into a deep wooden trough and munched noisily. A tall brown stallion with white socks and a star on his forehead looked straight at Eliza, locking eyes as though he recognised her from somewhere. Eliza touched the window pane with her fingers, wishing she could run her fingers along the length of the horse's features and see for herself if his fur was as soft as she had dreamed it to be.

By now, Eliza had realised that she had taken a wrong turn into the house of the tavern's owner by mistake. But her curiosity stopped her from turning back. She heard the sound of voices from inside the house and took a few quiet steps on the carpeted floor in that direction. A closed door stood in between her and the voices. She sank to her knees to peer in through the keyhole. A man and a woman sat at a table on either end. A young boy sat between them, the same one she recognised from the charcoal sketch in the sitting room, except he wasn't as chubby or child-like anymore but a few years older. The table was full of more food than Eliza could imagine. Loaves of bread, yellow butter, a board laden with cured meats, a jar of pickles, tubs of cream, slabs of cheese, roasted vegetables in a metal tray, a gravy boat full of thick brown sauce, a pie with a crisscrossing pattern on the top. Although she had just stuffed herself with bread and cheese, Eliza half-wished she could tumble through the door and join them at the table.

She watched as they chatted easily about this and that. The young boy told his parents about the fish he'd caught with his friends the day before. He stretched his hands wide to show how big the fish was.

'Are we to believe your stories, little lad, without seeing this big fish of yours?' his mother said, spreading a thick layer of butter on a slice of bread.

'I let Jo have it. His Pa's out of work so I thought he'd benefit from it.'

'Good lad, now there's the human spirit that is famed across the land. The spirit of generosity and sharing. Well done, son, well done.'

Eliza felt a lump in her throat arise. For years, she had longed to prove that she possessed the human spirit. She had spent hours each day trying to locate it within herself without quite understanding what it was. Hugo, staunchly Bardorian in his constitution, believed the human spirit lay in innovation. Augrives, the seat of the old kingdom, had thrown up this character who believed that the human spirit was marked by generosity and kindness. It was evident to Eliza that there was no specific characteristic that underscored the human spirit other than the fact that it was a human who possessed it. No matter how hard she had tried, this was something she could never have accomplished.

And yet, seeing this human family eat a meal together pulled at her heartstrings. The mother reached out and brushed crumbs off the sleeve of her son's coat. The father patted his wife's hand affectionately. Eliza looked at the scene with longing eyes, wishing she could swap places with this boy for just a day. She couldn't even imagine what it would be like to sit with a family, a Ma and a Pa who would ask after your day, load your plate with hot food, eat meals together and jest all the way. Over the years, she had cultivated a habit of not letting her mind wander to her parents. Who were they? And why had they left her in a tower? Had they wanted to abandon her, or had they failed to protect her? Were they alive somewhere, pining for her? Or were they dead and gone, eternally a mystery to her?

Hugo would never answer any of her questions about her parentage. He only said that his own Ma was a cold woman and his own Pa used to beat both him and her and that sometimes, people were better off without their parents. He had told her she was lucky she would never be disappointed by the shortcomings of her Ma and Pa. 'The hardest thing in the world is to come to an age where you see that your parents aren't heroes, but just ordinary, flawed humans with as much bad in them as good. You're lucky you never have to go through such upheaval, Eliza; I've spent me life feeling indebted to people who were no good to me.'

And Eliza had believed him. She had believed that parents were a mixed bag and that she was better off without living through the feeling of being disappointed again and again by the very people who had left her behind. But now, as she watched the mother cut an extra large slice of pie for her son despite his protests, she knew she would have accepted a million daily disappointments for the chance to be looked after and cared for like this.

The man stood up, having heard a knock at the back door. Eliza watched him get up, open the door, exchange greetings with someone, and return to the table with an envelope. When his back was turned, she noticed the insignia on his cloak and recognised him to be the first man they had met in the morning, the man with the pipe and the horse.

'Good news, Mary. The search party has been informed and will be here soon,' he said, dropping the opened letter from the envelope on the table.

'Oh, John, are you sure it's worth their trouble? You know how mean those Bardorian soldiers can be. If they think you've sent them off on a wild goose chase, they'll steal our horses in the dead of night.'

'I'm fairly certain, as certain as one can be. I asked them about the late Lord Cannaby, and I'll tell you - they had no inkling that he was long dead. The whole town of Otterdale was present at his funeral; there's no plausible way that the schoolmistresses wouldn't know of his death. And mushroom picking so far away from town doesn't add up, does it, Mary? I'm inclined to believe that these are the escapees from Bardoria.'

'And what if they're not, John? What if they really are schoolmistresses and young girls, and you've set the worst soldiers in all of Elatonia on their tracks?'

'If they've got nothing to hide, they'll be free to go, won't they? It's easy enough to prove whether or not you're a schoolmistress from Otterdale. And imagine if they are the escapees, just imagine that! There's a reward of a whole bag of gold coins promised in exchange for any useful information pertaining to their capture. We could put a new roof in the tavern, send Billy on a fishing trip with the other lads, and get you a new gown for the Yule dance. You'd like that, won't you, Mary?'

'What does the letter say?' Mary asked, suitably appeased at the thought of a new gown and perhaps some jewels to match with it.

'It says the soldiers have been informed, and they've changed course. They'll be here by late afternoon, I reckon. With the troops on horses and the whisperlings on foot, they'll catch up to them in no time!'

Eliza had to hold her palm over her mouth to stop herself from gasping. She got back up and hurried out of the house, her heart pounding in her chest like a hammer on a stubborn nail. In her rush, she knocked over a lamp in the sitting room. It fell to the floor with a resounding crash. Her breath stopped for a second. She was sure the family would hear it and chase after her. Once they entered the tavern, they would see the escapees they had apprehended dining right there, waiting for their capture like sitting ducks. She flung the door open and ran into the cold stone corridor. Shivering, she made her way back to where the others sat and made a beeline for Tierza.

'You've been gone a long time,' she said crossly.

In a shaky voice, Eliza told her everything. 'We have no time to spare. The family will be out any minute now. If they see us, they'll never let us go!'

Tierza nodded, pulled a few coins out from her purse, and went to the barkeep. 'We'll have to take off now,' she said. 'The rain might not stop for hours, and we've to get the girls back home by nightfall. We thank you for your hospitality.'

The barkeep, busy counting the coins, cared little whether they stayed or left. The girls hurried out through the doors and back out into the rain. The cold drops felt especially painful on their skin, which had become used to the warmth of the fire. Just as the door closed behind them, they heard a commotion in the tavern and snatches of statements that contained the words, young girls, escapees, reward.

'Run for the forest, daughters,' Tierza said, pulling her sword out from its holster, hidden behind her tunic. The blade reflected the grey clouds as well as Tierza's stern face. 'Lillian, you go with them. Riani, Kiani and I are match enough for a whole human town. We'll find you later.'

Without questioning her judgment, the daughters dug their heels into the wet earth and ran out of town and into the forest. Behind them, they heard the sounds of blades slashing through the air and loud groans. Within seconds, the rain drowned out everything, and all Eliza could hear was the sound of her own heart caught in her throat.

Chapter Nine

The shrunken party

The winter daughters and Lillian ran as fast as their feet could carry them. Once they reached the forest, Eliza began to breathe more easily. Although the rain had started to slow down comparably, it was still a heavy onslaught by usual standards. Their semi-dry clothes had turned to wet rags in seconds. The shrunken party forged into the heart of the forest, praying that they would be safer there than anywhere else. They didn't stop for a second until they had run deep into the woods. By then, all the girls had heard tidbits of what had happened, and Eliza could swear they all looked at her with accusing eyes. She knew it had been awfully clumsy of her to knock the lamp over. If she hadn't, the family would never have known that the escapees were under their very roof, and they would have made their way into the forest with the whole party without leaving anyone behind.

Thoughts of the very worst nature made Eliza's forehead wrinkle. What if Tierza, Riani or Kiani did not return? What if any of them was harmed in the fight against the family? What if they were captured? What if they never found their way back to the party? A heavy weight descended on Eliza's shoulders because she knew that it would be entirely her fault if any of these outcomes came to pass.

Lillian discussed the plan with them. 'We'll keep marching to Teragovia. We'll have to be twice as careful now that the Bardorian soldiers know we're in this neck of the woods. Tierza and the others will catch up to us in no time; we needn't worry about them.' Eliza thought the last sentence sounded unconvincing, but she said nothing, desiring little but to make herself as scarce as possible.

They walked on, the mood heavy and dismal. None of the daughters chatted to each other. Other than the sound of the rain crashing onto leaves, there was nothing else to be heard. And then that started to ebb, and the day turned to a dewey dusk, and still, there was little they could say to one another. The memory of the fire and the hot tea felt impossibly far away. When they built a camp for the night, they did so without their usual gusto. They buried themselves into the burrows, their sleep wafer-thin, the slightest sound giving them the hope that the missing members of their party had returned. Eliza sat by a tree, tears streaming down her face. She wished she hadn't let her own selfish desires make her linger outside the kitchen; she wished she could take it all back.

The morning brought with it a remarkably bright sky. The blue was almost electric, stretched like a freshly washed sheet without a cloud in the sky to stain its radiance. The sun was a pale yellow, beating down gently through the canopy, offering yet another day without expecting anything in return. And yet, the sense of loss hung so heavy in the air that not a soul took much pleasure in the sun's warmth.

When they cooked their morning porridge, Eliza was sure that everyone was being a bit colder to her than usual. Aoife didn't smile at her; even Nala had nothing to say to her. Eliza had been so consumed by her guilt and shame that she hadn't noticed that Amelie's manner had grown much more irritable since they had left Tierza behind. She was hard on Eliza, scorning at how long it took her to scatter the heather and annoyed that she never seemed to wake up without her aid. Eliza wasn't sure if this change in her behaviour was because she missed Tierza or whether she too, like everybody else, blamed Eliza for the state of affairs.

With Lillian being the only one overseeing their return to Teragovia, her usual pleasant manner was tinged with a hard edge. Amelie, the natural successor, took some of the weight off Lillian's shoulders. She was the only one who had grown up in these woods; she knew them like the back of her hand. She knew what every ring of moss revealed about the wind, she knew what every toadstool told about the pond, and without even looking at the sun, moon, or stars, she always knew where to find true north. Eliza was impressed at her ability to navigate through the woods. She never seemed to hesitate at forks in the path and always knew whether they should wade through a bog or go around it. Eliza understood then that Amelie's haughtiness was well earned. She hadn't carved up any illusions about her superiority - she was, in fact superior to them in almost every regard.

The Whispering Woods were different to the ones they had walked through in Bardoria. Although many of the trees shed their leaves here too, an equal proportion of them held on to their evergreen branches. The sun filtered through these leaves in cones of light and revealed small ponds of water between rocks. Frogs croaked, butterflies flew from flower to flower, and the air smelled lush and fertile, as though life was burgeoning in every corner. Eliza felt almost intoxicated, her head light and her fingers tingling whenever she touched the smooth pebbles or dangling ferns with the tips of her fingers. From the corner of her eye, Eliza was sure she could see movements in the bushes. She stayed alert in case they were Bardorian soldiers, but each time she turned her head, the movements halted, and she was left staring at a berry bush, certain that the fears that wrapped her mind into knots were at it again. And even though she knew it was all in her head, the sound of mocking laughter continued to haunt her, holding her back from enjoying the sunniest day she had ever seen.

When they stopped for rest, the winter daughters drank from a pond, letting the cool water flow down their parched throats. Eliza wandered off, wanting to be alone for a second, away from the hostile atmosphere where no one would catch her eye. She sat within earshot under a tree with low hanging branches. It bore a fruit she had never seen before, something orange and soft. She twisted it off its stem and inhaled its sweet fragrance. Debating whether or not she should eat it, she bounced it from one hand to another. She was so focused on her task that she did not even notice when a sleek brown creature walked up to her. It stopped a few paces in front of her and stared at her with brown eyes. Eliza's eyes widened. It was a spotted deer! She had dreamed of these creatures before. Its mouth and nose were carved delicately against its lithe frame. Eliza saw that its eyes were fixed on the fruit in her hand. She held it out, and the deer took one timid step towards her and then another.

'Come on now, I won't hurt you,' Eliza softly said. The deer understood and walked even closer, stopping just one step away. She waved the fruit from side to side. Tempted by this sweet fruit, the deer succumbed to the offer and took the fruit right out of her hand. 'You're my only friend in this world right now. Everyone else dislikes me. I don't blame them. I think I dislike myself too.'

The deer nuzzled against her palm, and Eliza tugged gently on its floppy ears. She ran her hands all over its spotted fur, and the deer walked closer, resting its head on her neck. They stayed like that for a few seconds, locked in an embrace that Eliza did not realise was extraordinary. And then Amelie's voice called her name from the other side of the bushes, and the sound of her treading through the understory frightened the skittish deer, who bolted out of sight before Eliza could even lift her head.

'Where have you been? We need to set off,' Amelie said curtly, poking her head from the bushes.

'I found a fruit tree. Are these any good?' she asked Amelie, pointing at the orange fruit.

'You didn't eat that, did you? They're terribly poisonous; you'll be dead by dusk if one of those things finds its way to your belly.'

Eliza felt her heart sink into her boots. She dared not ask if the fruit was poisonous for a deer too, afraid that Amelie would say yes, and then everyone would know that Eliza's thoughtless actions had put yet another innocent creature in harm's way.

Wishing she could disappear into the earth, Eliza got to her feet and followed Amelie into the bushes. The rest of the day felt long, and she dreaded that every day hereafter would feel like this. At night, when they slept in the heather bedding beside each other, Amelie turned away from Eliza, and they slept like sickles with their backs to each other. The open sky had brought in draughts of cold, and Eliza shivered her insides as cold and raw as she felt on the outside. She found herself wishing she could exchange spots with Tierza and the others. She knew they were more valuable to the mission than Eliza could ever dream of being. She knew in her heart that she was not the Midnight Daughter. She was just an ordinary girl whose entire life had been thrown into disarray because she had been birthed at the brink of winter.

Chapter Ten

An unexpected proposal

For three days, Lillian and Amelie guided the winter daughters through the woods. Without Riani and Kiani's watchful eyes, the forest seemed scarier, each rustle in the bushes implying danger close at hand. Although the Whispering Woods were friendlier and let in more sunlight, traveling with the shrunken party made them feel more desolate than the misty forest of Bardoria.

The deeper they walked into the woods, the more Eliza had the sensation of floating above her body. It was as though her spirit could not stay tethered to her limbs and threatened to evaporate into the shafts of light that poured in from the gaps in the trees. Increasingly, her head felt light, and her fingertips would buzz with some kind of charge. She did not know if this was merely a product of her moon cycle or something else. She wished she could speak to someone about it, but Amelie had retreated into a shell since Tierza's disappearance and no longer seemed to have the patience for Eliza's questions. She went back to her previous disposition, where she treated Eliza like a necessary liability and nothing more.

At night, after they made their bedding, Amelie would go to sleep right away, turning her face away from Eliza.

After everyone else had slept, Eliza often sat by the embers of the faded fire, watching the glowing coals fade into the darkness. She found that if she sat very still and slowed her breathing, the creatures of the night would come to her. Crickets sat on her fingers, gazing curiously at her as they chirped. Moths fluttered up to her nose, their powdery wings brushing her rosy cheeks before they moved on in search of the light. Once, while the embers still exuded some brightness, Eliza saw the shadows of a blunt reddish-brown snout poking through the bushes. She lifted her hands out the way she had done for the deer, but the fox was even shyer than the fawn. It only tilted its head in response to her gesture, appearing to neither distrust Eliza enough to run away nor trust her enough to come any closer.

On those long sleepless nights, Eliza watched the moon shapeshift whenever it greeted her from behind the clouds. It was waning steadily, as though someone with a hammer and chisel scraped a layer off each night. Pale and cratered, it glowed so brightly that Eliza couldn't look at it for too long. She found its glare even harder to withstand than that of the sun.

By then, Eliza had adapted to the ways of the woods. She rarely had cuts and scratches on her hands and rarely fell into the burrows of underground creatures. Although she still half-expected to see Tierza, Riani, and Kiani around every bend, Eliza had accepted the heavy tension that hung in the air as best she could and knew that her prayers would not be answered. 'Seven more days and seven more nights,' she told herself through gritted teeth as she tapped a spiky branch before clasping her fingers around the blunt stem. 'And then we'll be in Teragovia, and I will be able to separate from this party who rightly accuses me for our state of peril!'

She had all but forgotten about the mythstones that Tierza had mentioned on the day that she had freed Eliza. When they were three days away from Teragovia, Lillian announced that it was time to consult the mythstones. The space between the trees had tightened in that neck of the woods as though they were protecting something beyond their branches.

'Teragovia is the city of the free folk, the city where moonbloods from all over Elatonia are guaranteed safe refuge. It is where all the winter daughters will be groomed for their destiny. Such a city must be deeply concealed from the human eye. Since we do not believe in permanent enchantments that drain the life force of the trees, Teragovia is hidden by more ingenious means. Each moon cycle, the entrances to Teragovia change so that the site of the enchantment is shifted from one part of the woods to another. The Council of Elders does not have a say in which spot becomes the next entrance. Since the magic is lent to us by the trees, they alone decide. You might emerge in the Oracle's lair one time or through the trapdoor of the baker's storehouse the next! There are several such entrances that are hidden through the woods, smaller ones like these and larger ones for horses and wagons to pass through.'

Eliza gasped, something inside her opening up like a reluctant flower at the start of spring. She hoped that things would be different in Teragovia, that they would arrive and find that Tierza, Riani, and Kiani had beaten them to the city and would simply laugh it off when the winter daughters said how worried they had been. Eliza let the warmth of that hope wrap its arms around her.

'Do you see that over there?' Lillian pointed to an amber coloured rock, its texture that of dried honey. 'This will guide the way.'

The rock was as tall as Eliza's hips and covered in vines and leaves. Lillian knelt beside it and started to rub the dirt off of its surface until it began to glow from the warmth of her palms. A light appeared on the inside of the rock, illuminating its face wherever Lillian rubbed it. As the light grew brighter, symbols began to dance on the surface. Trees, fens, caves, wolf lairs scattered across the flickering brown rock. Like a serpent, a narrow path began to slither into existence from one corner. Lillian focused the full intensity of her gaze on it, drinking in the details of every turn and every resting place. The map stayed lit up for a few seconds and then began to fade as gently as it had come.

'That is a mythstone, winter daughters—a special kind of mythstone used for navigation alone. The trees transfer the directions to the entrance to Teragovia onto the mythstones that surround the invisible city walls. Only whisperer blood can tease the answer out of the mythstone. And that is how the city of Teragovia remains protected from prying eyes.'

Every time Eliza witnessed a display of whisperer magic, something trilled inside her like a songbird. She had no idea where her powers began or ended or even what she could do with them, but if it meant that someday, she would be able to do half of what Lillian and Tierza routinely pulled off, it was something to be optimistic about. This time too, she felt a sense of awe push past her dread and lodge itself firmly into her heart.

For the rest of the day's march, Eliza felt impervious to the uncomfortable silences and Amelie's cold shoulder. She pictured herself in Teragovia, anonymously fading into the city of free folk. This was the fresh start she needed; this was how she could truly leave the events of this week behind. She pocketed berries and popped them into her mouth gaily, stroking the waxy leaves of passing shrubs affectionately, and even smiled when her foot slid into a marshy puddle, and she got soaked with muddy water to her knee.

As usual, Eliza sat by the fire when the others went to sleep. She walked around the campsite, swaying lightly on her feet, finally free to express her joy without anyone there to scorn her for it. As she pirouetted and leaped around with her tunic swishing around her thighs, she almost stepped onto a fluffy little ball under a tree. Stopping just in time, she dropped to her knees to get a closer look at it. Beady black eyes peered at her through the soft cottony fluff, and a weak hoot escaped from a pinched yellow beak.

'Oh no, little one, have you fallen out of your nest?' Eliza murmured to it. The baby owl hooted back, trying to flap its wings to get off the ground. It barely hovered an inch above the bed of leaves it had fallen onto before it collapsed again. Eliza gathered the tiny creature in her palms and stroked it gently. She rubbed her nose against its downy body, and the bird seemed to nuzzle back up to her. She looked around at the nearby trees, scanning the branches for signs of a nest. On a thick oak tree, she saw a small cluster of twigs peeking through the branches. It was twice her height overhead. The tree's trunk was mostly smooth, with the occasional groove sticking out. Eliza looked down at the baby owl in her hands and back up at the nest. Ever since she had nearly fallen to her death on that rock face in Bardoria, the thought of scaling even the most modest of heights gave her the chills. The baby owl hooted and tried to flap its wings again.

Eliza swallowed, placed the baby bird safely in her pocket, and looked at the tree that sprawled away into the inky darkness. She stroked the tree trunk with her hands and begged it not to fling her down. There was no one to save her this time. Eliza lifted herself up into the tree, using the grooves as footholds. Their texture was rough, making it easier to hold onto them and climb up. She felt supported by an unseen force as she made her way up, as though the wind had curled itself behind her like a cushion, buoying her midair as she moved up the length of the tree. When she saw the nest at eye level, she perched herself in the V-shape where two branches conjoined. On her hands and knees, she made her way across the thick branch, careful to shift her weight gradually to avoid quaking the nest. Half a dozen baby owls with grey and white feathers cheeped from the nest. Their yellow beaks glistened in the moonlight. Eliza stroked the baby owl one last time and returned it to its nest, where it began to hoot loudly as if to tell all of its siblings about its adventures and caution them not to fly until they were sure they could make it!

Eliza backed away from the scene slowly and sat back in the curve of the V, her arms wrapped around one of the branches. This was what the campsite looked like to birds! The embers had all but gone out, and a chill was present in the wind. A smooth whoosh of wings cut through the air next to her. The mother owl had returned! She greeted her babies with food and pecked at them lovingly. She singled out the one that Eliza had rescued and then pecked at it with a greater sense of aggression. Her heart seemed to stop beating. The mother continued to peck at it and suddenly turned her gaze to Eliza sharply. They locked eyes for a few long moments, and Eliza tried to convey that she had done no harm; she had only picked the bird off the ground and put it back in its home. Eventually, the mother owl broke eye contact and looked at her ruffled offspring, and nudged it back into the nest with her beak. Eliza sighed with relief.

'It's rare for a mother bird to accept her young once it has been sullied by the hand of another,' came a voice from behind her.

Eliza turned with a start. A girl and a boy sat higher up in the tree. They had bright green eyes, high cheekbones, and wavy dark hair. Their edges seemed misty, dissolving into the night without any warning. She wasn't sure if she was awake in the middle of one of her outrageous dreams again.

'Who are you? Are you humans? Or whisperers?' Eliza asked, drawing her body back.

'Neither, whisperling. Do not insult us so, not when you're in the woods we have called home since the beginning of time!' said the female, her laughter cutting through the air like an arrogant breeze. It reminded Eliza of something she had heard before, but she couldn't quite put her finger on it.

'The fey of the forest! Oh, I've heard so much about you!'

'Terrible things, I'm sure,' said the male, idly tearing strips of bark from the tree.

Eliza said nothing.

'We've been watching you, little girl. We know everything about you!' said the female. 'We know you cry at night all alone by the fire, and we know you want to be a human and have your own pony, little girl.'

'Don't call me a little girl!' Eliza said. And then it dawned on her! 'Wait a minute! I recognise your voice. I've heard the sound of your laughter ever since I entered the woods in Bardoria. Why have you been following me?'

'We haven't been following you, little girl. We've only kept our eyes and ears open. You're the one who keeps coming to us.'

'No I don't! I don't even know what you're talking about!'

By this point, the boy had twisted the bark into the rope of a necklace. Without looking up, he said, 'you're not happy with your new friends. They're not really your friends, are they? No one knows how lonely you feel; no one knows how frightened you are. You think they see you as a burden...but the truth, little girl, is that they don't think of you at all.'

'That's a horrid thing to say!'

'Ah yes, you'll see, the truth rarely has any nectar in it,' the female said, flipping back her hair. Eliza noticed that the tunics they wore were made of a coarser material, not cotton but twisted bark woven together. Dried flowers and shiny stones hung from their necks, and their hair shone impossibly bright, reflecting light back like a mirror.

'Why are you talking to me now?' she asked, uncertain what she had done to be picked on like this by the fey of the forest.

'Little girl, you know you don't belong with the others, don't you? You're not like them. You're softer and more curious, and you like to play. You know, you could frolic in nature for the rest of your life.

'What do you mean?'

'You're off to Teragovia because you think the city of the free folk will give you what you need. But it will not, little girl because the city of whisperers only takes and takes. They treat you with some importance now because you might turn out to be the Midnight Daughter, but what happens when they find out that you are not? You will be discarded or made to serve the Midnight Daughter. We have looked into your destiny, and it will not do you well to ally so closely with the whisperers of Teragovia!'

'And who do you think I should ally with?' Eliza said impatiently, trying to create a mental shield so that the cruelly chosen words of the fey folk could not sting her. Why did she keep finding herself in these situations? Could she trust anyone at all?

'Only yourself, little girl. The fey abide by the laws of the forest. We are guardians and farmers, and medicine folk. We spend our days with animals and trees and water springs. We see that you share our gift. We see the way creatures come up to you and treat you like you are forest-born rather than moonblooded. Do you not wonder why?'

Eliza honestly had never questioned this until now. She had not known that her connection to the creatures revealed anything out of the ordinary. She looked back to the mother owl, who didn't seem bothered by the presence of the three bipeds on the branches and was busy with her chicks. Would she have been on guard if Esther or Nala were up here?

'Why?'

'Because you belong to the forest. And the forest belongs to you. The sooner you accept that, the easier it will be for you. You have no friends but the woods. Everyone else will betray you or leave you. Never the woods, never the trees.'

Eliza shook her head. 'I'm tired of people telling me I can't trust anybody. I'm tired of people coming to rescue me from threats. I don't want to be the Midnight Daughter! I just want to be left alone!'

'You will be left alone if you choose to retreat into the forest. Just say the word, and we'll hide you little girl. We'll take you away from the jeering eyes of those that blame you for their predicament. You can spend your days as we do, owning up to your true nature with the birds and the bees!'

Her stomach curled into a sticky mess as the weight of each word sank in. Was it that obvious that she didn't fit in? Were her skills so abysmal that it was evident to any onlooker that she was most certainly not the Midnight Daughter? Was she incapable of living up to any responsibility, destined for a life of play in the woods with strange creatures? Even as these thoughts bogged her down, another weight was lifted. Imagine that; imagine if she was free, truly free to do as she pleased. Suppose she could live in the woods without having to live up to any prophecy or be groomed for a grand destiny. If she could make friends with birds that would never blame her if she could feed the deer all day - oh what a life that would be!

'Think it over. We'll be around when you make up your mind. Just call out to us, and we'll appear,' said the male. He attached a dried flower to the centre of the bark necklace and held it out to her. 'Hold onto it. Consider it a gift from the fey of the forest.'

Before Eliza could conjure a response or even blink, the two of them had disappeared. She sat there, cushioned by the branches, holding the necklace in her hands, wondering if there was anything in this life that was as it seemed.

Chapter Eleven

What will Eliza do?

The next day, Eliza began to look at the forest in a different light. Instead of seeing it as a place she had to carve a path through in order to get to her destination, she began to see it as the final destination instead. She looked at the wide gaping hollows of trees and pictured what it would be like to wake up in one of those every day, feast on berries and roots all day, bound with the deer, win the trust of the foxes and fall asleep after dancing with moths under the moonlight. She didn't need whisperlings for companionship, did she? She had gone her whole life with only Hugo for company; she knew she would be just fine even if she went days without speaking to another person. Perhaps she could learn to be as stealthy as the fey, learn to keep a medicine garden from them, become privy to all the secrets of the woods.

It seemed idyllic and easy, but when Eliza looked around at the faces of the other winter daughters, the beads of sweat that clung to their foreheads as they marched stoically through the woods, she felt pangs of guilt in her belly. Even though she had become an outcast of late, there was something about being part of a mission that was larger than any of them that gave her a sense of belonging. If she could get back in their good books again and rekindle the familial feelings that had started to take root, perhaps she wouldn't feel so tempted to flee. After all, hadn't she craved a family more than anything her entire life? Was a life of further isolation in the woods really what she needed?

She thought of Tierza, Riani, and Kiani, somewhere far away in captivity - was their sacrifice something she could dishonor? If she escaped from this party after the lengths they had gone to in order for her to be safe, what would that say about Eliza?

Such was the muddled nature of her thoughts as she trudged along. At the rest stop, they stopped at a freshwater pond. The sun shone directly onto the water. As she walked up to it, she could see the rocky floor that held the water in place. It gushed through the pond and gurgled out of a bottleneck of boulders, where it trickled into a stream that disappeared into the understory. She crouched at the bank to wash her face, stained with mud and sweat. She almost jumped back with a start. She had never seen her own face reflected back so clearly at her. She had caught glimpses in stained windows and the surface of murky waters before, but nothing matched the clarity of the mirror-like water body.

'So this is what my face looks like,' she said to herself, taking in her small nose, large brown eyes, wavy hair, and high cheekbones. Her skin was browned from spending days marching in the sun, and a smattering of freckles had appeared. She turned her face from side to side and mimed talking to see what she might look like to other people. The experience was strange; it was hard to reconcile the person she knew herself to be with the disembodied face looking back up at her through the water. She had the passing thought that her features were fey-like. The oddity of it wasn't lost on Eliza - she was a whisperling who looked like the fey and had believed herself to be human all her life.

As night approached, Eliza felt a gnawing anxiety in the pit of her stomach. What if the fey turned up again? She had no idea what she would say to them, what she would choose. She tried to finish her bowl of stew by the fire, but her stomach resisted the sustenance, too busy coiling itself into nervous knots. The next day would be their final march, the last stretch before they made it to Teragovia, and the sense of anticipation was pertinent. The winter daughters chatted over dinner, brought together by the knowledge that their destiny was a shared one. They were all putting one foot in front of the other to walk into a city where their promised freedom would be brought to life. Eliza tried to partake in the sense of excitement that had started to buzz as the daughters began to share tidbits about what they had heard about Teragovia from Tierza and Lillian.

'I've heard that there is a statue made of solid gold in the center!' said Maud.

'Did you know that seven rivers flow through the city, and each of them is a different color!' said Nala.

'The biggest building in the city is the library. Not a manor or a palace but a library because of Teragovia's commitment to learning!' said Seena.

Could she really hold herself back from witnessing this fabled city? Eliza knew that she would never be able to find the entrance to Teragovia on her own. This was her one and only chance to see it for herself. Perhaps, if she didn't like it there, she could run away and find the fey again. Right as she had that thought, she heard the mocking laughter dissipating into the wind from somewhere behind her. She knew this was no coincidence. The fey seemed to have access to her thoughts before she had had the time to register their presence. And she knew that the laughter meant that this was her one chance to escape, and the fey would not be there to guide her if she tried to come back to them from Teragovia. She thought of the baby owl and how mother birds were known to shun their young when they had been sullied by the touch of another. Once they had the strong scent of another creature on them, they were easier to hunt. If they spread the scent to their siblings, the entire nest was doomed. She wondered why the fey had given her one chance only; perhaps they thought she would bring them doom if she returned with the scent of Teragovia on her once she had been sullied by the whisperers' ways.

Panic began to stab her insides as she pushed the stew around with her spoon. The fire crackled as the bubbles of water in the wood spat and hissed, and the glow lit up several cheerful faces. The winter daughters continued to discuss the city's marvels while Eliza struggled with the choice that lay ahead of her. She wasn't the only one silent. Amelie shoveled spoon after spoon of stew into her mouth, barely gave herself the time to chew it then disappeared into the trees before the others had even made a dent. Instinctively, Eliza left her half-eaten bowl by the fire and followed her.

'Amelie!' she cried out after her.

'What do you want, Eliza?' Amelie said, standing with her arms crossed over her chest.

Eliza paused for a moment. She knew that if she did choose to flee with the fey later that night, this would be the last time she spoke to Amelie. It was unlikely that their paths would cross again. She tried to weigh the words in her mouth before she spoke. Around them, the creatures of the night made their way from one tree to another, hunting, skulking, or simply observing. The moon was veiled by a thin layer of clouds, giving them a purplish glaze. The shadows of leaves fell on Amelie's face, partially obscuring it. Her golden braid hung like a weapon down her side.

'Well, have you got something you want to say to me?' Amelie said, tapping her foot.

'I-I just wanted to say I'm sorry. For everything. I know it's my fault that Tierza and the others have separated from us, and I know being sorry doesn't change anything, but I know you and Tierza were close, and I hate to have caused you such distress.' As soon as the words were out of her, Eliza felt lighter. Simply articulating the enormity of her regret felt good. She went on speaking, starting sentences without knowing how they would end. 'I wish it was me who had stayed back in Augrives, not them. I know it's awful, but I do miss Bardoria sometimes; I miss my tower and Hugo and how simple life used to be when I didn't have my freedom. I'd have done just fine in captivity, but Tierza and Riani and Kiani must be in a world of horrors. I should never have been rescued, then none of this would have happened! I know everyone blames me, and I understand why but it's awful not to have you to speak to from time to time. I know I haven't got the right to ask anything of you, so forgive me for even saying that, but Amelie, I wish you'd know how sorry I am for all of this!'

Amelie's mouth was open in a small o. She looked at Eliza with a puzzled expression.

'Eliza, you're being awfully dramatic. Nobody blames you for this. You're the reason we were tipped off about the soldiers. If it weren't for you, we'd have been apprehended by the Bardorian search party while we drank tea in that tavern!'

'But everyone's been so cold to me!'

'Nobody's being cold to you, Eliza. Everyone is struggling with the reality of losing Tierza and Kiani and Riani. You're taking their worry as some form of resentment directed at you. You've let your mind build up a story using your worst fears and then treated it as the truth.'

'Oh,' Eliza said, shifting her weight from one foot to another.

'Maybe I haven't been my usual self, but that has more to do with me not knowing if I will ever see Tierza again. She's my only family in this world, you know? She raised me to be a younger sister to her. I don't blame you for this, but I am angry that it happened. Angry at the world for letting it happen.'

At a loss for words, Eliza nodded weakly.

'Now, will you let me go to bed? It's tiring to navigate all day. I need all the rest I can get.'

Eliza watched her walk swiftly and disappear into the fold of the trees. She went back to the fire and looked around for her bowl. Her appetite seemed to have returned.

'I've got your bowl here,' Aoife said, holding it out. 'I didn't want the ants to get to it.'

As Eliza sat back down and paid closer attention to the others, she noticed that Amelie had been right. She had been so riddled with guilt and shame that she had assumed that all of the others shared her own view of herself. She smiled at Nala, who smiled back, and once again, Eliza felt the warm glow of their companionship wrap itself around her like an embrace. She helped them clear up after dinner, and instead of waiting by the fire until it fizzled out, she went straight to bed. She crept quietly under her cloak to avoid disturbing Amelie, who looked serene with her eyes closed. Eliza turned to one side and tried to push the fey folks proposal out of her mind.

'Try not to squirm too much if you have nightmares again, Eliza. I need to rest!' Amelie's tired voice came from the other side of the bed, its hardness replaced with a twinge of mischief.

Eliza smiled, huddled into the heather, and said, 'Don't you worry, I think I might sleep very well tonight after all.'

Chapter Twelve

Arrival in Teragovia

Eliza hadn't known when she woke up in her tower that it would be her last morning there. But when she woke up before daybreak in the bed next to Amelie, the butterflies in her stomach were frantically flying into one another because she had a larger than life awareness of what was to come. Now that she had made her choice, the fey's proposal seemed absurd and distant in her memory. She was half-convinced that she had dreamed it up. It had been her fear taking over, not her genuine desire. She rose before Amelie, scattered her bedding, and walked over to the embers of the fire where Aoife sat, waiting for the sunrise.

The two winter daughters watched the sun come up together, threaded together by the taste of freedom, the dawning of fresh possibility that each new day brought. After breakfast, the party set off from their campsite one last time to make their way to the city of Teragovia. The mood had shifted, everyone was nervous, but there was an uplifting even within that nervousness because it marked the end of their gruelling journey and the start of the next phase.

The day was gloomy and brought with it strong winds from the north. The dried leaves swirled into the air and spun in little circles before shuddering to the ground again. Eliza's body was covered in goosebumps, and the holes in her tunic meant that even her bones were cold and tired, but she didn't mind. One last day of hardship and then the city of the free folk would welcome her in. Even Amelie had a skip in her step, the thought of returning home proving to be at least a temporary antidote to her grief.

The last leg of the journey took them through a fen, not the sinister bogs of Bardoria but a lush landscape wherein red and purple grass danced in the wind around the thick mud. Butterflies used the marsh as a thoroughfare, telltale signs of there being flowers blooming in secret in the woods, even in the winter months. Eliza walked in between Amelie and Nala instead of lagging behind. Lillian led the way, her gaze searching for the last symbol that the map on the mythstone had revealed to her.

'Keep an eye out for a large tree with a hollow in the shape of a crescent moon,' she had told them once they entered the fen.

Eliza kept her eyes peeled, inspecting the oblong hollows for the slightest of curvatures. She picked up a stick from the ground and tapped it on the cold tops of the stones that dotted the overgrown trail. She could tell that nervousness was bubbling underneath the surface. What if the Bardorian search party was waiting to ambush them by the crescent tree? What if the mythstone had the wrong information, and they wandered through the fen for weeks in search of something that had ceased to exist? What if they did find the tree, but the entrance had changed since they last checked the map, and they would not know any better?

However, Lady luck was smiling down upon them that day since Seena spotted the tree after only an hour of trudging through the dewy grass. An oak tree with spidery branches extending in all directions stood before them. In the very middle of it was a hollow in the shape of a crescent, almost entirely covered by the branches that hung in front of it like a fringe. The party gazed at it with slack jaws. Almost there!

They secured their knapsacks and climbed the tree. Oaks were amiable like that; their branches grew stubby protrusions everywhere and made it easy for anyone to climb over. Eliza stroked the bark of the tree before stepping onto it and called for the same courage that she had called for when she had gone to return the baby owl back to its nest. Her call was answered, and as she stepped gingerly from branch to branch, she was buoyed by the same unseen force that had kept her safe that night. The branches were thick, and sprawled all around the tree. Once each of the girls was up on a branch at eye level to the crescent hollow, Lillian told them what was to come.

'I will open the passage for you, winter daughters, and then you must climb into the hollow. There will be footholds. I will wait for each of you to enter, and then I will follow, sealing the passage once again.'

Lillian placed her palms at the base of the crescent and whispered softly. The edges of the crescent began to glow ever so slightly. Amelie entered first, with Eliza close behind. The wood of the tree was warm, almost perspiring from the opening of the passage. They climbed down the flat of the hollow and dropped into the bottom of the tree, where several roots buttressed the damp earth. Eliza bent down to touch them and jerked her hand back. Something seemed to sizzle and sputter in those roots, and it caused a shock that almost rocked her bones out of their sockets.

Once Lillian had dropped down with them and lit up the Igneous Orb, the passage was flooded with light again, and Eliza saw a well-made tunnel open up in front of them. Mouldy roots spiralled around the roof and seemed to hold the earth in place, preventing the forest from collapsing onto their heads. Eliza's curiosity got the better of her, and she touched one of the roots again to see what would happen. She had to pull her hand away again as the sizzle and shock coursed through her veins and made her entire arm tingle. The tunnel rose and dipped and curved sharply. They soldiered on for over two hours, the dank smell of the earth wafting through their nostrils. The tunnel that Eliza had taken out of the tower had opened up into the forest, a pinprick of light conveying that the journey's end was near. But this tunnel did no such thing. It rambled on and on into the uncertain darkness, making Eliza wonder yet again if they had got the whole thing wrong and the real entrance to Teragovia awaited them elsewhere. She and Amelie walked a few paces ahead of the others. Lillian was in the middle, holding the light of the Orb up in the air so that everyone could benefit from it equally.

Eliza was out of breath as she tried to match Amelie's long strides. At the same time, they both took a few steps too fast, just out of reach of the Orb's glow, and smacked their noses right into a wall.

'Owww!' cried Eliza, rubbing her nose.

'We're here!' Amelie said triumphantly.

A round of cheers echoed through the tunnel. Lillian came forward and placed her palms on the stone, and whispered spells under her breath. The stone slab lit up, strange symbols in an ancient tongue crawling like worms along the surface. And then a deep groan emanated from the underbelly of the earth, and the stone shifted to one side, opening a narrow inlet just wide enough for them to walk through in a single file.

On the other side of the opening, the path sloped upwards, and there was a door at its end. Lillian knocked on the door three times.

'Who is it?'

'Lillian, accompanied by the winter daughters, reporting back to Teragovia to announce the completion of our mission.'

The door was flung open, and a beam of bright light fell onto the girls who were huddled together like cellar rats. A heavy-set silhouette blocked the light and said in a deep baritone, 'Well, well, look whom we have here!'

'Greetings from the Woods to you, Miriam,' Lillian said, dipping her head to the figure.

'We heard from the trees that you had made it to the mythstone. And then it got static again. We were worried that the Bardorians had caught up to you!'

'Ah no, not this time.'

As they stepped out of the door, Lillian filled Miriam in on the happenings in Augrives, and she nodded steadily. Hope was extinguished right then because Miriam confirmed that the missing party had not arrived in Teragovia yet. Eliza sought the comfort of their numbers and piled into the room with the others. It was a low ceilinged affair with stone walls and simple furniture, not like the raised roof of the tavern or the old man's home. There was a fire blazing quietly in the hearth and a set of round stools scattered all around the room.

'We had ourselves a wee meeting here, me and the teachers, once we got word that you lot were on your way. Rest assured, we are all ready to look after you, winter daughters,' Miriam said, smiling brightly at them, her grey curls bouncing around her face as she nodded. 'I'm Miriam, as you might have gathered. I run the lodging and boarding house across the river where the Council has reserved your stay. You must be tired; let's get you across, come on now.'

They filed out of Miriam's house and into the bright, shimmering vista of Teragovia! Audible gasps filled the air as they saw a bright pink river running fast along the bank in front of them. The water seemed to shimmer, and salmon jumped up as they fought the current to go upstream. Sunlight glazed over the rocks, and the grass seemed to giggle as it fluttered in the wind. They walked along the river until they came to a narrow point, where a wooden bridge had been built. It arched over the thundering water that pulsed beneath them.

Eliza wondered how far the current would carry her if she were to fall in.

Almost as though she had read her mind, Miriam said, 'try not to fall in, winter daughters. The current eases up by the time the river gets to town, but the water is colder than anything you've felt before.'

Beyond the bridge was a thicket, and once they made their way through it, they arrived in the front yard of a long stone house with a generously sloping roof. There were six red doors, five of them closed. They entered through the open one and found themselves in a dining room with a banquet table. There was a fireplace and a wall full of books next to it. Thick volumes with golden lettering were piled onto shelves that went from floor to ceiling. There were two large windows at the back of the room that revealed a pond, the fading light giving it a metallic hue. Next to it was an empty patch of land where the grass had been cleared in a circle. Head-high stone slabs stood around it at intervals, giving the circle some sort of significance. Eliza couldn't see what was written very clearly, but symbols had been scratched onto the ground at the centre of the circle.

They were ushered into their rooms—two whisperlings to each room. Eliza and Amelie walked into the one in the furthest corner. It had two twin beds with paisley sheets and a large window that overlooked the thicket. There was a single shelf on which they could place their belongings and a row of hooks for their clothes. It was simple yet elegant, and Eliza looked forward to waking up to the view of the forest as she had done for three weeks now. The thought startled her.

Three weeks had gone by quickly, and yet her days in the tower felt like something from a different lifetime. How had she gone her whole life without running her hands on the branches of trees, feasting on berries as she trampled through the woods, and befriending the creatures of the night and the day as they crossed her path?

They unpacked their things. At the very bottom of her knapsack, Eliza found Hugo's blue button. She clasped it between her fingers and held it close to her heart, wondering if she could forgive him now that everything had turned out okay, now that she was safe in Teragovia and not in some awful Bardorian camp for enslaved whisperers. But then she remembered his lies and the family he had promised her, and the raw ache in her heart throbbed again. She put the button back in the knapsack, not desiring to keep it out where she could see it every day.

They went to the dining room afterward, where warm pumpkin soup, fluffy bread, and a board of various cheeses had been kept on the table. Miriam stood at the door, welcoming each of the winter daughters as they took in the comforts that they almost couldn't believe were theirs to keep.

'Eat well and rest long, winter daughters. Tomorrow morning, I will take you into the heart of our city and present you to the Council. You will see the wonder of this city of free folk with your own eyes.'

The girls broke into chatter and wolfed down the meal in minutes. Now that they had arrived at their destination, the edge of hardness had been replaced by a much lighter curiosity. Their fears clung to the surface, and their full bellies churned from excitement every now and then. Just when Eliza was about to retreat to bed, Lillian put her hand on her shoulder and gestured to her to follow behind. They walked into the back garden and stood under the milky moonlight. The symbols looked clearer now, similar to the ancient tongue that had spread itself all along the entrance stone. Fireflies flickered in and out of existence around them, and the scent of the earth was rich and fertile.

'Eliza, there's no easy way for me to tell you this,' Lillian began, sending Eliza's heart straight into her boots. 'But your human tutor, Hugo, has been killed by King Grandalford for treason. He was hanged in the town square, and his wife and sons have been banished from town. None of this is your fault or responsibility, but I thought you might want to know.'

Her head spinning and her heart too numb for tears, Eliza opened and closed her mouth, unable to say anything. Her hands shook involuntarily, and she pinched the skin on her elbows to keep them steady. Her body felt too hot and too cold all at once. It seemed to her that she was prone to injecting more wrongdoing into the world, whether she wanted to or not. No matter what direction she stepped in, it seemed like she had left a trail of destruction in her wake.

Chapter Thirteen

The Council of the Free folk

After a breakfast of eggs and hard bread the following morning, the winter daughters were escorted by Miriam into the city centre. The air was abuzz with excited chatter, and no one noticed that Eliza had been walking around without any colour in her face. The previous night, when she got back to the room, she had teetered on the edge of spilling her heart to Amelie, but something had held her back. Never having lost someone before, Eliza had no notion of how to grieve them, and she surmised that if she never told anyone or said the words out loud, the gaping despair might plug itself like marsh did when a pebble skid across the path and sunk into it. A ripple or two, and then the phlegmy water would swallow it whole. So Eliza put on a brave face and decided that she would never think of Hugo ever again, much less speak of him. She allowed Amelie's brightness to spill over onto her, fully ignoring the leaden weight of her heart.

As they walked closer towards the heart of the city, more and more stone houses started to appear. The houses were small like Miriam's, with round windows and small squarish doors making the walls look like upturned faces. Sheep bleated from pastures, and rolling hills yawned along in the distance. The clouds were high in the sky, racing past the blue as though they had a strict appointment elsewhere that they were late to keep. From the houses, faces peeked out to see the famed party troop through town. Some of them recognised Amelie and called out to her.

'Welcome back, Amelie! Little May and I have both missed you! You'll still teach her to climb, won't you?'

And Amelie blew a kiss to little May and promised that she would come for her soon. The baker told her that her supply of jam biscuits had been going to waste ever since Amelie had left with the freedom fighters of Teragovia, and Amelie swore that would no longer be an issue. She agreed to call at an old lady's house and take back an old cloak that she had patched up for Amelie. At every bend and turn, someone would emerge that had long awaited her return and was overjoyed to see her. Amidst them, Amelie's manner was mild and warm. She seemed at ease, her unguarded self. Eliza realised then that Amelie had never intended to appear haughty with the other girls; her heart was simply too full of people to cram a whole set of new ones into it, especially when they had done nothing in particular to deserve it. This must be what it is to have an entire village raise you, Eliza thought, her mind repudiating all paths that led to the thought of who had raised her.

The centre of Teragovia was unlike anything Eliza could ever have imagined. Rivers of every colour wound their way through the city, and wooden bridges were built over them. There was a marble fountain at the centre that shot colourful streams of water, one from each of the rivers, high into the sky and swirled it around with a flourish. Around the fountain was a morning market, where whisperers laid their wares on tables. Men and women called out the prices for fresh pumpkins, hard yellow cheese, fey spices and roots, ornaments from human towns, and fresh produce from their own farms and gardens. When the winter daughters passed them by, a few of them paused their sales and came up to them to press tidbits into their hands. A dark-skinned woman, barely older than her, pressed a clear piece of quartz into Eliza's palm. 'It'll enhance the effect of whatever is in your heart, winter daughter,' she said. 'The realm needs the fullness of your heart and your head.'

Eliza wanted to say that she had walled off her heart until further notice, but she accepted the gift and held it close to the beat of her chest. They walked through the market and past the grand library. It was a large brick building with white columns and the ancient symbols scratched on a stone banner.

'It says knowledge is power and power is freedom,' Amelie said, noting Eliza's glance.

They continued walking along the cobblestone pathway. Children chased each other and shouted loudly. Cats mewed and scampered along the roofs and walls of houses. The atmosphere in the town square was lively, but all activity halted whenever the winter daughters fell into people's line of sight. Some gaped; others cried out. Miriam smiled and waved at them, and the girls tried to make sense of the fanfare. All of them but Amelie had spent their lives in towers and cells and dungeons and had never thought themselves to be of significance to anyone until their respective rescues. The prophecy about the Midnight Daughter had seemed like a distant tale that could not change their lives very much, but as they walked past these people who believed them to be the saviours of the realm, each of the girls realised with a jolt that there was a good chance that the long arm of destiny could come for any of them, any minute now.

The entrance to the Council was glorious yet simple. An archway of bougainvillea vines that were perpetually in bloom welcomed them in. They walked through the garden, where fruit trees grew wildly, and bees swooped in circles over their heads. The statue of a woman with a crescent mark on her forehead stood at the entrance. Her eyes and hands were lifted skyward, and a singular ocean wave rose behind her.

'Goddess Ayla, the first whisperer,' Amelie said, unable to keep the awe out of her voice. 'She is the one who opened the moon channel thousands and thousands of years ago. All whisperers are her descendants. That's why we are called moon blooded. The magic of the moon flows through our bloodlines. It is said that in the start, humans and whisperers were not too different, but the more distant the groups grew, the more different they became. No human now could access the moon channel, you know.'

Eliza stared at the statue for several long seconds. Even in this inanimate form, Ayla was the most beautiful woman she had ever seen. Past the statue, they walked down a long stone corridor. On either side of it, paintings of Council Mistresses were hung on the walls. Eliza saw her own history opening up around her. With every step she took, yet another thread of her story was revealed, teasing her to just stop for a second and pull at it.

At the end of the hallway, they reached an open air courtyard with a circular wall of berry shrubs all around it. Two sentries, similar in their stolid disposition to Riani and Kiani, stood on either side of the entrance, staring straight ahead, a sceptre in one hand.

'Blessed be, guardians,' Miriam said, tipping her head to the women.

'Blessed be, Miriam,' they said to her in unison.

'I've come with the winter daughters. They must be expecting us.'

'Aye. I will ensure that the Council is ready to receive them.'

She disappeared inside. The girls looked at each other with wide eyes. They knew that this was the last time they would walk into a room as former prisoners of Bardoria. From now on, they would have to step into the role of the winter daughters, whatever that entailed.

'The Council will see you now,' the sentry said, returning a few minutes later.

Miriam led the girls through the maze of the berry bushes into the courtyard, where a semi-circle of women of varied ages sat on stone benches. The one who sat right in the middle bore a crescent mark on her forehead, just like the Council Mistresses in the paintings. She radiated an air of authority. Her hair was silvery like Tierza's but long and straight, running like a shaft all the way down her back. She wore a black tunic, all of them did, and her olive skin was smooth and soft-looking.

'Greetings, winter daughters,' said the Council Mistress, rising and placing her hand on her heart. The others rose after her and followed suit.

The girls looked awkwardly at one another, not knowing how they should offer greetings to the Council. The Council Mistress sat down, the others doing the same after her.

'I am Zara, the seventy-first Council Mistress of Teragovia. The city of the free folk has awaited your presence for many moons, winter daughters, ever since the prophecy came to light. We hope your first night in the city was steeped in peace and rest. Winter daughters, we know that you have endured many hardships in your life on behalf of this realm. You have been unfairly imprisoned under severe conditions for most of your life. We have been lucky to be able to break out all of the winter daughters that the prophecy could pertain to. Although we have prioritised your rescue, there are countless whisperers and whisperlings that have been interned in Bardorian camps all over the north. They are our kin, and yet, we are unable to stop the suffering that is amassed daily in the name of Bardorian vileness. We believe that the good of the realm of Elatonia relies on reversing their fortunes and bringing them into the fold of freedom. Winter daughters, I assure you that the easiest portion of your journey has ended. From here on out, we will ally together to fight the forces of the foolish King Grandalford and liberate our people from their bondage. Together, we rise for Teragovia and the bastion of freedom that has always been our greatest asset.'

Eliza swallowed, thinking of all the cuts, scratches, and nights of shivering she had endured on the journey to Teragovia. If that was the easy part, then what would come after? A couple of plump bees buzzed into the courtyard and raced from one end of the courtyard to another in search of a flower whose corolla they could bury their bodies into. Not quite satisfied with anything, the bees eventually landed on Eliza's shoulders, their tiny wings resting idly on their backs as they built up the reserves for another quest.

'I don't intend to frighten you,' Zara said, her silvery mane glistening in the weak winter sun. 'I intend to prepare you. Although the prophecy is about the Midnight Daughter, there is an equal chance for any of the winter daughters to be the one. We do not know yet the nature of the dormant powers within her, so we must groom each of you as though it is your personal destiny to save the realm from the heinousness it has long endured.'

Eliza glanced at the faces of the other girls. Some were openly scared, others determined, and some confused. Only Amelie looked serene as ever, the novelty of this information lost on her as it was something she had always known. Eliza wondered what emotions her face betrayed. She wished she could glimpse it again, her features drawn on a clear surface of the water, her own face, her own markings, the one thing she could use to hold onto her sense of self while everything else slipped away.

'Ever since the old King Leon of Augrives perished, the harmony in Elatonia has been compromised. I remember a time when fey, whisperer, and human all lived in peace. We had business dealings and danced together during the harvest. The humans ruled their lands their way, the fey ruled the forest their way, and we whisperers ruled our waterfront cities our own way. We might not have been kin, but we never hurt or exploited one another. We never had to hide away in our separate enclaves as we do now. Whisperer cities were built on the banks of rivers and all along the southern coast. The moon channel is the strongest when there is water nearby, and it was understood that we had the first right to the land by the oceans. Although the fey have historically been considered to be the holders of the sun channel, the reign of King Grandalford has challenged that notion. In fact, it has challenged all that we know and revered in Elatonia.' Zara paused to take a breath. Her voice had begun to crackle with emotion.

'A hundred years ago, when King Grandalford came into power. We heard about his menace in Bardoria, but it was against the code for us to enter into the internal affairs of others. So we let the tyrannical ruler of the marshland of the north lay waste to his own city. We watched idly, hoping that King Leon would intervene in the matters of his fellow humans, but he was old and frail and perished before he could tame the waywardness of Grandalford. King Leon's son was but a teenage boy when he ascended the throne, and he proved to be no match for

Grandalford. The best he could negotiate was the freedom of Augrives in exchange for total passivity while Grandalford continued to pillage and plunder all of Elatonia.'

Eliza shivered involuntarily as the dark history of Bardoria came to light. She wondered if Hugo had known all of this if he had been aware of the damage that the Bardorian rule had caused in the rest of the realm. She realised that she would never be able to find out since he was no longer there for her to ask. She pushed the thought out of her mind roughly and stared at Zara with a steely disposition.

'In his quest for total dominion, Grandalford has wreaked havoc on the set order. He does not believe that the fey hold the secrets of the sun channel; he thinks that it is the humans that do, or at least he wants everyone to believe it. The Bardorian people have been brainwashed to believe that Grandalford has unlocked the sun channel and that the sun's power has turned Bardoria into an advanced civilisation. Very few know of the whisperers that have been interned in camps, forced to use their powers to do Grandalford's bidding, powering Bardorian mines, factories, and hearths. And so, thousands of innocent people have become complicit in one of the greatest crimes against the creatures of this realm. To make matters worse, Grandalford has convinced his people that whisperers are evil beings that want to use the moon channel to bring darkness and destruction to the land. He has extinguished most whisperer cities. Many whisperers now live in hiding, in communes and caves in the south where they are far from Grandalford's reach.

Very few dare to cross into the Whispering Woods to search for Teragovia, as all the human towns around the edges are replete with Bardorian informants who are quick to turn in any suspicious individuals. You have had the misfortune of coming into contact with one such informant in Augrives. We have sent scouts to search for Tierza, Riani, and Kiani and hope to have word from them soon. Anyhow, those that are able to make their way to the Whispering Woods and find Teragovia are welcomed into our fold without question. We are the last city of whisperers that stands tall to this day, but we are worried that our luck is running out.'

The faces of the other Council members, which had so far been calm and dispassionate, now flickered with strains of worry. Eyes flashed, and lips flattened into thin lines as Zara continued to speak. Each sentence of hers sent a shockwave through Eliza's body as whatever kernels of her past life that she held onto with fondness were rapidly disintegrated.

'Grandalford has taken the destruction of the realm too far. He has become delusional, believing that everyone in the realm challenges his power. He wants to destroy all creatures and claim all of Elatonia for Bardorian conquest. He knows that the fey are tethered to the sun channel through the trees, so he has begun to fell them indiscriminately. He knows that whisperers speak to each other and the trees through the mycelium that connects the woods underground. He has begun to turn former forest land into desert all around the Whispering Woods so that none of the whisperers that hide in the south can communicate with us to find Teragovia. We're not sure when his next attack will be or what it will look like, but it is sure to come sooner or later. Teragovia can hide from the Bardorians only for so long. The time will soon come for us to break out from the veil of enchantment and meet the Bardorian forces head-on. And the Midnight Daughter will guide us into battle and use her powers to restore peace to Elatonia. And so it is!'

'And so it is!' echoed the voices of the Council members.

They were then told that their lessons would begin in the courtyard behind their lodging the next day. Details were shared about what they could expect from the studies and who would be teaching them, but Eliza's mind had absorbed so much new information in the last twenty-four hours that she had become immune to the emotional consequences of it all. Every new thing she learned seemed to break her a little more. She thought of the ancient symbols at the entrance. Knowledge is power, and power is freedom. That was probably true, but no one had warned her that knowledge was also the greatest burden of all.

Chapter Fourteen

The prophecy

That evening, Eliza accompanied Amelie on some of her visits to see old friends. The city centre was transformed in the milky dusk. The square where the market was held in the morning was now empty of sellers. Instead, a live band had taken over. Men and women with fiddles, violins, and tin whistles stood to one side, bouncing on their feet and nodding their heads as they played to a transient crowd. A woman with long dark hair stood in the centre, singing a ballad about a whisperer lost at sea on a dark moon night. Her powers were diminished, and a storm blew around her, cleaving the ocean in half. The lyrics were sad, but the melody was upbeat, and the crowd jigged with insouciant energy.

'Wait till the Solstice dance. In a few weeks, this square will be utterly transformed. It's the longest night in the year, which means that the moon reigns over the sky for most of the day and night, and our people rejoice in her glow.' Amelie glided past the dancing throng over to a house in the corner where a ginger cat guarded the door.

Eliza followed her, transfixed by the celebrations that were underway on such an ordinary night. The door opened and one of the Council members took Amelie into her arms and squeezed her so tight that she had to beg to be released. Eliza stood next to her, awkwardly raising her hand in a wave. The Council member ushered them in and poured them both a cup of tea. Colourful flower petals floated in the amber liquid, and steam rose from the surface rapidly. While the other two chatted and caught up on Amelie's adventures, Eliza stood by the window, her arms cupped around the warm mug, watching the dancing folk. She had never celebrated anything in her life, not an ordinary day, not a special occasion. She wondered what it would be like to simply walk into the heart of the crowd and begin to dance with them. Would they welcome her, or would she be shunned? Did she have to practice beforehand, or would her limbs know how to sway to the beat? The ginger cat strolled up to her and rubbed its fluffy body against her legs. Eliza hunched down to pet it, and it purred like an engine.

'No word from Tierza then?'

'Not yet.'

'But you have hope?'

'I must, or I will break.'

Eliza pretended to be immersed in the happenings outside the window. She picked up the cat and perched on the sill; the mug placed next to her. Although her eyes were fixed outside, her ears were keenly tuned into the conversation at the table. Amelie rarely spoke to Eliza openly about what was going on in her mind. Perhaps she didn't think that Eliza had it in her to find the right words to say. Or perhaps her secrets were a gift that she dispensed only to the worthy, only to those who had proved themselves to be up to the task of keeping them safe over the years.

'And the rescues, do they seem promising then? Or is it as we have always thought it would be?'

Amelie paused for a long moment. 'Aye, there are some with elegance in their crafts. Time will tell, I suppose.'

'Ah, but you're far too modest for your own good. We've watched you grow, Amy, and we all know it's you.'

Eliza took in this information and tried not to feel a thing. It came as no surprise that the whole of Teragovia believed that Amelie was the Midnight Daughter. She had sojourned with Amelie for three weeks through bracken woods and bogs and thick forests, and she had yet to find anything that Amelie could not do better than others. Their lessons would commence the next day, and no doubt Amelie would surpass them all. This was common logic, something rudimentary and to be expected, and yet Eliza felt a pang of jealousy. Not of Amelie's powers but of the fact that an entire city rallied behind her. What did one have to do to receive such consistent support?

When they walked back to their lodging, Eliza was stricken by how much faster the clouds seemed to move through the skies of Teragovia. In Bardoria, they were dense and unmoving, a permanent part of the landscape. Here, they raced one another to an invisible finish line and opened rivulets of stars that splashed across the sky. A sea of twinkles that existed only to delight!

The next morning, Eliza asked Miriam whatever had happened to Lillian! They hadn't seen her after their arrival at the lodging. Miriam told them that she was resting. Being the sole whisperer guiding the winter daughters, performing all the magic on her own, and roughing it out in the wilderness had taken its toll on her. She would reenter society soon enough; she just needed a bit of rest first.

Miriam waited for them to finish breakfast and then escorted them to Oracle Moonfall's nest. It was in the opposite direction of the city centre, plunged deeper into the thickets and rivers, a lone standing cabin overgrown with moss and ivy. There was no clear path guiding them through the field and to her door, so the girls walked through the wet marsh grass and found their way across. Miriam knocked softly on the door.

A few long minutes passed before the Oracle opened the door. She was a wizened old woman with long grey hair that had been plaited down to her hips. Her earlobes stretched down to her chin, and the wrinkles on her skin gathered like wax on a candle. Her eyes, however, were youthful and alive, flashing brightly as her gaze hovered on each of the winter daughters briefly.

'We'll go to the back,' she said, leading them around the house and into an open courtyard, similar to the one they had in the lodging. An oak tree with hanging limbs covered it partially, casting a long shadow on the damp earth. It was a crisp morning; the wind blew in from the open fields and bottlenecked at the point where they stood, the last patch of open land before the thicket took over.

The Oracle was dressed in colourful shawls, with red, blue, and green patterns that merged into each other, giving her an esoteric air. A row of long beaded necklaces hung from her neck. Thin glass bangles clinked on her wrists whenever a strong gust of wind blew past.

'Winter daughters, I have felt your arrival from the moment you set foot in the Whispering Woods.' Her voice had a cavernous quality about it, as though it emanated from deep in her belly. 'The trees told me of it even before, but oh, I felt it on my skin when you ran into the woods on the day of the storm. The Midnight Daughter is coming; the Midnight Daughter is coming, every pinprick of my flesh erupted in awareness. And now, with all of you standing before me, I have the same sensation again. My skin is alight with knowledge. She is among us, she who will bring peace to the realm.'

Eliza felt her own skin tingle when the Oracle spoke. Birds swooped onto the branches of the old oak as if to listen to what the Oracle had to say.

'Before you commence your lessons, it is vital for you to know the prophecy, winter daughters. When the whisperers were first interned in the camps of Bardoria, I retreated deep into the forest to ask for guidance from the moon. She is fickle, but she is not fallow, as you know. She is fertile for wishes to take root if you plead with your best intentions. I closed my eyes and meditated for a whole moon cycle, paying homage to both sickle and shield as the moon went from a crafty shadow to her finest form, brighter than the sun in the sky. At last, when she was directly overhead, a passage opened up, radiating from her core into my forehead, passing on the certain knowledge of the prophecy to me.'

The Oracle's gaze shifted from face to face as the full weight of her words descended upon them.

'The moon spoke a poem to me in an ancient tongue. I whisper it to myself every night when I see her, and she nods at me to say, yes, the words still contain truth within them. Our fate is an ever-moving breath of wind, liable to change in every direction. And yet the prophecy had remained a steady gale, immutable, unseen and evergreen.'

Lifting her hands to her heart, the Oracle closed her eyes and said, her voice half-whisper and half-song,

'At the very brink of winter,
the daughter of the earth is born
Her power simmers underneath
Until the shadows rise from above and below
She is the Midnight Daughter
She who holds both keys
Bringer of peace, holder of unity
This is the winter daughter's realm.'

The girls listened with bated breath, the exact words that had guided their fortunes dancing before them for the first time. They looked at one another, each syllable rising overhead before sinking into their bones. Eliza sneaked a glance at Amelie, wondering how she kept a straight face, how she had it in her to humour these proceedings when she knew full well that she was the Midnight Daughter. The more Eliza thought about it, the more right it seemed. It had to have been a stroke of good fortune that had prevented Amelie from ever being imprisoned when so many whisperlings had faced such a treacherous reality. It had to be because the unseen forces of the realm had known that she was special. She was different, and it was vital to safeguard her within the city of the free folk wherein she could spend a lifetime amassing the knowledge that she would need to save the realm.

The Oracle continued to speak in her deep, rumbling voice. 'The meaning is clear, is it not? Ah, I see how it bounds and sways amidst the verse, but it is so very clear to me. The key piece of the puzzle here is that the Midnight Daughter holds both keys. What keys, you might wonder? They're not literal keys. You cannot actually hold them. But they will hold you, do you see what I mean?'

Ignoring the blank looks on their faces, the Oracle's passionate soliloquy continued. 'The keys, winter daughter, the twin keys, the opening of the sun channel and the moon channel. The Midnight Daughter must be attuned to both. That is the unity that is spoken of. It makes perfect sense, does it not? In a realm splintered by disharmony and the cruel dominion of one creature's rule, it is the allyship of both forces within the Midnight Daughter that will have the power to shape things anew.'

Nala asked the question that was on everyone's lips. 'But we are whisperers, Oracle Moonfall. We only have it in us to commune with the moon. How are we ever to gain access to the channel of the sun?'

The Oracle smiled, a droopy smile that stretched her wrinkles tautly across her features. 'That is the hidden power of the Midnight Daughter, winter daughter. Unbeknownst to us all, invisible to the naked eye, she has the capacity to commune with both sun and moon. It is a rare gift; it is not something that we have seen before in this realm after the time of the Gods and Goddesses came to an end. But this time of terror is a marvel in its own right, for it has forced the hand of the world so that it must birth a saviour equally luminous. The light that drowns out the darkness. She is among us, our Midnight Daughter, saviour of the realm!'

Chapter Fifteen

Eliza goes to school

Eliza had humble ambitions as far as the lessons went. She wasn't hoping to unlock any great accomplishments regarding the sun channel, but she did hope to emerge as a somewhat decent whisperer whose ability to commune with the moon was at least above average. The prospect of going to school was exciting. She had learned about human schools in Bardoria through the literature that Hugo brought her. She had longed to go to a human school all her life, press books into her satchel, pack an apple to eat at snack time, and spend her days cultivating knowledge that could be condensed into reams of parchments.

The schooling of the whisperlings was done in a different fashion. There wasn't much importance given to the sort of learning that could be gleaned from parchments. Whisperers learned by doing. And the schooling of the winter daughters, in light of the consequences it would have for the realm, was a site for accelerated learning. Not only were the girls taught the ancient tongue, enchantments, and societal affairs, but they were also expected to hone their skills in woodwork, forest survival, archery and warfare, to name a few. And there was the matter of special lessons with the Oracle, which would begin only when the girls had a reasonable level of mastery in the other arts. Only then would they have the reflexes and mental strength to withstand the most crucial lesson of all: learning to derive ancient knowledge by speaking to the trees.

The next few days were full of lessons in the courtyard behind their lodging. The girls would rise at dawn, eat breakfast, and stay out in the cold until their morning lessons were finished. During woodwork, they would learn to carve tools out of sticks. From spears and sceptres, their goal was to be able to craft entire bows and catapults out of wood. During archery, they learned to shoot arrows into targets that were mounted on tall poles. The arrows were light feathery things with pointy metal tips that sliced through the wind. From then on, Eliza learned to associate the zap of the arrows with the sound of the wind, ducking whenever a draught blew in unexpectedly. Eliza was unable to shine at either of these tasks. She took little pleasure in creating weapons and shooting them. She was afraid that she lacked the requisite grit to truly harm anyone or anything, even when push came to shove. She tried to picture the Bardorian soldiers when she pinched the arrow between her thumb and forefinger, pretending that shooting the target would bring Tierza, Riani, and Kiani back, but the tactic didn't serve her as well as she had hoped. Her arrows barely made it past the halfway mark. Next to her, Aoife and Amelie shot arrow after arrow into the bright red centre of the target, often slicing the previous arrow down the middle.

In the afternoons, after lunch, they would gather around a large slab of slate that their teacher would scratch symbols onto with skinny sticks of chalk. Learning the ancient tongue was a droll and tedious task enjoyed by none. Eliza wasn't quite sure why they had to learn to speak it, given that they only ever used the common tongue with one another anyway. Aside from inscriptions on old buildings, she was yet to see the use of the ancient language anywhere else. However dull it was, it was undoubtedly relatively easy, simply a matter of internalising the patterns created by similar strokes and ascribing meaning to them. The post-lunch hour was no time for Eliza to have her wits about. With a full belly, Eliza often found it hard to concentrate. The symbols would start to swim around before her eyes in a dizzying fashion.

Once the day had darkened, they would sit on the cold earth in the courtyard and work on their enchantments. Eliza had been especially keen for these lessons, picturing herself lifting her palms to the sky as she had seen Lillian and Tierza do. She knew that, above all else, this was the most important lesson there was to learn. She cared little about forest survival or warfare - she knew that those were skills that would be valuable to the Midnight Daughter and her army. She knew that for her earthly aspirations of becoming a regular whisperer, this was all that counted - wielding the power of the moon channel.

It was not at all like what Eliza had expected. Their teacher, a young and muscly woman, named Aga, told them that they wouldn't be casting any enchantments for a long time to come. Many steps had to be checked off along the way before they could even think of drawing in the power of the moon channel. Aga made them sit cross-legged on the ground with their eyes closed. Her voice was silky and sanguine, and she asked them time and time again to focus on their breath. Enchantment was a two-way street - not only was it about drawing in the power of the moon but also about creating space within yourself to receive it.

'If your mind and heart are full of clutter, there is nowhere for the moon power to go. It will simply ricochet from your foreheads if there is no space within you. Breathe in and exhale any fears, worries, or concerns you might have. Picture an open, unending space within you. This is where the moon power will go and until you have mastered the art of emptying your mind, your attempts to whisper will be met with failure.'

Eliza tried her level best. But every time she closed her eyes and counted her breaths, images would travel to the forefront of her mind from whatever recess they were buried beneath and make her quake and sweat. The dreams from the tower and the memory of the last time she saw Hugo combined with new images of terror. She would suddenly picture Tierza lying face down in a bog, sinking slowly and irrevocably into its clumpy maw. She would see blood and dirt coursing through the rivers of Teragovia, the enchanted blues and pinks, and yellows of the candied water turning a coppery red. She saw the library going up in flames, the images of the Council Mistresses being stacked one on top of another as they were set alight, and the town square empty, covered in a sheen of soot as there was nothing left to celebrate ever again.

Eliza went from looking forward to the lessons in enchantment to dreading them. She grew breathless and sweaty every time she tried to clear her mind. It seemed that there was simply too much going on and Eliza's strength lay not in emptying her mind but in filling it up with even more clutter. She didn't know where to put the horror images if not for the back of her mind. How was she to unmake them? How could she forget what she had endured and what might come to pass?

At night, after dinner, the girls would either make a fire and chat around the flickering flames, or they would go into the city to dance at the square. Eliza found herself too exhausted by the toll of the enchantment lessons and struggled to keep her eyes open even at dinner. As soon as she had licked her plate clean, she would sink into her bed, falling into a deep sleep that made her appear dead to the world. In the mornings, she would sleep through the breakfast bell and have to be shaken awake by Amelie, who had been doing this for so long that she did not complain about it anymore.

Each morning at breakfast, there would be anecdotes from the other girls about new songs they had danced to or other Teragovians they had met. New characters sketched out against the ever-growing plane of their new lives. They met fisherwomen and dancers and scouts and other whisperlings. They came back with seashells and feathers and biscuits. Although they shared them with each other, Eliza felt ashamed as she never had anything to offer. She vowed each morning that she would not succumb to her weariness, and yet, as soon as dinner was served, she found herself wolfing it down and collapsing onto her bed.

It seemed that all of the others were not only surviving here, but they were thriving. No one seemed to struggle quite as much as Eliza at lessons, and they had surplus energy to go out and meet people and make merry. Things that were routine and easy for others felt doubly taxing to her. Why, she wondered, did things always have to be so much harder for her than anyone else?

Chapter Sixteen

The Old World

Their woodworking teacher fell ill one day, and they had a free morning. Eliza's heart skipped a beat when Miriam told them they were to do as they pleased until lunch. She walked into the city centre with the others, bouncing on the balls of her feet. The fog never quite hung over the fields the way it did in Bardoria. The days were clear and cold, and it mostly rained at night when they were asleep in bed. Eliza would sleep through it all and only know about the night's downpour because Amelie had been kept awake by the pitter-patter of the raindrops on the tiled roof. The ground was mushy underfoot, but the sky was open in a broad smile, bars of light beaming onto the undulating landscape. The market was underway, and several of the girls went to the stalls where they knew people. Nala was chatting to a whisperling who sold fey spices with her mother, and Seena and Esther were examining human ornaments on a neatly laid table.

'Try a bit of this pie, dearie,' a voice called out to her. Eliza spun on her heel to locate its source. A table full of tarts, pies, and biscuits sent a homely, tempting fragrance through the air. Behind it, a plump woman and her son stood, fanning the goodies with a piece of parchment to enhance the spread of the scent.

'Oh, I'd love to, but I'm afraid I haven't got any coin of my own!' Eliza said, looking down uncomfortably.

'Ah, that is a trifling matter for a winter daughter, is it not? I won't be taking a coin from anyone who puts their life on the line for this realm!' She held a piece of apple pie in front of her and beckoned to Eliza with her other hand.

Eliza accepted the gift, not quite sure how she felt about anyone believing that she was about to put her life on the line for Elatonia. There was something quite haphazard about stepping into a role that other people had been aware of for ages but that she herself had only learned of a few weeks ago. Her attachment to Elatonia and what it stood for was something she was still assessing, and matters of living and dying for a cause were best left to the Midnight Daughter. However, the pie was delicious, and Eliza licked her lips, making sure not to waste as much as a single crumb.

'And how are you finding Teragovia, dearie?'

'I love every bit of what I've seen so far. The skies are always clear, the people are friendly, and the rivers are most wonderful indeed!'

'I haven't seen much of you around town. The other winter daughters come by on most days; why don't you come with them and make yourself at home with your fellow citizens?'

'Oh, I've wanted to come by more often, but I find myself utterly exhausted after our lessons!'

'Fair enough, fair enough, it's no ordinary learning, is it now? What are they teaching you?'

Eliza told her, and the woman nodded wryly. 'It seems to me that your education has been pointed at the future alone. I understand the rationale behind such a choice but have you been taught about Elatonian lore and legend?'

'Not yet, no.'

'A crying shame! Every whisperling grows up listening to these stories. Why don't you come by my house for dinner tonight, dearie? Little Dion and his sister Lou do love to make a fire afterward and hear their Pa telling stories. I have a feeling you'd like it too.'

Eliza could barely believe the kindness being offered to her without cause. 'Oh, are you sure? I'd hate to impose!'

'I'm certain, dearie. The free folk will do what they can for Elatonia. You must know all about the realm that you have been born to protect, eh?'

Eliza agreed to go there straight after her enchantments lesson and walked through the rest of the market with a skip in her step. She noticed that the scene around her was in stark contrast to the tiny glimpse of human civilisation she had got in the tavern in Augrives. Only men sat with beers on the barstools and cared about little but their coins. Here in Teragovia, it seemed to be women that claimed the square and coin was secondary to kindness. She ran her fingers through the fine fabric on sale, watched the children dare each other to run into the fountain, and stroked the cats that seemed to come out of nowhere and mew at her feet.

During her enchantments lesson, she diverged from the instructions to empty her mind and instead distracted herself with pleasant reveries of the evening that would follow. She excused herself before dinner and followed the instructions to get to Tina's house. It was one of the stone houses on the path, halfway into town. She knocked on the door, and it was opened by a stout man, presumably Tina's husband.

'You must be Eliza!' he said, signalling her to come on inside. Similar in shape and build to Miriam's home, the low ceiling and round windows made for a cozy dwelling. Small wooden toys were strewn on the floor; a wooden rocking horse stood in one corner. The muffled sounds of laughter trickled out from the kitchen.

'Dinner's ready!' called Tina, poking her head through the kitchen door.

The table was laden with roast chicken, baby potatoes fried with fresh sprigs of rosemary, and a fresh salad from Tina's own garden. Her husband tended to their garden, chickens, and children while Tina went to the market to sell her baked goodies and attended city meetings that were mandatory for all the female folk of Teragovia.

'Not like human society, is it, where the men lord over their women. Amongst whisperers, we honour those that bring life into the world above all else. You'll see that women hold much of the power in whisperer society,' Tina explained, heaping potatoes onto Eliza's plate generously.

Eliza bit into them hungrily and listened as their buttery skin melted in her mouth. Lou was a couple of years older than Dion and considered this the most significant fact of their family history. She told Eliza so right away and made it a point to tell Dion to finish his salad before asking for more potatoes and even threatened to confiscate his rocking horse if he didn't comply. When Lou wasn't looking, Dion would quickly place a potato onto Eliza's plate and smile at her conspiratorially, his blue eyes lighting up in mischievous delight. Eliza winked at him, grateful to have some kind of role within this family, and gobbled up the potatoes before Lou could notice his sleight of hand.

After dinner, Tina and the children led Eliza into the back garden while her husband cleaned up. There was a brick fire pit in the middle. The children both took Eliza by the hand and opened the door to a shed that was stacked with dry heather. They collected it and placed it in clumps around the fire pit so that each person could have a cushion of heather to sit on. Tina got a small fire going, and they sat around it, watching the pieces of wood light up one after another. Her husband joined them shortly after and began a night of storytelling. Eliza noticed that no matter how much Lou and Dion bickered, they had placed their heather cushions side by side and were now squished together, Dion's head on Lou's shoulder. The affection between the two of them was unmistakable.

'Who wants to hear the story of the Old World?' he said, rubbing his palms together. Both children squealed in excitement. Eliza leaned forward and nodded excitedly.

'Hundreds and thousands of years ago, when the Gods and Goddesses lived in Elatonia, the realm was rather different. It was a time of peace and prosperity, and all those who lived were demi-gods in their own right. There was no separation between the sun and the moon, they would dance across the sky whenever they felt like it, so it would go from being light to dark and light to dark again in a matter of minutes. Can you picture that, Lou, darling, no day or night, just a long stretch of eternity with moments of light and shadow?'

His voice was deep, and he spoke slowly, drawing out the syllables so that they had time to visualise every element of this story.

'The King and Queen of the Old World were blessed by the sun and the moon. They came from the ether and began to create the world with each breath they took. The only thing older than them were the trees. Before there were people, there were only trees. The King and Queen built the first houses, lit the first fires, and ushered the first people into existence. They were kind and loving and ruled their subjects with honour. There was no mayhem or madness. In many ways, it was a perfect world. Some say that the sun and the moon were present in both of them, that they shared the ancient magic, and that the world as we know it would never have existed had they not partaken in these powers equally.'

From the corner of her eye, Eliza saw that Dion had curled up next to Lou, his head on her lap as the two of them listened in rapt attention, hanging on to every word even though they had heard this story a hundred times.

'And then once they were satisfied with the world they had built, they had children, a boy, and a girl, just like you two. They were twins, evenly matched in skill and beauty and fervour. Beloved to all in the realm, they were taught the ancient magic by the trees themselves, for this was a time before there were teachers and lessons. They wielded the power of the sun and the moon together. It seemed that the Golden Age would never end, that they would surge into eternity like this, but the King and Queen decided one day that they were weary of living and wished to ascend into the heavens. They wanted to leave the realm to their children, but the question arose of what would happen when their children found love and made children of their own? How would the realm be governed? For the first time, tensions arose between the brother and the sister. They began to fight amongst one another, declaring that one was superior to the other. The peace of the times bygone was extinguished in the blink of an eye.'

Eliza shivered and moved closer to the fire so she could warm her hands. It wasn't any colder tonight than on any other night, but the tale gave her goosebumps.

'The King and the Queen did not want to ascend into the heavens without restoring balance to the realm. So they did the unthinkable; they parted the powers of the sun and the moon and gave one to the son and the other to the daughter. The son, Riaz, became the God of the Morning, taking over the realm at daybreak and the daughter, Ayla, became the Goddess of the Evening, taking over the realm at dusk. The brother and the sister never spoke again and confined themselves to their division of the realm. Day and night were splintered into two, and aside from the few fleeting seconds each day that the sun and the moon rise and set, there is never a doubt about who rules the sky.'

Eliza remembered the marble state of Goddess Ayla in the Council House, the crescent moon on her forehead, the ocean wave rising in a calm fury behind her. She was the Goddess of the Evening, the great mother of all whisperers, the holder of the moon channel. It was her power that they were summoning from the sky when they closed their eyes. Suddenly, the realm felt like a breathing, quaking thing that extended not only around her in space but also in time, reaching far back to the very beginning of everything, a time when there was nothing but trees. She looked up at the moon and pictured a ribbon of light entering from that ancient source into her, and for the first time, her forehead burned where the crescent mark should be.

Chapter Seventeen

The Solstice Dance

The days went by with a considerably greater sense of ease for Eliza from there on out. Although she still struggled with most of her lessons and the awareness of her ineptitude pricked her sharply, her friendship with Tina and her family helped her derive satisfaction from something outside of her capabilities as a whisperer. She would excuse herself before dinner every few days and skip over to Tina's house. Lou and Dion had begun to treat Eliza as a mediator when they argued over the toys or whose turn it was to help their father with the harvest, so she settled their disputes and enjoyed every bit of it. Tina was always relieved to have her around as it gave her some time with her husband. She always sent Eliza home with jam rolls or custard pies, fussed over her hair, and taught her how to darn the holes in her clothes.

'It's like having a family, Amelie,' Eliza said happily, using her fingers to wipe away a dribble of custard that slid out from the corner of her mouth. 'I don't think I've wanted anything more.'

Amelie smiled vaguely, as though she couldn't fully comprehend why Eliza's needs were so uninspired.

'I can't wait for all of this Midnight Daughter business to be over so I can stop with these lessons and have a shot at a normal life,' Eliza said.

'You seem quite certain that you won't be roped into the conflict, Eliza. I mean, it is only the greatest war of our times, so it's not like we need all hands on board or anything!'

Eliza flushed. 'I just mean to say that once the dust settles, I'll be thrilled to build myself a small stone house and learn to keep a garden. Oh Amelie, we could be neighbours!'

'We could. And our sheep could be friends too. Now there's only the matter of survival to ensure first,' Amelie said, with a twinkle in her eye.

Another thing that Eliza found respite in was the lore and legend of Elatonia. At first, she waited with bated breath for those fireside tales and then started to grow impatient as her mind hungered for the knowledge that most whisperers already seemed to possess. On their next free morning, she sped into town right away. She barely waved at the marker vendors or stroked the cats and made a beeline for the intimidating structure of the library. Up the grand marble stairs at the entrance and in through the columns. She wrote her name down on the official registry and entered the enormous room. It had books from the floor to the high ceiling and ladders on wheels that could be moved along the walls of books to get to the ones at the top. She spent an hour walking around the library, going up the stairs and discovering room after room full of books. Picking just one to take home with her felt like an impossible feat. After hours of fingering the spines of aged volumes, Eliza found one titled *'Children's Stories from the Realm.'* She brought it home with her and began to read one story every night, hoping to find a captivating tale that she could share by the fire in Tina's house the next time.

Before she knew it, it was time for the Solstice Dance. Nobody said much about it for days until, all of a sudden, it was all anybody could talk about. Eliza was thrilled; it would be her first real celebration of anything! But there were matters to attend to. Over the weeks, the others had been stocking up feathers and ornaments that they could use to glamourise their tunics, but Eliza had done no such thing and had little to wear except the necklace given to her by the fey folk that still lay at the bottom of her knapsack. She pulled it out one night and examined it, expecting it to be in a state of potent decay. But the fey magic held it together as though it had been bound together only hours ago. While sifting through her belongings, Eliza also found the piece of clear quartz given to her on her first day in Teragovia. She slipped it into her pocket and took it to Tina, who attached it to a piece of hide and tied it around Eliza's wrist. It hung delicately and glimmered whenever it caught the sun.

On the day of the dance, she went into the woods with the other girls and picked flowers to put in her hair. She gathered a handful of small purple flowers and strung them together with strips of bark to make a delicate wreath. She washed and brushed her hair neatly, so it fell in soft waves below her shoulders. It wasn't much, but it was something, and Eliza was beside herself with excitement as they walked into town; all of the winter daughters, clad in flowers and stones, ready to celebrate the longest night of the year!

Amelie had been right; the square had been totally transformed. A raised platform had been created for the live band, who were all decked up in velvet robes. Fat waxy candles hovered over their heads and illuminated the square. Gossamer ribbons hung from the trees and fluttered in the cool evening breeze. Women with bushels of burning herbs greeted everyone as they walked into the square, brushing the air around them with herbs in a purification ritual. The air was thick with a cloying smell. On one side of the square was a long table full of food - jams, butters, rolls, fruit, roast chicken, gravy, sandwiches, potatoes in every form, and so much more. On the other side of the square was a makeshift tavern that served mulled wine and beer. People picked at bites of the food as they passed through and had a goblet of drink in their hands at any given time. On the opposite side of the square, a fire burned brightly, large and surreal, appearing to be suspended in thin air as the logs that crackled beneath had been turned invisible by an enchantment.

Eliza gaped at the scene around her. Everyone was in a cheery mood. She saw Tina walking around with a pitcher of mulled wine, topping up the goblets of whoever passed her by. The children were present too, laughing and playing and dancing together. Some of the older ones begged their mothers to let them try the mulled wine but to no avail.

'I'll hex big ugly warts onto your nose if I catch you so much as sniffing an empty goblet,' she overheard one mother say to her daughter.

People flooded the square in twos and threes. The band sang ballads about the moon, and Eliza drifted on the periphery of the dancing mass of people, swaying on her feet, greatly interested in the stories that were being revealed to her. The song was about the Old World, when the moon was a maiden that came and went as she pleased, lifting her skirts to cast bars of moonlight onto the rolling hills and pastures of Elatonia.

She walked to the fire, where a group of whisperlings, much like herself, flung small objects into the flames. She asked the girls what they were doing, and one of them replied, 'only a burn ritual, winter daughter. We're ridding ourselves of what no longer serves us!'

'And how do you know when something no longer serves you?' Eliza asked, her eyebrows arching in perplexion.

'Why, you must decide that for yourself! Your spirit will always know when it is ready to let go of something.'

Eliza thought about the weeks bygone and how topsy turvy her life had become since that day in the tower. Was she ready to let go of her life before she had been freed? She thought about throwing Hugo's button into the maw of the fire and felt an instant barrier form in her chest. No, not just yet. She fingered the fey necklace around her throat and wondered if she should rip it off and cast it into the flames. Yet again, her body clenched in horror. To throw away the necklace signalled a sort of finality, a pledge of sorts to her commitment to being a winter daughter. As far as Eliza was concerned, she wanted little to do with a dramatic life of war and bravery. All she wanted was a family and an idyllic life by the woods, and although the fey may not take her back if she escaped into the forest now, the necklace was a reminder that she could run away at any given moment and leave behind this life if she so desired.

'And what if there's nothing I wish to let go of just yet?' Eliza asked, squishing her toes nervously inside her boots.

'Then you must join the merry mob of dancers!'

'I don't know how to dance! I've never danced before!' Eliza cried, shivering a little despite her proximity to the fire.

'The more you think about it, the harder it gets. Come with me; I'll show you!'

A whisperling with dark green eyes, curly brown hair, and a lithe build like Amelie's took her by the hand and led her into the pulsating nucleus of dancers. She wore a golden silk tunic, and her hair bounced on her bony shoulders when she walked.

'I'm Mina,' the whisperling said.

'I'm Eliza.'

The two girls smiled at one another, and Mina grabbed Eliza's hands so their arms were linked like two chains. She lifted them up and then swung them from side to side.

'Match your movements to the melody,' Mina said, picking up the pace when the band got more raucous and dropping it slightly when they sang a slower verse or two. 'Close your eyes, Eliza; it's easier when it feels like nobody's watching.'

Eliza did as she was told. With her eyes closed, she could ignore the feeling of other bodies moving a pace or two away from her. She could opt out of the field of their perception by canceling them from hers, and the result was uplifting. Her body felt less like a wooden toy with metal screws in the joints and more like a unified beam, lifting and dropping with the music. Mina, noting the shift in her confidence, began to add movements. She kept Eliza's hands clasped in hers and swung her around, slowly and gently at first so Eliza could orient herself and then faster and faster. She spun her around on her heels as the music picked up, the song conjuring up images of a lost whisperling discovering the wonder of the Whispering Woods on her own. Eliza pictured herself perching on branches like the child, observing the life cycle of a frog in a pond, collecting flowers to make tea, and learning to use the delicate fibres of bark to darn the holes in her clothes.

For a few minutes, it was like there was a spell cast on Eliza; her breath and body were alight; she thought little of her fears, little of whether she belonged to Teragovia, little of whether she was a competent whisperer, and little of Hugo and the fact that he had lost his life trying to save hers. Mina had been right; the less she thought about the physical act of dancing, the more she actually found herself dancing.

And then the band ended the song, announced that they'd be taking a ten-minute refreshment break, and Eliza was pulled back into the jarring reality that persisted once she opened her eyes. She touched her face, and found it warm and covered in beads of sweat. She looked at Mina shyly and saw that she was smiling broadly.

'See, I told you that anyone can dance!' Having proved her point, Mina walked away back to her friends, leaving a stunned Eliza in her wake.

The formerly dancing crowd moved towards the bar and the table, using the break to line their stomachs and fill them with drinks. Eliza scanned the crowd for signs of Amelie and saw her standing with a group of young whisperlings, most of them male. Something about the presence of males of her own age made Eliza rather coy, and instead of walking up to Amelie, she took distinct steps in the opposite direction. From the corner of her eye, she spotted Lillian for the first time since they had begun their lessons. Just over two weeks had passed since their arrival in Teragovia, and Lillian had only just emerged from rest. Eliza was about to greet her when the band came back on stage. Lillian disappeared in the throng of people that milled back to the square with drinks in their hands.

The band played slower numbers, songs that made people want to move their bodies gracefully. Eliza watched a handsome young boy follow Amelie into the square, looking at her as though he couldn't fully believe that she was letting him have this dance. Amelie wrapped her arms around his neck and let him hold her by the waist. They moved together elegantly, both of them tall and attuned to the music, their limbs moving off their own accord even as they kept their eyes locked the whole time. Amelie's expression was its usual steely one, but her eyes had softened, and Eliza knew that this meant that her guard was down. The boy was openly beaming, his features reeking of contentment as he got to spin the girl whom everyone said would save the realm. As Eliza looked at them, she realised that there were so many forms of love that could be exchanged between people. The thought made her both happy and sad. On the one hand, there was so much love she had the chance to acquire, and on the other hand, it was unclear how she could go about staking her claim onto any of it.

Lost in thought and unabashedly staring at the blissful duo, Eliza was startled when someone grabbed her by the shoulder. She yelped, her instincts from the Woods still alive, sure that a Bardorian soldier had broken through the enchantment and succeeded in finding her.

'Oh my word!' cried a middle-aged man, gripping her shoulders as he exhaled a gust of his smoky breath around her. 'It is you! It has to be!'

Eliza looked at him quizzically, confident that he had mistaken her for someone else.

'Why, it's the same nose and smile and eyes. You're the spitting image of him, you are!'

Her breath caught in her throat as she spoke, 'a spitting image of who?'

'Of your old man, of course. My word, I can hardly believe that I'm speaking to Josef's own daughter. I never thought you'd make it out of there, but there you are, little Eliza, sweet one. I grew up with your father; we

were neighbours, you see. Ah, we must sit down, little
lady; there is much I yearn to tell you!'

Chapter Eighteen

The story of Josef

T he man, who introduced himself as Naoise, was tall and dark-haired. His skin was freckled, and his hands rough from working in the sun. He had a deep voice that shook when it was full of emotion, and throughout his conversation with Eliza, it seemed as though he was on the verge of tears. Eliza herself was dumbfounded. Not even in her wildest dreams had she expected to uncover something about her past, let alone meet someone who had grown up with her father.

'Oh, Naoise, tell me about my Pa! Tell me everything you know!'

'That's Uncle Naoise to you, little one, or Uncle Nano, which is what most whisperlings call me. Go on, bring Uncle Nano a pint to nurse while he talks to ya,' he said, gesturing in the direction of the tavern.

Eliza barely felt her own legs as she walked up to the tavern and asked for a pint. Her hands trembled as she grabbed the mug by the handle and brought it back to Uncle Nano. They walked away from the bright bustle of the Solstice Dance, away from the music and festivities, and sat on the library's stairs. The white marble gleamed in the moonlight and was cold to the touch.

'You grew up with my Pa?' Eliza asked, clasping her fingers together.

'I did, oh I did. We were joined at the hip, some would say. Peas in a pod, real brothers in arms, you know that type of thing! We didn't grow up in a fine city like Teragovia. No, little one, me and Josef, we're village folk. You probably haven't heard of Earlford, have you? Even at the best of times, it was a grim little place. And ever since the Bardorians decided to scorch the earth between the Woods and the sea, there's nothing left of Earlford anymore. Even in its heyday, the village was no work of art, I'll tell you that much. Our houses were small and stuffy and close together. Our streets were narrow, and rats scurried along the drains without a care. But the sea, little Eliza, the sea was in our front yard, and what a mighty beast she was. The bluest thing you ever saw, with great waves crumbling at the shore when the moon was full. The sand was white as snow and littered with shells from half a world away. That was what made Earlford special, that sea, that haunting beauty.'

Uncle Nano paused to take a large swig out of his beer while Eliza waited for him to get to the point in memory lane where he began to reveal more about her father.

'We spent most of our time there, catching crabs, digging up mussels, climbing great rocks, and trying to cast spells that were too great for us. Ah Josef, he was a mad bloke, with his great love for enchantments! He was always trying to bring fossils back to life! Luckily, he never succeeded, but one time he managed to enchant the skeleton of a sea snake to move. Gave me a proper fright, it did; he was always pulling my leg like that, your Pa was.'

'Did you say you were neighbours, Uncle Nano? What was my Pa like?'

'He was grand, Josef was. Aye, we were neighbours and did most things together. We were the same age, and our Ma's took us to the woods together to forage berries and mushrooms, and our Pa's took us fishing together. Josef was gifted though; he was always better than me at everything. He could sniff out a berry bush from a mile away. The biggest fish succumbed to his net. Even at school, he put in almost no effort. No effort at all, yet he was out there, mastering enchantments before the rest of us even comprehended what it meant to free your mind. Despite his obvious superiority, everybody loved him; Josef was always sweet-talking to the baker's wife and getting biscuits pressed into his hands. He always showed the youngins how to catch crabs, swimming further and further with them each time and making the pennies in the wishing well jump out of the water like dolphins. Real showman he was, and everybody loved to watch him; all that was missing was a stage!'

Eliza wasn't sure why but something had begun to stir uncomfortably in her stomach as though she had drunk a glass of curdled milk. 'He sounds impossibly perfect!'

'He was. And loyal to the bone. For most of us, all we ever wanted was to grow up and get out of Earlford.

We wanted to go to the East, where the grandest, wealthiest, and oldest whisperer cities were located. Grand places, like Teragovia, but so very ancient. Touched by the hand of Goddess Ayla herself, some say. There's statues and remains of thrones and jewellery pieces that all belong to her. As soon as we came of age, I told Josef, let's go, let's get out of this dirty old town. Let's go into the world and become rich men. But Josef wouldn't hear of it. He was aghast that I even suggested we leave. No, he was a real Earlford lad; he wanted to die where he was born and then be buried at sea. The thought of watching the moonrise anywhere else in the world was shocking to him.'

Gasping, Eliza shook her head. How could someone love any place so much that they would refuse to give it up for a decidedly better one? Her hands wandered to the fey necklace, her reminder that there was always a backup plan, always another place she could flee to and call home if the current one failed her. She was the happiest she had been in Teragovia, and yet, she couldn't picture being anywhere without one foot in the door and one foot out.

'We parted ways then, little one. It was the hardest decision I'd ever made. I had no desire to leave Josef behind, but I knew that Earlford was no good for me. I wasn't a particularly competent whisperer, and I didn't like the cold lick of the sea. I was made for grand cities, wide streets, and a leisurely life as a shopkeeper. And that's what I did when I made it out to Fionnos, the oldest city of whisperers. I put my coins together to purchase a small shop and sold wares from human towns, spices from the fey, and bits and bobs from the artisans of our village. The coins flowed to me steadily, and there was great potential to expand. I wrote to Josef again and again. Just come for a visit, I told him. Just come and see what you're turning down before you turn it down completely. But Josef was not a lad to be reasoned with once he'd made up his mind. He was adamant that there was nothing outside Earlford that would please him.'

'Was he upset with you for leaving?'

'To be honest, I don't know, Eliza. I wonder about it to this day. I wonder what it would have been like if I had stayed, if I had stuck around long enough to warn him when the tides started to turn, when the Bardorian filth started to spew closer and closer to home. I reckon I was the only one who might have succeeded in getting him to escape, only for your sake if nothing else. But with me in Fionnos, there was no one left at home whom he would listen to. Ah, but I'm getting ahead of myself now!'

Uncle Nano drained the contents of his mug and sent Eliza back to the tavern to bring him another one. Wiser this time, she came back with two, and he chuckled in appreciation.

'That should keep me going for a bit,' he said, slurping from the mug noisily.

'Did you see my Pa after you left for Fionnos?' Eliza asked, hugging her arms close to her chest.

'I did not, little one. In the early days of being in Fionnos, I never had a spare coin to travel homewards and back. Everything I made went back into the shop. I was happy there; I won the love of a good woman and married her soon after. I wrote to Josef to ask him to come to the wedding, but his Pa had passed on about then, and he couldn't leave his Ma alone. He became the breadwinner then, taking the boat out to sea, fishing through bright shoals of fish. He was at peace when he was in the water. The cold spray, the grey chop, the harsh wind - it never bothered him. Josef was a rare example of a man who belonged exactly where he was born. He knew his purpose from the second he stepped into the world. I wasn't fortunate like that, was I now? I had to leave the land behind and make a place for myself elsewhere. And although I was gutted to be getting married without Josef by my side, I carried on. We lost touch for a bit; you know how it gets. I was starting a family and managing the shop, my wife worked in the court of Fionnos, and then she got pregnant, and I had to do her share of the household tasks as well as mine. It was only once my son came out into the world and cried himself hoarse that I was able to write back to Josef. Amid all this chaos, I had missed Josef's wedding too!'

Eliza's heart caught in her chest. This was the first mention of her mother. Her eyes welled up with tears.

'Oh! My mother, my mother! What do you know of her?'

'Not much, I'm afraid. Josef didn't say much; he only wrote to say that she was from a faraway land and it was a delicate matter but that I would love her the second I met her. I was determined to make it back to Earlford for a visit. I hadn't seen my folks or Josef in years. I had made arrangements to go home for a few weeks, all was in motion, and then my wife announced that she was pregnant yet again. I was overjoyed naturally but also distressed because this meant it'd be a few more years before I was able to get to Earlford again. Despite all the grandeur and wealth of Fionnos, I had begun to crave the stuffy alleys of Earlford and the sheen of the sea in the summer and my mother's rhubarb pie and sitting in a tavern with my best mate. For the first time, I started to see the cost of leaving home. Everyone I had ever loved was getting on with their lives, moments big and small were happening day after day, and I wouldn't be around for any of them. This began to eat away at me. I fantasised about going home for good, shutting down my shop in Fionnos, and taking my family to Earlford. I spoke to my wife about it, but she wouldn't hear of it. She did fine work in Fionnos, very important work, far more important than what I did in the shop. She couldn't just walk away from that. Fionnos was a better place to raise children than some rank old village at the edge of the world, she said. She was cruel, but she was right. Still, I quietly tortured myself every day, convinced that my sense of purpose was shattered and that I'd only be able to put it back together in the land where I was born. And then Josef wrote to me saying that he'd had a baby daughter and named her Eliza. And that broke something inside me for good, the first of the breakages that were to come. My word, I cannot believe that I am narrating my sorrowful tale to Eliza, Josef's own daughter. Ah, if only he could see us today, he would be glad, so very glad.'

'You never made it back to Earlford, Uncle Nano?' Eliza asked softly, feeling the weight of his sadness thick and heavy in the air, gnawing at her skin, threatening to flood her insides too.

'I very nearly did, but not in time, little one. My own indecision cost me everything. My life back in Earlford seemed like a distant dream that I looked at through rose-tinted glasses. I had become a sad man, a negligent husband, and an absent father. Around this time, evil was afoot in the realm. We received tidings of Bardorian dominion. At first, we paid it no mind because it was unprecedented for any one creature to attempt to defy the order of Elatonia. As time went on, the news got darker and darker. Entire cities of whisperers on the northern shores had fallen. Those that resisted were murdered, and the others were taken away. We didn't know yet that the whisperers were being interned at camps and forced to do magic to bring Bardorian cities out of their filth and poverty. Bardoria used to be the most repugnant and vile place in all of the realm when I was a boy. Terrible crime, cruel people, and abysmal levels of poverty. Grandalford wanted to reverse that; he wanted to be known as the man who changed the fate of Bardoria for good. And his way of doing that was to pillage and plunder whisperer cities, steal our treasures and imprison our people. Fionnos is the southernmost whisperer city in all of the realm. Even when the worst of the rumours were confirmed, we never thought the Bardorians would make their way over to us. There were countless towns in between as well as the Whispering Woods. There were endless opportunities for others to put an end to this. So we dined and danced and planted our crop without any fears or worries. We never expected the threat to come to our door. But that's what life is

Eliza; it's all the things that happen while you're busy looking the other way.'

Eliza's stomach had taken on the texture of glue. Thick and viscous, it had begun to roil unpleasantly. She knew the story was coming to a close, and she did not want it to end. She wanted to sit on the marble staircase for days and days and pick Uncle Nano's brain about the times he had shared with her father.

'When city after city began to fall to Bardorian forces, panic kicked in. It seemed like any day now; we would be next. People had begun to flee into the Whispering Woods. There were rumours of a city of free folk but no one was quite sure how to get there. There were chances of running straight into Bardorian hands if you took one wrong step in the Woods. Even the fey had severed all relations with others, burrowing deep into the earth, waiting for the terror to pass before they could rise again. My wife and I were perplexed; we couldn't believe that our quiet lives were thrown into disarray like this. And while we fretted about whether to go or to stay, all I could think of was Josef. Earlford would have no chance against Grandalford's soldiers, and I had a terrible feeling that he would stand his ground and choose to die on his own land rather than flee into the Woods. I was worried for him and his wife and his young child. I wrote to him again and again but received no response. I decided that I owed it to Josef to go back for him. I thought, if I take a horse and ride it day and night, I can be in Earlford in three days. I could bring Josef and his family with me, and we could disappear into the Woods and find Teragovia together. I was determined. Josef was my anchor to home, and even though we hadn't seen each other in years, we were bound together in some irreversible way. Despite my wife's protests, I set off one morning. I kissed my son and daughter on their foreheads and promised them I'd be back in a week. I told them to pack their things and wait for me. I'd be coming back with someone who was like a brother to me. Ah, little did I know how terribly wrong I was! Little did I know the extent of the loss I was inviting into my life!'

A single hot tear fell from Uncle Nano's eyes. He gazed into empty space as though the memories had made something come alive for him that he had long since buried. Eliza felt wretched for making him relive this agony, but he seemed to have forgotten that she was there, addressing the ether rather than her, his eyes vacant and dull, slightly glazed over from the beer.

'I borrowed a horse from my neighbour and shot into the wilderness. I rode past the coast road for three days and three nights with barely enough bread and berries in my belly to tide me over till I saw my beloved hometown again. I was almost there, an hour's ride away from town, when I recognised the brackish stench combined with the smell of cow dung wafting through the air. I smiled to myself; a short lived joy, for the next thing I heard was the sound of hooves roaring down a path parallel to the one I was on. I backtracked and hid inside a secret cave on the coast and watched as hundreds of black warhorses with steel-clad human soldiers disappeared in the direction of my village. I knew right then that I was too late and that I had failed my friend and family. There would be no escapees or survivors.

There was no sense in waiting. I jumped on my horse and yanked the reins, changing course so we would go back the same way we had just come. For another three days and three nights, we charged along the route. My eyes were blurred with tears the whole time, and I barely registered the great navy blue of the sea weeping in tandem with me.'

Eliza gasped and covered her face in her hands. Her cheeks were cold like the blood had drained out from her face.

'And then, as I galloped to Fionnos, I saw horrific plumes of smoke rising from the city walls. The air smelled acrid like death had taken over everything. Soot landed on my face; my hands turned black in seconds. I entered a city that had been ransacked and plundered to the last coin. The statues of Goddess Ayla had been toppled over; homes had been broken into, the wares from every shop stolen or flung onto the street. And the bodies. They were everywhere. Those that resisted, those that fought back against the Bardorians. The fountains that once had birds bathing in them were sullied with blood. I ran from corner to corner in search of my family. I checked every body, every home and saw no sign of them. It seemed they hadn't been killed, which meant that they had either escaped or been captured. All because they waited for me to complete a quest that I had failed to make good on. I rode off into the distance, thinking I could save them all, and in the end, because I couldn't choose one or the other, I managed to save no one at all. Everyone perished, and I was the only one who could have done anything about it. I failed them all, Eliza.

Your Pa, your Ma, my wife, my children. Everyone. And you, taken into captivity as a child, living your whole life in Bardorian chains, for crying out loud!'

Eliza opened her mouth to assuage his guilt, to tell him that her life hadn't been all bad. She had known companionship and nursed dreams and been happy. But Uncle Nano continued to speak, the half-empty pint forgotten in his hand.

'You can't know how much relief it brings to my weary old heart, little one, to see you sat there, safe and sound. Josef's daughter returned to me in one piece. I might have been a victim of my own foolishness time and time again and caused immense sorrow for everyone I know, but thank goodness I held on from one day to the next until I lived to see you with my own eyes.'

Eliza searched for the right words but seemed to have nothing to say. She whispered a soft thank you under her breath. Uncle Nano shook his head.

'You needn't say a thing, little one.'

The silence crept in as both got lost in their own murky thoughts, distraught and relieved, trying to be there for each other while also holding their own. Bars of music drifted in from the square, slow and drawn out, signalling that the end of the celebration was near.

'Let's go back there. It's your first Solstice Dance; you mustn't waste the entire night listening to a sad old man tell his story.'

They walked back to the square, which was alive and raucous. Beer and mulled wine coursed through everyone's veins, and the crowd danced together, tipsy on their feet. The band started a new song, a slow number with an upbeat swing. The crowd raised their drinks to the sky as the song was about the parting glass. Halfway through, fireworks began to explode in the sky. Whizzing flowers of pink, yellow and white lit up the night. The moon glowed brightly from behind them. Eliza saw that she was rotund like a pregnant belly, full and radiant. The longest night of the year stretched on all around them, with hours and hours to go before Ayla relinquished her festivities and handed the sky over to Riaz. Even after the music died down and the fireworks subsided, people would linger in the square, drinking in the milky light of the Goddess, gazing at the moon for hours. They said it was a night when dreams came true; even casual utterances came to life. Tina had cautioned Eliza to set only the purest intentions and make only the kindest declarations. However, as Eliza watched the bright black of the night stir itself into the tepid morning light, she found that for the first time, her mind was strangely blank, truly free of everything.

Chapter Nineteen

Eliza and Amelie

For several days, Eliza felt like she was floating on a cloud. She once had a father, a man named Josef. He was intelligent and loyal and loved the sea. She had his features on her face. Eliza lingered by the pond in the backyard for long minutes at a time, looking at her face in the reflection, running her fingers down the bridge of her nose, the high cheekbones, the large watery eyes that had been passed on to her by her Pa. What part of her had come from her Ma? Would she ever know anything about her? The urge to link herself to her family had only been a vague throbbing pain at the back of her heart so far because she had no straws to grasp. Having met Uncle Nano, she began to conjure up images of Earlford and its mesmerising sea, her Pa as a young boy digging up mussels and bathing in the foamy white spray. When you go your whole life without knowing who your Ma and Pa are, when you don't even know the name of the place where you were born, you can traipse through life feeling entirely unmoored. Eliza had uncovered the first big chunk of her own personal history, which tethered her to the world in a real way like never before.

She was so elated that not even the raging dreams during the full moon got her down. Eliza went home and crashed in the wee hours of the morning after the Solstice Dance. The sun had come up already, but the moon took her time to bid her people farewell. Eliza tossed and turned in bed, waking up as soon as she drifted away because her mind would plunge straight into the darkest dreams of derelict landscapes. She would see images of Earlford in ruins, her father's home broken and shattered, his garden reduced to embers. She saw the grand old city of Fionnos ravaged to the ground, its statues and busts splintered and stained with blood. She saw whisperers fight for their freedom and be brutally murdered. Those who surrendered were tied by the neck and led into Bardoria, where they would spend the rest of their short lives working in camps. The images that Uncle Nano had given her were seared into her mind, and she could not shake them off. Her dreams still troubled her, they still made her choke and whimper and become riddled with anxiety, but she did not know how to make them stop.

Eliza preferred the waking hours which she spent daydreaming about her father's strong arms, how he'd row a boat, the way he'd whistle as he strutted through the dank alleys of Earlford. It wasn't the same as actually meeting her Pa, but it was the closest she would ever get, and for the moment, it was more than enough.

Along with this came an inescapable sadness. Now that she knew for sure that her Ma and Pa had perished in Earlford along with the entirety of the village, Eliza knew that there was no hope of ever reuniting with them. She wouldn't just bump into them somewhere in some forgotten whisperer city and discover that they had been pining for her since the day she'd been taken. Uncle Nano's story added a sense of finality to the question of her parentage. Eliza's heart was a bittersweet medley of emotions as she rejoiced and grieved in the knowledge that had fallen into her lap out of nowhere.

Now that she knew who her father was, an unexpected pressure came to fill his boots. Eliza had long since let go of any desire to excel in her lessons, but each time she failed to free her mind during the enchantments lesson, she felt a burning sense of shame - what would her father think! The prodigal Josef, loved and revered by all, and his daughter was an imbecile who couldn't shoot an arrow beyond a few paces. She couldn't free her mind for more than a few seconds, let alone long enough to cast a spell. The others were progressing rapidly. Amelie and Aoife were neck to neck, using the power of the moon to lift leaves into the air and make them hover for a few seconds before they danced to the ground in a lazy hum. Afterward, Aoife would sit with her head in her hands and complain of a headache while Amelie looked unfazed as ever.

Eliza wasn't sure why, but a kernel of resentment had lodged itself into her heart. Every time she saw Amelie shoot an arrow into the middle of the target or carve a dagger in the time that it took Eliza to find a suitable piece of wood, something in her heart grew cold and icy. She accompanied Amelie on her visits into town, watching children flock to her with toffees and slingshots. There was an aura about her that made people want to please her, to shower her with gifts and treats, and admire her skill and strength. Little whisperlings would cartwheel on the grass to impress her and older ones would give her their blessings freely. It was like Amelie could do no wrong, and she did so without making any effort at all. Eliza, who struggled a million times before getting the smallest thing right, began to resent the ease with which Amelie attracted things into her forcefield. All this time, Eliza had been content to hide in Amelie's shadow and revel in the dreams of an ordinary life in the free world. Now that she was Josef's daughter, she longed to be extraordinary too, so that if he were to see her now, he would be proud to call her his blood.

'Do you know who your Ma and Pa were?' she asked Amelie one night as they lay in their beds after dinner.

'I never saw any reason to find out,' Amelie replied curtly.

'You never wondered where you came from and what makes you who you are?'

'The people of Teragovia have raised me - it takes a village, remember? And I know who I am. I've always known.'

Although she didn't explicitly state it, Eliza knew she was talking about her destiny as the Midnight Daughter. She took issue with Amelie's air of being too important and too loved even to need a family. Surely she was lying. Surely she didn't actually think she was too independent to have been a product of other people.

171

Telling her about what she had learned about her Pa felt vapid after this, so Eliza kept silent and found that she enjoyed keeping secrets from Amelie. It gave her a sense of power that she could keep for herself without Amelie's intrusion.

Eliza kept an eye out for Uncle Nano whenever she walked through town, hoping they could sit beside one another again so she could ask him to share more anecdotes about her Pa. But he was nowhere to be seen, and when she asked Tina about his whereabouts, she scrunched her nose and said that he was probably in some tavern at the edge of town, staring at the bottom of the bottle. It seemed he had a reputation for being a sad drunk and only showed up in town from celebration to celebration when the booze flowed freely.

On one chilly evening, Eliza hurried to the library to trade in her book on the mythical creatures of Elatonia for one about the history of the fey folk. She was so distracted by mental images of water horses and cloud falcons that she almost didn't see the winter daughters perched on the marble staircase. They had a bowl of berries and another one of biscuits in between them. Aoife, Seena, Nala, Maud, and Esther.

'Eliza! Where are you off to?' Nala asked, waving to her.

Startled, Eliza looked at them, as merry as can be despite the gloomy overhang in the sky. 'Just the library.'

'Quite the bookworm, aren't you?' Aoife said, gesturing to her to sit down. 'You might as well eat a few biscuits with us; the books won't go anywhere!'

Eliza sat down on the stairs, aware that the last time she had done so, she had spent hours with Uncle Nano, listening to stories of her father for the first time. The girls chatted about the whisperlings in town they fancied. Maud confessed that she had snogged a warrior-in-training named Britta just the night before. They had met in the Woods after hours and explored each other's bodies. The girls oohed and aahed, and all agreed that the warriors were the most beautiful women in Teragovia. Eliza felt coy, unsure how to respond to these comments as she could not imagine having the pluck to sneak into the woods and explore anyone's body.

'What about you, Eliza?' Seena asked her sweetly. 'Is there a lad or a lass who's caught your fancy?'

Eliza shook her head and shrugged her shoulders, hoping she appeared mysterious rather than foolish.

'Out with it, Eliza, it's not as if you're blind. Or are you impervious to the beauty surrounding you?' said Maud, poking her teasingly. 'Too good for the Teragovians, she is!'

The only face that swam to her mind was that of the boy who had danced with Amelie at the Solstice Dance. She wasn't sure if she had noticed him because she had found him attractive or because he was dancing with her friend. Amelie herself had made no mention of him, so Eliza saw no harm in using the boy as a convenient scapegoat to avoid further embarrassment. A series of low oohs went around the group.

'Amelie's boy! I bet she wouldn't like that, would she now?' said Seena, smirking as she reached for a handful of berries.

Above them, the clouds hung in a thick grey sheet. The sun hadn't shone for days and days. There was a fatigued yellow spot in the dark mass where the sun hid. There was a nip in the air, and Eliza shivered.

'I suppose not,' Eliza said, hoping they would move onto a different topic soon.

'Tell us, Eliza, what is Amelie like behind closed doors? Does she ever loosen up? Or is she too busy showing off her powers to have time for fun?' said Aoife. Eliza detected a twinge of disdain in her words and was surprised by it. She hadn't considered the idea that there might be anyone out there who might share her growing resentment towards Amelie.

'Well, she's very kind and helpful, to be honest,' Eliza said, her sense of loyalty triumphing over her resentment. In any case, she didn't want to be gossiping about Amelie behind her back, least of all with the other winter daughters.

'Is she being helpful, or does she simply like to hand out advice to reiterate that she is better than you?' Esther scoffed. 'There was someone at the Bardorian camp who used to do that. One of the humans. She liked to pretend to be our friend so that she could talk down to us without feeling like an absolute wretch!'

Eliza's face flushed. She thought back to the start of her friendship with Amelie. She realised that it had only begun when Amelie saved her life on the rock face, thereby locking them in a dynamic wherein Amelie was superior, and Eliza was indebted to her for everything. Amelie did like handing out advice, and she was often dismissive of Eliza's struggles, chalking them off to Eliza being too whingy about stepping outside her comfort zone, which she claimed was the library.

'You lot don't seem to think very highly of Amelie,' Eliza said. 'Everyone else in town seems to worship the ground she walks on.'

A group of young school girls climbed up the stairs and disappeared into the library. The sounds of vendors advertising their wares came through from the town square: Saffron, mint, cloves, thyme - the freshest from the farms. Birds fluttered past overhead, the swooping noise of their wings like a soft sigh. Eliza looked around, still sometimes stricken by how much there was to the sensory experience of life, how many colours and sounds and textures.

'It's not as though we think she's not talented or skilled,' Nala said fairly. 'It's a bit of a struggle to get on with someone who clearly believes that they're better than you!'

'Britta told me that most Teragovian locals believe Amelie is the Midnight Daughter. I bet she's grown up with people telling her she is oh so special. She never spent any time locked up like the rest of us. It's no wonder she thinks we're beneath her!' said Maud, flicking her sheet of long brown hair to one side.

'You don't think she's the Midnight Daughter then?' Eliza asked, considering the possibility for the very first time.

'I doubt it. I'd put my money on Aoife if I had to,' Seena said, crossing her arms.

'You're a born flatterer, you are,' Aoife said, punching Seena lightly on the shoulder. Seena winked and blew her a kiss.

'Amelie doesn't have the temperament of a leader. The Midnight Daughter shouldn't see themselves as superior to their peers but equal to them. Her role isn't to tread on others but to lift them up. Can you really picture Amelie doing that?' Nala asked, raising her eyebrows.

'Aoife's the only one who can keep up with her in lessons. Rather than enjoying the challenge, Amelie is abrasive towards her. What does that tell you?'

Eliza found herself unable to defend her friend. With a horrific jolt, she realised that Amelie probably saw Eliza as an imbecile, too unimpressive in her skills ever to be a threat to her title. She had the feeling that she'd been picked not for any merit of character but the lack thereof. The realisation hit her like a ton of bricks, and she felt shattered under its weight.

'Though if fairness and kindness are the main criteria, I'd say our Nala is the Midnight Daughter,' said Maud, squeezing Nala's hand.

Nala shook her head and said, 'it doesn't matter though, does it? Regardless of who is the Midnight Daughter, we're all going to be a part of this war. The Midnight Daughter might have the hardest job of all, but we're in it together. We're being trained together for a reason. It's not about who leads and who follows. Fact is, we're not going to free our imprisoned whisperer families without defeating Grandalford, and that means we're going to have to band together in the effort. Even if Amelie does turn out to be the Midnight Daughter, and we're stuck with a leader who thinks we're nowhere near good enough to be her army. We're the winter daughters, and our fates have been sealed together long before any of us met. And what we do, we do not for the Midnight Daughter, but for the realm.

We're the only captives to have ever been freed from Bardorian clutches. Those that still remain deserve to go back out into the world and taste freedom. To feel the sun on their skin and build homes on grassy river banks. To grow old without the fear of the Bardorian whip on their back. Remember, that could have been us, but we were born on the brink of winter, which brought our safe passage into the city of free folk. It is our duty to balance the scales and bring as many as we can into the fold of freedom. What do you think, sisters? Are we not in this together?'

The reveries of a stone house, a pond, and a garden full of herbs began to fade from Eliza's mind. Nala's words sat heavily in her bones. A life of peace seemed impossible if Nala was right. The Midnight Daughter might have the biggest task of all, but all of the others would have to fall in line and buttress the mission. Without noticing, her hands crept to her throat, where the necklace from the fey hung. Perhaps the fey had been right then; perhaps they had looked into her destiny and seen that she was not cut out for the life of a hero in Teragovia. Maybe they knew that the surest way for her to be happy was to have an unremarkable life nesting in nature. And she had turned them down and sealed her fate as a warrior, even if she was the weakest link in the chain. She had severed her last chance at escape, and now she had to fight a war against the mightiest force that the realm had ever seen.

Chapter Twenty

Around the fire

Eliza's evenings at Tina's house were the only things that did not chip away at her sanity. In the clang of pots and pans and the subsequent uproar of Dion and Lou's quarrels, she felt a tranquillity descend upon her. She had learned to make a fire from Tina, who now left it up to her and Lou to get the flames going before they settled in for story time. Her patch of heather was always set in between Dion and Lou's, and they both snuggled up to her as the story went on. Neil had started to show her how he tended to his garden. The rows of turnips intercropped with kale and winterberry. The patch of herbs whose growth slowed down considerably in the winter months. The plump tomatoes and sparkly green basil grew side by side and longed to stew in a pot together in the afterlife. She tried not to think too much of Nala's words. After the initial shock wore off, she reasoned that there was no real urgency in the matter. The powers of the Midnight Daughter were yet to be revealed, a plan of action was yet to be formulated, the Bardorians showed no signs of striking upon Tergaovia, and so on. It could be several years before chaos broke out. In the meantime, Eliza could tend to gardens and start to build a home of her own. Who could fault her for that?

Eliza ushered the chickens into their coop one night and latched the metal grill so that the foxes wouldn't take them at night.

'They like you better, Eliza,' Lou said, her arms folded over her chest. 'They never go in so quickly when I tell them to!'

Eliza flushed. There was the rare little thing she was naturally good at, and so starved was she of compliments that even this morsel offered to her by a child satiated her.

'They like you just fine, LouLou; it's just that the chickens don't always support you talking down to Dion. They know when you're scolding him for the right reasons and when you're not. Try going easy on your brother for a day and see how quickly the chickens fall in line. They'll be racing each other to get back in the coop faster, just you see!'

Lou looked skeptical but offered no resistance nonetheless. Eliza was reminded of Hugo and how he'd try to get her to stop her endless questioning by inventing causal links between her excessive curiosity and the grey of the sea and sky. She waved the thought away and turned her attention to the firewood. Tina and Neil arranged the heather in a circle around the firepit. Next to them was a fat porcelain pitcher filled to the brim with steaming hot chocolate. They poured it into chipped mugs and passed them around. Eliza took her seat and blew on the liquid slowly.

'What story shall we listen to tonight?' Neil asked, cupping his palms around the mug.

'I want the story of the enchanted rivers of Teragovia!' cried Dion.

'But we just heard that one last week!' Lou said, glaring at Dion. Eliza raised her eyebrows and gave her a pointed look.

'Fine, but we'll take only the short version!' This was a noble compromise as far as Lou was concerned.

Niel launched into it. Eliza had seen a mention of it in the book about the mythical creatures of Elatonia but didn't know the whole story.

'In the time of Goddess Ayla, the Woods were filled with creatures that no living whisperer has ever glimpsed. Golden deer, luminescent water horses, large grey falcons, silver mountain goats, and wise old serpents. Each of these creatures was as old as time, created by the trees in the same aged breath with which they created the King and Queen. Throughout the Golden Age, they frolicked freely. Back then, the rivers had no colour, they simply took on the colours of the sky. And remember, the sky went from day to night in seconds, giving the waters a dynamism of their own. Metallic blues went to peachy pinks in a heartbeat. The fish that lived in these waters evolved and grew with the flickering shadows and beams of light. All was well in the realm. But once the quarrels broke out between Goddess Ayla and God Riaz, the ripples of this disruption flowed deep into the rivers. With the moon and the sun sharing the sky in such a tightly wound battle, all the creatures in the Woods and the Water had to change their ways to keep up with the new way of the world. Alas, they could not do it on their own. The fish began to die, and the forest creatures began to worry. Why should the fish and all the creatures that feasted on the fish pay the price for battles fought between two-legged beasts? So the ancient creatures got together and conspired to find a solution.'

The wind whistled around them, bringing sounds from further away. The gurgle of the rivers seemed louder now that they were being talked about. The hoots of owls and mews of cats penetrated the night. The rustle of leaves indicated that the smaller creatures were going about their business. At any given moment, Teragovia was teeming with life and activity, every being moving in tandem with the others, watchful, present, and wholly immersed in their own tiny dramas. Although they had never been seen, Eliza suddenly felt the presence of ancient creatures in the woods, slithering and galloping and bounding around them.

Neil continued. 'Not too far from where we're sitting, they all gathered together. The creatures were tired of the quarrels of the Gods and Goddesses and did not invite them to the conference. But since they conducted it in the home of the fey, the very first fey folk to have emerged from the earth, they were obliged to extend an invitation to them. And so the fey showed up, lines of concern etched onto their faces, for they were the ones that tended to earthly matters while the daughters of the moon tended to matters up above. As the first descendants of the sun channel, they had a duty to safeguard the balance of the earth, to ensure that the divine dance of life was eternally ongoing. The ancient creatures were impressed by the love that the fey had for the land, and all its beings, and they vowed to work in unison with them. A pact was formed between the two, the oldest alliance in the realm's history.'

Eliza shivered. Lou, despite her initial impatience, was deeply drawn into the tale and cared little that it was no longer the short version she had insisted upon.

'The ancient creatures knew that all life came from water. They knew that the health of the rivers and the oceans was considered the utmost sanctity for all life to be preserved. If the water creatures died out, that would affect the health of the soil and the trees and the crop and all the creatures that depended on it for sustenance. The fey decided to use their powers from the sun channel to enchant the waters and protect them forevermore from the actions of those that lived on the land. It was pouring all around them, and the trees had bent their branches together to form shade, for they knew that important work was being done. The fey summoned the sun through the rain, and the intensity of their magic was so strong that the first rainbow appeared in the sky. A crescent of seven different colours, made of dust and light. One for each of the rivers of Teragovia. The colours fell from the sky with the rain and pulsed through the waters to form a binding enchantment so that as long as the sun was up, the creatures of the water would gain all their sustenance from the bright yellow and white light.'

Eliza gasped, knowing that she would never look at the rivers in the same way again. 'The sun channel protects waters in the city of whisperers! How absurd!' she exclaimed.

'It seems absurd now that we have splintered into such separate existences, Eliza, but keep in mind, when the first whisperers and the first fey were born from the lineages of Ayla and Riaz, their instinct was not to combat but to combine. There was little distinction between cities of whisperers and humans and fey. Each had areas where they dominated, but the duty to rule and the right to enjoy the yield was shared by every creature that called any place their home. Over the centuries, every creature began to think less and less about the welfare of the whole and only about their own species, their own families, or only themselves. And that is why we have such a great divide in how we live. The Bardorians have been rearing their heads for decades, yet fey and whisperer have not been able to work hand in hand. Now I'm no Council member or scholar; I'm only a farmer who tills his wee square of land. But I know this - if the realm is to be saved, it is not for one group to defeat another and secure victory. No, the goal must be to get all the groups to work together to see the foolishness of this divisive spirit. Mark my words, Eliza, it's not the Bardorians who are the real enemies but this idea that we've all nurtured over the years that our differences bear more weight than our similarities. Anyhow, let's get back to the tale, or else Lou will give me a dressing down for deviating off course again!'

Pleased with the allusion to her authority, Lou sat up primly and looked over at Eliza.

'So the fey magic protects the rivers in the daytime when the sun shines brightly over all of the lands. But what about the nightfall? What would happen then? The ancient creatures spoke up. They were born before the Gods and Goddesses and bowed neither to the sun nor the moon. Their allegiance was not to any group but only to the balance of the world. They released themselves from the bondage of the world up above and called in the ancient magic so that they could become one with the water and live beneath its bubbling surface. They would sleep in the day while the magic of the sun ensured that the water was able to safeguard all the life that dwelled in it. And at night, the creatures would open their eyes and drift through the water, breathing life into all the things that moved and crawled and slithered at the bottom of the river. And thus, for centuries, the magic of the fey has worked in tandem with the ancient creatures to safeguard the rivers of Teragovia!'

Her brows crinkled; Eliza asked, 'I thought whisperer magic was bolstered by water bodies. How do we access the moon channel if we're cut off from the magic of the rivers?'

'But we're not, Eliza, we're not. That is the beauty of this enchantment. It's not an inhibitory thing; there's no malice in it. Whisperers can still draw moon magic from the rivers on dark moon nights when our direct access to the moon is cut off. The enchantment only seeks to protect the life already in the rivers. Between the fey and the ancient creatures, the motive was to secure the balance in the waters so that the affairs on land would not disrupt the life forms that lived beneath the water. You see what I mean, Eliza - it's never been about fey, whisperer, or human. It's only ever been about how our powers can work together to safeguard the earth, to maintain the balance, and live in harmony. I might be old-fashioned, but that's what I think.'

The words had barely rolled off his tongue when a sharp rap on the front door startled them all. They were not expecting visitors at this hour. Tina went to answer the door, and Eliza picked up the empty mugs to bring them back to the kitchen. As she entered the house, she saw Tina open the door to two sentries whose faces were stony in their seriousness. They spoke in low tones, and Tina let out audible gasps. The exchange was brief, and she returned with a spark in her eyes.

'Eliza! Tierza, Riani, and Kiani have returned! They're with the Council now. An emergency meeting will be held in the square now; come on, let's go!'

Chapter Twenty One

Bad tidings

Eliza barely had time to collect her thoughts before they rushed off into the darkness, followed by several others from neighbouring houses. Neil stayed behind with the children, much like the other fathers. The meeting was mandatory for the women. They walked down the mud road into the town square, Eliza was breathless with excitement, for this was the one piece of news she had wished for with all her might.

As soon as they arrived in the town square, she hunted down the other winter daughters and stood close to them, for they knew how deeply important this event was. Amelie was nowhere to be seen; it was likely that she had been summoned by Tierza already. Eliza stood in between Aoife and Nala and waited for the empty platform in the square to fill up with Council members. While they waited, all the womenfolk of Teragovia assembled. The square grew full and warm, nervous chatter breaking out everywhere as everyone discussed what news would come to light at the meeting.

The moon was like an orange segment in the sky, shapely and bright, looking on without care at the trifling affairs of her descendants. The Council Mistress walked onto the platform and addressed them in a booming voice. Her silver hair had been plaited into a long weave that tapered down to her hips. It looked more like the tail of an ancient creature. 'Blessed be, Teragovians,' she said, bowing her head slightly. The crowd responded to her greeting. 'My deepest apologies for rousing you from your hearths at this hour. A most essential matter has come to my knowledge, and I felt it was right to bring it to you right away. The Council operates with full transparency, and we, the city of the free folk, have every right to all and any information that may affect our safety.'

The crowd broke out into soft murmurs, weighing their conjectures against their neighbours'. Eliza's eyes darted from one end of the platform to the other, hoping the three missing women would emerge sooner than later.

'Most of you have heard by now that our beloved Tierza, Riani, and Kiani were separated during the completion of their mission to rescue and bring back the winter daughters. After freeing the last of the winter daughters from a Bardorian wasteland, they were on their way back to our city when their identity was given away by one of the informants in Augrives. They stayed back to fight off the humans while Lillian could escape with the winter daughters. Not much has been known about their whereabouts or circumstances since then. They did not communicate with us using the trees, so we feared the worst and scarcely let ourselves hope for the best. However, against all odds, the three women have returned, battle-scarred and bloodied, but in one piece.

They bring back bad tidings, Teragovians; they say that evil is at our doorstep. There's no sense in me telling their story when they are here to tell it themselves. Before we dive into serious matters, let us take a moment to greet the freedom fighters of Teragovia back into our fold.'

Strong applause rang out amongst the crowd as the women cheered the unexpected returnees. Tierza, Riani, and Kiani walked onto the platform, still dressed in the tunics and armour they'd had when Eliza had last seen them. Each of their faces was pockmarked with scars and bruises. Their clothes suffered wear and tear, unpatched holes gaping through their thighs and bellies. They were in a poor state indeed, yet their expressions were stoic, stern, and tough, a reminder that the life of a warrior was what they had chosen, what they had been born for.

Tierza stepped up to the front, her arms behind her back, and bowed low to the crowd. Her silver hair was matted and dreaded, held back loosely in an ineffective bun.

'Greetings Teragovians. Despite the circumstance, it is a pleasure to be home and look at each of you. It has been a couple of years since we left on the mission, and I have longed for this moment ever since. Although we were captured towards the end, I consider this to be a highly successful mission. We were able to free and deliver each of the winter daughters to Teragovia and begin their training soon after their moon cycles commenced. Zara tells me that the Midnight Daughter is yet to reveal herself, but I believe it will happen soon, for the darkest days are nearly upon us. Aye, I speak the truth not to strike fear into your hearts but to caution you so that we can work together harder than ever. Elatonia needs you, each of you. The great war is coming. Let me begin at a more appropriate point so you can hear my tale and decide for yourself if my warning is entitled to some merit.'

Eliza noticed that her breath had become short and shallow. She tried to slow it down and placed one hand on her heart. It thudded like a wild thing in a cage, rattling against iron bars in an attempt to break free.

'I believe everyone was privy to our story until we arrived in Augrives. While we took cover from an unforeseen storm in the human town, our identity was compromised, and we were forced to flee in a haphazard fashion. The loathsome men in the tavern didn't care for much beyond the bounty that hung over our heads. They wanted the fat sack of Bardorian coins promised in exchange for any information about the winter daughters. We stayed back and fought them off so that the winter daughters could follow Lillian into safety. The humans were determined to take us captive and present us to Grandalford's soldiers when they arrived, and we were outnumbered ten to one. Ultimately, we were incarcerated, and when the Bardorians rocked up on their black warhorses, they seized us and left the humans disgruntled, for they left them no coins in exchange. That's what you get for trusting the words of a Bardorian. Anyhow, we were taken on horseback back to Bardoria, a brutal journey without food or drink. We arrived in the dead of the night and were presented to a warlord by the name of Mattias who was in charge of the whisperer camps. For many days and nights, we were tortured by him in a dark cell where not a single beam of moonlight was allowed to enter.'

A series of angry shouts erupted through the crowd. People shook their heads and stamped their feet. Eliza clutched her throat and felt her stomach churn mercilessly, for it was clear that this was only the beginning of their tale of agony.

Tierza continued, her face betraying no sign of struggle or overwhelm. 'We kept silent; there was no way we would reveal anything to the Bardorian's that would aid their conquest of the realm. They questioned us most harshly, which is all I will say. Even though we were battered and bruised and weary to the bone, I would close my eyes and think of the moon until I could feel a crescent-shaped burn on my forehead. This gave me peace even on the most trying days, even when my skin singed and my blood boiled. I knew then that Ayla was watching over me from the moon that she was witnessing my sacrifice and preparing me for what was to come next. I half-wish that I had stayed in that chamber for a lot longer because what came next was interminably worse.'

A collective gasp emanated from the crowd. People shook their heads and covered their mouths. Eliza spotted Amelie rushing into town from the mud path that led to the forest. Her expression was frantic, her hair tousled, as though she had dragged herself out of bed while still half-convinced that this was all a dream. She waved to her, but Amelie's eyes were fixed on the platform.

Tierza continued her tale, her voice laden with angst and hardness. 'I thought I knew what evil Bardoria was capable of, but I was wrong. Nothing could have prepared me for what was to unfold. The state of those camps was utterly miserable, truly not something I even wish on the Bardorian's once we overthrow them. In dungeons deep underground, where neither the light of the sun nor moon can enter, the whisperers are forced to do the bidding of King Grandalford. Entire factories and mines exist beneath the earth's surface, unbeknownst to the common Bardorian villager. Thin trickles of water are pumped through aqueducts so that whisperers can access some portion of the moon's energy, but this water is neither fully charged by moonlight nor adequate for any whisperer to wield, so she might break out of her shackles and make her way to freedom. No, there is only enough of the moon's energy in those aqueducts for the work that Grandalford needs doing. Our sisters and brothers are trapped underground, taking weak currents of energy from oily aqueducts and putting them into mythstones that power Bardorian homes. For every Bardorian who dwells comfortably in a modern home on top of the earth without a care, at least five whisperers underground are working tirelessly in squalor. Two measly meals per day, a drink of water three times, and crowded rooms where as many as fifteen people sleep in appalling conditions. And we all know what happens to whisperers when they don't see the moon for this long. Our lifespans are halved; we perish in the prime of our lives. It is the moon that gives us our lifeforce; we cannot be kept away from her for so long. But in Barodorian dungeons, whisperers are not treated as people. Nay, they are mere objects, tools to be used for their utility and then discarded without a care in the world. In the time we were there, we saw at least five whisperers younger than us succumb to the insanity of these camps. I never thought I would say this, but I fear death might be a kinder alternative to what I have seen whisperers endure in those wretched camps!'

Tears were flowing freely from Eliza's eyes. All around her, women were dabbing at their eyes using their sleeves and scarves. Eliza could barely believe the words that were coming out of Tierza's mouth. She had grown accustomed to the knowledge that the Bardoria that Hugo had told her of was not the Bardoria that whisperers knew it to be. Still, the horrors exacted by this level of cruelty were unfathomable. Whatever became of the famed human spirit? Its generosity? Its nobility? This was dastardly and grim, lacking any fervour except the will to bloody and brutal dominion.

'We were lucky to have fully charged mythstone pendants with us that the guards didn't recognise and left on us. We stayed only a handful of days in the dungeons, enough time for us to gather information and figure out the best escape route. The prisoners there helped us; they created a distraction so we could use the moonstones to blast our chains and get away. We hid in the dungeons for days, right under the noses of the guards, because we knew their search parties would find us right away. And then, when we were certain that the search parties had traveled too far already, we broke out. The prisoners cheered us on; they put on brave faces and told us to bring an end to Bardorian rule. They wanted little from life except to see the moonlit sky once again.' Tierza paused to wipe a tear from her eye.

'I wish these were the worst of our tidings. But there is more cause for alarm. We befriended a few whisperers who filled us in on what they knew of Grandalford's agenda. The guards there are the vilest creatures and are prone to regaling tales of Grandalford's cruelty to torture further the whisperers that are trapped in the dungeons. When we'd break for lunch, they would clang their staffs against the metal bars of the railing and belch out whatever horrors Grandalford had been up to with so much mirth that I fear I will never be able to look upon a human face with kindness. They told us that Grandalford not only plans to conquer all of Elatonia but that he will stop at nothing to incapacitate and enslave both fey and whisperer so that we are forevermore bound to him. His tactic has always been to thwart the ancient magic that strengthens us and then attack. He plans to do the same to the fey that he has done to us. Through his whisperer camps, he has legions and legions of moonbloods that power his civilisation. Now he wants dominion over the sun channel. He wants to ensnare the fey so that they can give him all the earth's secrets. And then he wants to domesticate the land, destroy the forests and bring them all under cultivation so that Bardorian bellies can be full of seasonal delicacies all year round. He wants fey medicine to be encoded and kept with his people so that they can grow taller and stronger and sharper and bow not even to death. He has begun to fell trees mercilessly and rip mycelium from the earth. Without the trees, the fey cannot harness the sun.

Without the mycelium, whisperers cannot speak to one another across great distances. In this fashion, Grandalford is not only emptying our reserves, but he is also destroying the ancient magic that holds the world together. Who knows what will happen when that magic is gone? Will we even recognise a world without trees? When we are at our weakest, he will strike. The longer we sit here and do nothing, the more time he has on his hands to destroy the pillars of our world. We cannot bide our time any longer, Teragovians. The time has come to bring the Bardorians down and liberate the innocents that live and die by the Bardorian sword. We must not be afraid; we must lead the realm back to times of peace and balance, when all its creatures drank from the same pond without a care when we wished nothing but wellness and prosperity for one another. It is a terrible paradox of this world that sometimes the only way to peace is through war. But we must not let ourselves forget that we did not choose this course. We did not destroy the realm with our selfishness and ambition. We did not usurp the ancient balance that has governed all the creatures of Elatonia. We are the ones who have been wounded most by Bardorian vileness. It is time we stopped tolerating it. It is time we gathered our troops and met the forces of Bardoria head-on. It is time to rise, Teragovians; it is time to rise now!'

Tierza's voice rang like a church bell, echoing through the town square, ricocheting off the hardened bones of the furious citizens who were all white with rage. Eliza found that her hands were shaking. War was no longer a distant notion, but it was right here, and if they didn't march to it first, it sounded like it would come to them instead, an outcome that seemed far worse. Eliza looked up at the sky and saw that the moon had turned ominously red as though her capillaries had burst, and now the blood was flowing everywhere. Aoife took her hand and squeezed it. She squeezed it back and saw that the winter daughters had formed a chain of linked arms, no one else realising what this declaration meant quite as profoundly as they did. They would be at the frontlines; they were the ones who were prophecy-bound to persist with this mission until their last breaths. Eliza squeezed hard on Aoife's palm and searched for Amelie again. Her resentment had flatlined for the moment, and she wanted nothing more than to clasp the hand of her first friend, the Midnight Daughter, the one who would save the realm. But Amelie had disappeared; her long blonde hair was impossible to miss as it fluttered wildly in the wind. Tierza had left the platform too, and Zara had taken over, her eyes flashing furiously despite the calm arrangement of her features.

'Thank you, Tierza, for saying your piece. The Council will meet at daybreak to discuss this matter further. Until we conclude the best course of action, I would like all Teragovians to prepare themselves physically and mentally for the perils that lie ahead. The winter daughters will commence their lessons in Ancient Magic with the Oracle. The warriors will be recruiting new soldiers. We are not at war yet, but I imagine we will be soon enough. We will summon you once again as soon as we have arrived at a decision. Until then, peace be with you Teragovians, and may you drink in the days of quiet that follow. They might be the last ones we see for a long, long time.'

Chapter Twenty Two

Lessons in Ancient Magic

Miriam took the winter daughters to Oracle Moonfall's dwelling right after breakfast. The girls were nervous; most of them reported not having slept a wink the previous night. Eliza had managed to catch Amelie before they left the lodging. Her eyes had been blank and confused, as though she too was exhausted by the constant whirlpooling of reality.

'You must be delighted to have Tierza back!' Eliza had said warmly, desiring nothing more than to bury the resentment and converge with all the daughters as a united front.

'Of course I am!' Amelie had snapped, her eyes flickering over Eliza without registering her presence in any particular fashion. 'Always one to state the obvious, aren't you?'

Wounded, Eliza had turned away without asking Amelie why she'd been late to the meeting. She had her suspicions but did not want to make assumptions until she'd heard the news from the horse's mouth. She remembered what Maud had said about whisperlings going off to the woods to explore each other's bodies.

Perhaps Amelie had been doing the same with the boy from the dance. The most handsome youth in Teragovia was carrying a torch for Amelie; there was no surprise in that. Despite the threat of war lurking around the bend, Eliza's mind was caught in petty matters. Her own worries felt real and tangible - the realm was still an abstract notion to her. A set of towns and villages strung together by networks of trees and mycelium, where ancient magic ran through the rivers and fell from the sky and wafted through the air. In it, different groups of people warred and fought and lived in fragments so they could each honour their pasts and forge their futures in their own unique way. Eliza kept contrasting Tierza's fury with Neil's temperance. Tierza had been reared as a warrior and saw no resolution to the conflict but the annexation of Bardoria and a toppling of their power. Neil seemed to believe that the problem was buried far deeper, covered by one veneer after another of social norms that made people forget that they had more in common than apart. And yet, only one of them could be right. Which of them was it? After listening to the horrors of the Bardorian camps, even Eliza's residual love for her erstwhile homeland had disintegrated. That love had chafed her heart and held her hostage for too long. But were anger and hatred a suitable fuel for her drive? Did she want to become someone who acted out of revenge and rage instead of fairness and compassion?

These were the questions on Eliza's mind as they trudged up the lonely path to the Oracle's home. It was unnaturally warm that day. The air had the nectarine odour of springtime, and the sun shone so brightly that

Eliza had to squint in the light. The air was warm and licked her arms, and the river glistened like a thousand diamonds were caught in each ripple. And yet it felt unnatural, for it was the middle of winter, a time for wind chill and frost.

Miriam knocked on the Oracle's door. She took even longer to open it this time. The purple grass shook in the wind, bent this way and that by the weight of the small insects that used it as a thoroughfare. Eliza wiped the sweat from her brow and fanned herself with a broad leaf from the ground.

When the Oracle finally answered the door, she did not say a word but gestured to the area behind the house. They walked to the clearing under the shade of the spider oak. The Oracle wore a purple shawl draped around her shoulders and a wreath of feathers on her head. More feathers dangled from her earlobes. Her forearms were bare, exposing faint tattoos all along their length. Strange symbols, ancient runes, and unusual designs marked her arms in fading black ink. Eliza wondered if her entire body was covered in tattoos.

'I have been instructed to commence your lessons in Ancient Magic, winter daughters,' the Oracle said, gazing at each of them long and hard. 'I have been instructed to do so, and I shall honour the decree, for I am but a subject of Teragovia, obliged to follow the rules much like anybody else. But I have made it clear to the Council Mistress that Ancient Magic is not something that can be taught overnight. It is a long and slow unraveling, it requires total submission and total surrender. Have any of you gained mastery over your mind? Have any of you succeeded in casting enchantments that are more than party tricks?'

The girls flushed and shook their heads. The fresh sense of determination they had gathered after the previous night's revelations took a hit with the Oracle's words. Did she not think that the daughters were ready? If she who could tease answers from the past and look into the eye of the future believed that they were not equipped, then how could they even consider going to war?

'That's what I thought. Ancient Magic is taught to whisperlings after years and years of lessons. This very clearing that you find yourselves on is hallowed ground. Generations of whisperers have stood here and purged their souls to connect deeply with the Ancient Magic. I have seen how much they struggle and how few can truly surrender and open up the channel for the magic to pass through their blood. Every whisperer, fey, and human contains seeds of this magic within. But it takes something different for each seed to sprout, winter daughters. For the seed of a tomato, a day of rain and the dropping of a snail is adequate. For the seed of a tobacco plant, which lays dormant and waiting for decades, it takes a forest fire. Which will you be?'

Deflated, Eliza took a seat on the mossy ground. Amelie's brow was wrinkled, the enormity of the task ahead appearing unassailable even to her. The Oracle stood in the middle, the girls arranged around her in a crescent shape.

'The Ancient Magic that we will attempt to wield is not your ordinary magic. It is not about the trifling enjoyment you gain when you pelt a stone a few meters away to scare your sibling. It is not about the larger than life matters of life and death either. The Ancient Magic is about honouring a code, winter daughters. It is about reaching deep into yourself, bathing in self-knowledge, cultivating awareness of who you are, and embracing that self authentically. This becomes the foundation stone, the base atop which all else is built. Without this self-knowledge, you will sink into the quicksand of your own shadows, the tantalising lure of all the things you wish you could be but are not. This is a trap we all fall into early on, the greed to live a hundred lifetimes in one, the wish to be both hero and hermit, monk and majesty, farmer and fiend. Such a desire is innocent, evidence of an untrained mind. You are not to be blamed for wanting the world, winter daughters, but you are expected to look past the smoke show of distractions and ask yourselves: who am I?'

The Oracle instructed them to close their eyes and ponder upon the question for a few minutes. Eliza, who had long since begun to avoid the fervent chatter of her own mind, took a deep breath and half-heartedly did as she was told. Who am I? What a peculiar question; what sort of an answer was she to put together? She was a whisperer, a winter daughter, Josef's child, Lou and Dion's adopted sister. Was it meant to be that easy, or was she missing something?

'And what did you arrive at? Who are you?'

'A winter daughter!' said Maud.

'A woodcarver!' said Seena.

'A warrior!' said Amelie.

'A daughter of the moon!' said Aoife.

'A weapon against the Bardorians!' said Esther.

The Oracle shook her head. 'You must strip back these tangible labels. Inspect your life closely. Really, think of who you are. What defines you, what drives you, what makes you feel whole and complete and truly yourself?'

They closed their eyes and sat with the question again. Eliza's mind drew blanks. Was there anything in particular that defined her? When she had first been rescued, she had been plagued by the notion that she was a human who had been mistaken for a whisperer. Through the course of the journey to Teragovia, she had discovered her affinity for the woods and its creatures and considered abandoning the promise of a new life to sequester herself quietly in the woods. Upon arriving in Teragovia, she had been swept away by the simple lives of those who lived at the edge of the city, planted bulbs, read books, and tended to their sheep. Then she had learned of Josef and his mammoth abilities and longed to be extraordinary in some way, to be fitting of a father who was larger than life in every sense. It seemed that at every moment, the defining force in her life was to be anything but what she actually was. To be greater, better, stronger, faster, or be someone else entirely. What did that say about her now?

The Oracle asked again. 'Who are you?'

'I am a young woman born at the brink of winter whose fate has been sealed by the prophecy,' Amelie ventured.

'Ah, but until the prophecy is proven to hold true for you, you cannot tether your fate to that of the Midnight Daughter. You are presently in a state of great potential. What else defines you?'

'I am a whisperling who has been chained and made to work in a Bardorian camp until my rescue,' said Esther quietly, her voice devoid of its characteristic hardness.

'Are you defined by your past alone, winter daughter? Will that tragedy forever determine who you will be?

Eliza, who had been silent thus far, said, 'I am a creature who wants what she does not have. I am driven and defined by my impulses.'

'Now that's a good start, winter daughter; what sort of impulses are these?'

Not expecting to be prodded further, Eliza took a few moments to gather her thoughts. Her cheeks burned hotly as she said, 'the impulse to belong, the impulse to be safe, the impulse to care for someone and be cared for.'

The Oracle smacked her palm on her thigh and said, 'Aha! There's something we can work with. We're only scratching the surface still, but oh, this is a precious place to begin! You might wonder why this question matters at all, winter daughters. You might wonder what this question of mine has to do with anything. But if you understand the Ancient Magic to be the bare bones of the earth, the most intrinsic and fundamental part of the world when all pretenses and layers and masks are dropped, then you will see that the only way of interacting with such a force is to also drop your pretenses and layers and masks. The greater the sum of the distractions around you, the greater the distance between you and your truest self-knowledge. If you do not know who you are, how might you expect to recognise the sturdy, undying, noble force of the Ancient Magic that dances right under your nose? The more deeply connected you are to yourself, the more deeply you can connect with anything else! To talk to each other using the mycelium underground, to speak to the ancient creatures that live invisibly amongst us, to receive guidance from Ayla, to interpret the dreams sent to us from the moon, to do all of this and more, you must first foster the deepest possible connection with yourself.'

The Oracle's words hung heavy in the air. For girls that were in the midst of the fifteenth winter of their lives, they had neither the experience nor the knowledge to know how to even begin a task as endless and demanding as knowing oneself. Every day, they were brought in front of the Oracle, who would put them through various tasks to bring them closer to their personal truths. Some days, she would float around thought experiments devised to get them to think deeper about their own desires and drives. She would ask them to envision a place where they felt safe, to imagine every detail of it, the colours and sounds and smells, and where in their body they felt the contentment. And then she would declare that a flood had forsaken their safe place and cackle wildly as they sighed. The Oracle enjoyed shaking up their thoughts, drawing them into comfortable snares, and then snatching the rug from under their feet. She would make them sit around a clear pond and gaze at their reflections. 'Are you seeing yourself? Do you feel connected to the face in the water? Is that who you are?' she would call out, laughing to herself as though she had displayed top-tier humour.

Eliza found these exercises to be more peaceful than the others. She had a tendency to overthink in any case, and this was the sort of lesson that rewarded contemplation. She found herself speaking up and responding to the Oracle's questions more and more. The Oracle rarely rebuffed her, which did a great deal for Eliza's confidence. Although she was no closer to sending messages through the mycelium, it seemed as though she was headed in the right direction, that one of these days, something would click, and lo behold, she would be a mistress of Ancient Magic! She kept thinking back to the story that Neil had told them about the rivers of Teragovia. Whenever she walked past the rainbow hues, she took a moment to gaze at the gurgling greens and violets and reds to search for the ancient creatures that lay under the water's surface, to summon them over to her so she could feast on them with her own eyes and confirm that they were in fact real!

The heatwave continued for days, and sweat dribbled down their noses. And then, one morning, they woke up to the sight of everything covered in frost. A thin glaze of white ice perched on every blade of grass, every rooftop, and bare tree branch. The Oracle lit a fire in the clearing, and they closed their eyes and contemplated their question of the day - what is my biggest strength.

The Oracle didn't pay mind to linear progression. Some days, she would have them meditate and mull over questions that were constructed to produce self-knowledge, such as, what makes me feel alive? What are the values most dear to me? And other days, she would have them read poetry from dusty manuscripts and write their own. One time, she even blindfolded them all and cast an enchantment on the birds in the trees to create a long, fluid song, and the daughters were made to stand up and dance in the clearing, dance to their heart's content because there was no one watching! These lessons grew to be so enjoyable that Eliza almost forgot that they were somehow being prepared for war. That these lessons would form the cornerstone of the skills they needed to cultivate in order to beat the Bardorians. It seemed that the Oracle had so far only begun the process of breaking them out of their shells, prising them out of their comfort zones, and forcing them into unknown pastures. This was indubitably one small step that preceded several much larger ones, and yet; it was unclear whether they would ever move beyond it.

And then, out of the blue one day, the Oracle led them past the clearing and into the woods. She sang a song of some kind under her breath, a low hum punctuated with deep notes from her belly. Her voice drew out curious hares from their burrows and floppy otters from the river. They gazed at her keenly as though they recognised the tongue she spoke in. The Oracle paid them no mind and continued walking deeper into the woods, her twisted wooden staff supporting her weight with each step.

She stopped in front of an oak tree, bigger than anything Eliza had seen in her whole life. It had a hollow so large that all of them could fit inside it. It was more like a cave that happened to have branches growing out of it than a tree! The Oracle led them into the cavernous space and giggled wickedly, the twinkle in her eye visible even in the dim light. There were cobwebs hanging from the sides, and some of them had spiders with shiny metallic bodies stationed at the centre of the web, their long silky legs frozen in time. Eliza wondered what peculiar task the Oracle would have them do this time.

'Winter daughters, I believe you have been stretched, pulled, and kneaded plentifully over the last few days. I'm not expecting much to come out of this, but I intend to check the pulse of this congregation and see where we stand now. Today, we are going to do something exciting.' The Oracle rubbed her palms together and stared at them gleefully, unbothered by the smell of bat scat around them. 'Today we will attempt to use the mycelium to communicate! It'll only be a short distance, from this end of the tree to the other end. One daughter at each end, sitting on the ground with her eyes closed. Communicating in specific words is much harder, so let us start with images. I want one of you to hold an image in your mind, it can be of anything at all; the simpler the better. And place your hands on that bit of tree root that is jutting out of there. Clear your mind, connect to yourself and visualise this image traveling from the root to the mycelium below and up the root on the other end. And lo behold, we should have the image zapped into the mind of the daughter sitting over there!'

The girls were split into twos. Amelie stood next to Eliza, assuming they would be part of the same pair.

Eliza frowned, for Amelie thought nothing of being rude to her and seemed to believe that Eliza would be willing to partner up with her regardless. But there was no point in protesting because the other winter daughters had paired up already, and there was no one left for her to team up with.

Aoife and Nala went first. Nala sat on the receiving end, and Aoife sat on the other side. Aoife closed her eyes and held onto the dusty curve of the root that stuck out from the damp earth. She inhaled and exhaled deeply and had her eyes scrunched in concentration. For several long minutes, nothing happened, nothing at all. And then Nala seemed to shudder a little before whispering, 'was it the sun? Were you picturing a sunrise?'

Aoife nodded and pumped her fist in the air. 'Oh yes!'

'It was the faintest image, barely a glow, but maybe it's because I know you so well that I could tell it was a sunrise?' Nala said, tilting her head.

'We'll never know!' said the Oracle happily, gesturing at them to switch places. With Aoife on the receiving end this time, the girls repeated the actions. The others looked on expectantly, but the minutes ticked on without a flash of recognition on Aoife's face. Finally, Nala removed her hands from the root and touched her forehead. 'My head hurts!' she said, closing her eyes again.

The Oracle gestured to Amelie and Eliza to go next. Amelie confidently walked over to one end and left Eliza to be the receiver. A cold sweat had gathered on

209

Eliza's brow. She knew that her prowess in the lessons so far was seconds away from being demolished. Her experience as someone competent at lessons was short-lived, she had always known this, but reverting to the class average after growing accustomed to being at the top would be no fun at all. Eliza sat on the receiving end and held onto the root with closed eyes, sure that it would be a matter of seconds before Amelie sent an image whipping through the mycelium and into her head.

Eliza waited and waited, opening her mind to the best of her ability, waiting for something to appear. Other than the flurry of images from her own mind, images she knew to be distinctly her own concoctions, nothing else came to her. She knew Amelie was stubborn and not the type of girl who quickly admitted to failure, so she was sure they would sit there for hours. Luckily, the Oracle intervened and said that they should switch places and try it the other way.

Even with her eyes closed, Eliza could feel the waves of anger radiating off of Amelie. Her resentment was primarily directed at herself for not excelling at the task at hand but also at Eliza, lest it was a blockage on her part that had prevented her image from traveling across the distance between them. Eliza paid it no mind and sucked in a deep breath. She felt the cool air enter her windpipe and make its way all the way down to her belly. She touched the root with the tips of her fingers and tried to connect with herself, as the Oracle had said they should. She pictured her face in the pond the first time she had seen it. Her still features looking back at her through the clear water. Her dark hair, lifted cheekbones.

Who am I? The question ran through her mind over and over again. Eliza felt a deep longing surge from her chest, the longing to have a life of peace, quiet and unassuming excellence, even if it was only in knowing just when to rip a carrot from the soil. The image of the carrot, long, sturdy, and orange was embedded in her mind and became what she was sending through the root. She could picture the fine hairs that hung from its skin, the wispy green leaves that sprouted from the head. She could even taste it and hear the crunch it would make when she bit into it. Her cheeks warmed up, and something began to swirl inside her. At first, it felt like a single leaf blown by the wind and then proceeded to a swift circular motion, as though the leaf had been caught in the whip of a raucous storm. The energy made her feel bloated like she would explode if it didn't leave her body soon. A sharp pain started to stab at her forehead, and she bit her lip to stop herself from crying out loud. A ringing sound went off in her ears and drowned out the distant calls of birds and the hum of the bees. Her hands began to shake on the root, and Eliza wasn't quite sure what was happening.

As her head grew lighter and lighter, she heard Amelie's stiff voice calling out from somewhere far, far away. 'Is it a carrot, Eliza? Did you really send me an image of a carrot?'

That was the last thing Eliza heard before her thoughts withered away, and her mind fogged up. Before she knew it, she had fallen to the ground in a dead faint.

Chapter Twenty Three
Who is the Midnight Daughter?

Eliza could have forgotten about her fainting spell in the woods if it was only an isolated incident. However, it was hard to get on with it because it happened every single time. Eliza was out cold for a long time that first time, and their first session was cut short in this fashion. In the next session, Eliza and Amelie were made to go last in case Eliza fainted again and disrupted the class. The other winter daughters struggled to send images to one another, and the Oracle cackled and stomped her feet as though it was all rather funny. Amelie had no luck after the first lesson and remained stagnated in her attempts. Eliza and Aoife were the only ones transmitting messages through the mycelium. Still, the joy from the success of this endeavour was contaminated by the shame Eliza felt from dropping to a dead faint every single time. She had begun to send across more and more complex imagery - dancing swans, the moon darting behind clouds, a fat worm crawling up the length of the stem of a plant to get to its juicy green leaf. The energy would bundle up in her body, and each time, right when she was sure she would explode, the image would ping through the mushroom network and, in doing so, drain the energy right out of her.

This meant that Eliza was exhausted a lot of the time. She wished she was strong like Aoife, who, although she was only sending out still images, at least didn't have the day's energy sucked out of her. Aoife would have a mild headache that lasted maybe an hour afterward, but then she'd return to her spritely self. Amelie said nothing to Eliza, didn't mention the fainting spells nor the fact that she could do something that Amelie could not.

The atmosphere in the city was tense. The Council was yet to present a plan to them, so the city folk were suspended in the collective holding of their breaths. When they walked through town, Eliza saw legions of warriors marching through the streets, surveying any weak spots in the city walls, practicing fight sequences with spears and enchantments, and stopping to speak to any whisperling over the age of sixteen who wished to become a part of the war effort. The farmers began to store the grain they harvested in silos underground in case the city was besieged. Whisperlings everywhere spoke of nothing but stories from Bardoria that had been passed on from someone's aunt's cousin's wife who had once visited Bardoria before King Grandalford had taken over. The music in the evenings continued in the town square, lively bands helping them attain the desired level of normalcy. The ballads had changed track; they were now about Aaron the Archer and Wilona the Warrior. The songs of heroes rang through the crisp evenings, and people sang and danced. When the winter daughter came into town, the fuss around them was trebled. People insisted on handing them bows crafted by their great great grandmothers and helmets that belonged to their forefathers, family heirlooms that had brought about luck. Although Eliza was grateful for the support offered by the Teragovians, she began to dread going into town as each visit added yet another bar of pressure onto her slacking shoulders. She began to put her hood on whenever she walked to the library so that she would not be intercepted by too many people.

Her visits to Tina's house were what kept her sane. Lou and Dion did not regard her as someone burdened with the fate of saving the realm but as their long lost sister, the sweet, calm, loving presence that they had always wanted to diffuse the tension between them. They kicked a ball around in the backyard, made fires, and looked at the stars together. In those moments, Eliza didn't have to wonder who she was; no words were needed for her to embody the warmth of self-knowledge that came when she and Lou were subjecting Dion to tickle torture.

One morning, after breakfast, instead of walking over to the Oracle's homestead, Miriam informed them that they had been summoned by the Council. The girls spoke in hushed whispers, uncertain of what was to come. Surely a war plan had been created, and they were being summoned so they could be informed of their roles in the plan. Reality had crept in despite the best of Eliza's defences, and the porridge in her belly threatened to come back out.

They walked into town, past the library, and in through the corridor of framed photographs that still sent goosebumps down Eliza's skin. They were met by the same sentries outside the courtyard and then led in through the maze. The faces of the Council members were calm and serene as always, but Eliza could detect tension in the air. Overhead, the clouds had gathered in a mass of grey, bulging with moisture, ready to implode at any minute. The sky hummed dully as low rumbles of thunder were belched out. Eliza shivered and pulled her coat tightly around her.

Zara stood up and greeted them. They bowed low and returned her greeting. For a second, no one said anything; they observed Zara, who seemed to have gained the first wrinkles on her smooth face. The anticipation of war alone added years to a person's body.

'Winter daughters, as you know, the Council has been deliberating the most appropriate course of action for eleven long days and nights. Ever since we heard Tierza's tale, we have known that the worst is on its way to us, and we have to choose whether to defend or attack. We have explored every plan, contingency, route, threat, ploy, decoy, and outcome. Yet, the most crucial piece of the puzzle remains out of reach: the Midnight Daughter!'

The girls shivered uncomfortably. This was the elephant in the room after all! Despite all their optimism and unitedness, they all whispered to each other the same questions: who is the Midnight Daughter? When will she reveal herself? Is there a way we can find out on our own?

Zara continued to speak, the weariness evident in her voice. 'That is the one thing that is out of our hands. It is unclear how we can identify the Midnight Daughter, how we can look at this group of fine young whisperlings and single out one for the easy task of leading the realm into victory. After deliberating this time and time again, we thought the simplest thing might be to bring all the winter daughters together and ask you the simple question: do any of you have an inkling as to which of you is the Midnight Daughter?'

The silence that followed this question was so perfect and long that whispers from the faraway woods could be heard in the courtyard. The girls shifted uncomfortably from one foot to another. Eliza made eye contact with Nala and broke it quickly, looking over at Amelie, whose face looked ashen.

'Winter daughters, we understand that this is no small matter. I am not assuming that you will irrevocably declare yourself as Midnight Daughter, and we consider it set in stone. All the Council asks is that you take the pulse of where you're at so we can assess the situation appropriately.'

Still, nothing. The girls looked at each other and looked away. Someone coughed, and another person cleared their throat. Finally, Maud piped up.

'I reckon it's either Aoife or Amelie, Council Mistress,' she said in a small voice whilst looking down at her feet.

'The same has been reported back to us by your teachers. Tell me, Maud, why do you say so?'

'Well, they're ahead of everyone at lessons. They grasp things effortlessly. They're most likely to flourish on a battlefield as far as skills go.' Maud's voice became more confident with every word.

'Ah yes, winter daughter, I see what you mean. But much of this war will be fought off the battlefield. It is not our intention to elect a General or a Chief for the battalion. It is our intention to find someone who can join the Council, be able to vote, and help us hone in on the best possible course of action going ahead.'

A murmur of whispers began to reverberate through the courtyard. All this time, the winter daughters had imagined their role to be on the bloody and brutal battlefield. Cutting the throats of Bardorians, marching into camps, and freeing prisoners. This was something else altogether.

'And how do you feel about these nominations, Aoife and Amelie? Do you suspect that you are the Midnight Daughter?'

Amelie spoke in a hard, confident voice. It was the first time Eliza had heard her admit to her fate in no uncertain terms. 'Council Mistress Zara, you know as well as I do that I have been groomed for this fate since the day I was born. The people of Teragovia have already put their faith in me. If I am the Midnight Daughter, I know I will wear the title with honor and pride. It is not for me to make any declarations on the matter, but it should suffice to say that I will be neither surprised nor overwhelmed when the truth is revealed.'

Many of the Council members nodded their heads and exchanged glances that seemed to say that this had been the raging consensus amongst them too. Eliza saw Esther's face harden and Nala's eyebrows furrow in a picture of concern. She herself felt uneasy, as though hearing these words out loud presented a kind of finality that none of them could contend with. How could anyone trump Amelie's words? If any of them did turn out to be the Midnight Daughter, would they be disappointing all of Teragovia?

'And Aoife, what do you have to say?'

Aoife tucked a loose red curl behind her ear and gazed at Zara with impossibly calm eyes. 'Only to state the obvious, Council Mistress. As you said, the Midnight Daughter is not merely someone who can lead us in battle but provide something exemplary to the Council and the People. I have no doubt that I am an asset in any battle, but whether that necessarily means that I am the Midnight Daughter, I do not know. I believe that Nala has the wisdom and temperance to offer worthy counsel. I believe that Seena has the ability to scout and survive anywhere in the wilderness. Esther has the vigor and courage to march into an enemy camp and attack them head on. I believe that Eliza is closer than any of us to the Ancient Magic. I believe that Maud is a master of decoys and traps and could easily defeat a legion without shedding any blood. There is no way of knowing who the Midnight Daughter is unless something new is revealed. From where I stand, I believe that any of us could bring something crucial to the Council if we were the Midnight Daughter.'

Zara nodded knowingly, one finger on her chin as she took in each of Aoife's words. Unspoken communication was exchanged between the Council members as they attempted to put together a response.

The wind picked up around them, its breath coming out in brief, strong grunts.

'Your words ring true, winter daughter. The Council respects the stand you have taken. It is clear to me then that none of us are any wiser than the others about the identity of the Midnight Daughter. The next full moon is in a week's time. The Council proposes to conduct a special ritual calling out to Ayla to guide us, give us a sign, and help us name a leader who will bring back glory and harmony to the realm. We will begin the preparations with Oracle Moonfall. You may resume your lessons as before.'

Chapter Twenty Four

An encounter with Oracle Moonfall

T he evening before the Full Moon ritual, Eliza went for a walk in the woods. She followed the violet stream all the way to the point where it disappeared underground. A ring of rocks sat atop the source of the river, giving the impression that the river stemmed from deep in the belly of the Whispering Woods. Hares scuttled about in the understory and peered at her with curious eyes when Eliza drew closer. A couple of the little ones came up to her, rubbed their velvety brown ears against her ankles, and scurried off again. Eliza sat on a small rock by the river's edge and watched the fish swim with the current. The weather had been erratic all week. The freezing cold and mist would change to a languorous burning heat in a matter of minutes, as though someone was going out of their way to make sure that she dressed incorrectly every time she set foot outside the house.

Eliza closed her eyes and attempted to free her mind. She went over some of the visualisation exercises that the Oracle had made them do. She envisioned her face in the pond's reflection, sent her breath billowing through every segment of her body, and tried to push past the distractions to see if she could connect with her most authentic self. The fainting hadn't gotten any better, but Eliza saw that each time she practiced by herself, she was able to unlock more and more of her instinct.

'Maybe you could try something different this time, winter daughter?' said a voice.

Eliza's eyes opened with a start, and she saw Oracle Moonfall standing there with a small basket of mushrooms in her arms. She moved a few paces closer to Eliza and then sat on a rock in front of her. The magic she contained was so powerful that the moss on the stone began to glow brightly as soon as she sat on it.

'Different how Oracle?'

'By facing whatever it is that you are terrified of, winter daughter.'

'Terrified? I don't know what you mean, Oracle!'

The Oracle giggled and pointed to a fish that leaped out of the water and pirouetted before flouncing back in again. She turned her attention back to Eliza and said, 'why do you think you lose consciousness when you are attempting to communicate using the mycelium, winter daughter?'

Quietly, Eliza said, 'I fainted the very first time I touched the earth, Oracle. I am not sure why this happens to me.'

'Ah, but you know. You know in your heart why. You don't lose consciousness each time because you are weak or inept, winter daughter. You lose consciousness because you have opened up almost the entirety of the passage that connects you to yourself. Almost the entirety of it, yes, all but one corner of it. Something in there is so tightly wound up and hidden that you have built a fortress around it. The walls are so thick that they almost block the entire passage. The Ancient Magic has to squeeze through a tiny sliver. Think of it as you having bottlenecked your own powers. In doing so, you have made it so that it costs you grievous amounts of energy to push the magic through so it can do its job. Now, if only you were to crumble those walls to dust, open up the door to the fortress, and face whatever it is that you are afraid of, you would be opening up the passage for the magic to pass through you. You wouldn't be getting in your own way, then, would you?'

Eliza looked at the Oracle, bewildered and nervous. The Oracle's gaze had turned back to the fish, pirouetting in twos and threes, shooting through the air like dancers.

'I don't know what you speak of, Oracle. There's nothing that I'm particularly terrified of. I mean, I'm hardly excited at the prospect of war, but I don't believe that it's something I'm particularly anxious about.'

'I don't believe so either. But I am certain that something lurks beneath the surface. Something that might not seem as great and life-threatening as the war but is somehow far worse than that. What could it be, winter daughter?'

Eliza looked at her uncertainty, not sure how to answer the question. She shrugged her shoulders.

'Well, meditate upon it, and the answer will come to you. The day it does, the day you decide to face your deepest fear, you will open yourself up to the Ancient Magic. You have an affinity for it, winter daughter. You have an affinity for it, unlike any of the others. It would be a shame to let it go to waste, to stand so firmly in your own way, would it not?'

Eliza nodded. 'I have noticed that forest creatures come closer to me than they do to anyone else. They seem to feel safe with me.'

'Precisely! This is no coincidence, winter daughter. Forest creatures are the wisest of us all. They can sense that you are more sensitive to Ancient Magic than the average whisperling. Something about you must feel familiar to them; something old is alive within you, winter daughter.'

'I find that hard to believe, Oracle. I find it hard to see myself as significant in any useful way.' Eliza's cheeks flushed as she said these words out loud.

'Sometimes you have to see yourself through the eyes of another to know your true worth, winter daughter.' With these words, the Oracle stood up and gathered her basket. 'Fear is not a foe, winter daughter. It is here to tell us that there is still work to be done. It is only in facing your fear that you will become aware of your shortcomings and how to strengthen them. When you are ready, you must let go of the fears that no longer serve you. Blessed be, winter daughter, blessed be.'

As quickly as she had come, the Oracle was gone, leaving a stunned Eliza lost in thought on the river bank. When Eliza looked over at the water, the fish had disappeared back under the surface. There was no more pirouetting to be done.

Chapter Twenty Five

Ayla's ritual

The ritual took place in Oracle Moonfall's backyard. She hadn't been embellishing the truth - it was hallowed ground indeed. The moon was high in the sky, an incandescent disc that dominated over the wispy clouds. Stars flickered next to each other with reckless abandon. The ground was wet from the day's torrential rain, though looking at the clear sky now, one wouldn't have imagined that a single cloud could have interrupted the serene vista of the nocturne.

The Council, the Oracle, Miriam, and the winter daughters were gathered together in the clearing. Eliza's breath was hot and shallow. She wasn't quite sure what to expect, but she did know that something would be done tonight that could not be undone easily.

A fire crackled merrily in the pit in the centre. The Oracle sat on her haunches next to it, carving ancient symbols onto the wet earth with a sharp stick. When she was done, she picked up a mixture of flower petals, nettles, and herbs from her basket and scattered them onto the symbols. Then she rubbed a powdery mix of ash, ground-up roots, and enchanted berries onto their foreheads. She poured a small sip of mushroom tea from her flask into a wooden cup. She walked from one winter daughter to another, whispering a prayer under her breath as they raised the cup to their lips and swallowed the vegetal tea. The Oracle issued larger sips to the Council members. Once everyone had been initiated, she unveiled a large gong from the darkness. She struck it once. The sound reverberated through the night, causing birds to fly away in the sky, leaving the bald branches empty of observers.

'Take your seat on the heather,' the Oracle said.

Everyone sat down. The fire was small but glowed brightly, its flames reaching high into the sky, creating a bright circle of warmth around them. Eliza sat across from Amelie, who was looking up at the moon conspiratorially as though the two of them had been plotting sagely all week.

The Oracle beat the gong again and again and again. The sound traveled to the inside of Eliza's bones, causing her to shudder involuntarily. They were instructed to close their eyes. The sound of a flute came next, soft and lilting, a prayer and a blessing all at once. And then the Oracle's voice, a deep and booming call into the wild. She made guttural noises and beat the gong, her words echoing through the trees. Eliza's skin vibrated like a drum as the Oracle chanted in the ancient tongue, a language that she could not comprehend but reverberated through the inside of her body.

Eliza closed her eyes and stopped trying to find meaning in the jagged syllables that the Oracle uttered. She pictured the statue of Goddess Ayla in the Council house and the crescent moon, marked on her forehead. The reflection of her own face swam back to her. And then, one by one, the faces of the winter daughters played in the reel of her mind, followed by the faces of all the other Teragovians she had come to know and felt affection for. Lou, Dion, Tina, Niel, Miriam, Zara, and Uncle Nano. Their faces glowed brightly in her mind. And then, out of nowhere, her mind brought forth the image of Hugo, his mustached grin as he scolded her for her incessant questions. Eliza's mouth went dry, and she blinked back hot tears. She drove the thought of him away from her mind and felt her insides clam up as she did so. She half-opened her eyes to gaze at the others. They were all sitting with closed eyes, swaying slightly, palms folded, bars of moonlight falling all around the glade.

The fire was the same size as before, but its flames soared further and further into the sky each time the Oracle hit the gong. The forest creatures had come to watch. Foxes and hares stood next to each other without fear. Ravens and owls perched silently on the branches. Mice and squirrels, and moles peeked out from their burrows and hollows to bear witness to the Ancient Magic that was casting a hypnotic glow in the clearing. And then the bars of moonlight began to quiver. Instead of falling like long and straight lines, they began to ripple and curve and flutter like the ends of ribbons in the wind. It seemed like Ayla had heard their call and was reaching out!

Eliza knew that she should close her eyes and tune into the Oracle's chants for the ceremony to be successful. But her lids would not close; she was enraptured by the dance of the moonbeams. Waves of drowsiness coursed through her, followed by moments of ecstasy so profound that it made her want to burst into a stream of giggles. The Ancient Magic had a playful touch to it, as though to say that creation had always been in a state of play. The elements, and the creatures all engaged with each other predominantly through a playful dance. It seemed abundantly clear to Eliza as she watched the way the forest creatures began to dance in synchrony with the flickering moonlight that people had misunderstood their relationship to the earth. Was life meant to be a scary and serious thing? Or was it meant to be a joyful celebration of the magical and the mundane?

All around her, the foxes leaped into the air, and the squirrels jumped from one branch to another, their bushy tails cutting through the sky like the tails of comets. Even the sinister ravens fanned their feathers and swayed on the spot. The mice squeaked in soprano tunes, and the hares ran in circles around the clearing, occasionally stopping to jump gleefully in the air.

In Eliza's mind, pieces of a wildly colourful puzzle were snapping into place. Everything and everyone around her appeared to be illuminated like there were tiny fires burning bright inside them. Something within her was beginning to burn too; her belly grew so warm that it almost made her nauseous, only for the feeling to disappear in a split second and be replaced by the honeyed warmth again. The sky overhead was clear, but the stars had changed. They appeared to break formation and make different shapes in the sky. Eliza looked on as the stars split and rejoined as dancing swans, boats at sea, a tree shedding its leaves and growing them again. She could no longer suppress the urge to giggle. She didn't know how everyone else could keep their eyes closed. Some of them had rounded open mouths now. Others were more than just swaying, their fingers caressing what seemed to be an invisible ball and moving it around their faces and through the air and close to their hearts. Amelie was the only one who was still, statue-like, her porcelain features uninterrupted by the hum of the Ancient Magic that had taken over the senses of the winter daughters. It was as though the whole world around her was alive and breathing, a slow and languid breath that drew in sustenance from the world around them deeply and let it out slowly, long seconds passing before the lungs of the earth were empty. Eliza matched her inhales and exhales with this breath and found that it was easier to empty her mind when she did so.

Her eyes drew close, and she was sliding back ever so gently into the meditative state of before when the the ceremony suddenly changed. The Oracle's gong picked up the pace and her chanting grew more powerful, more emphatic. Eliza began to sway on the spot, her mind spinning like a top and the waves of nausea flooding and receding at quicker intervals through her body. And then Amelie cried out loudly. Eliza forced her eyes open, even though the drowsiness had taken hold of her already. Through half-fogged eyes, she saw Amelie clutching her forehead, the spot from where the moon channel opened up. For a second, worry squeezed Eliza's heart, and the hammering, coiled fear that the Oracle had warned her about seized her again. And then Amelie moved her hand away, and she saw that there was a broad smile plastered on her face. Weary but distinctly happy.

'I received an image; I did! I'm not sure who sent it, but I saw clear as the day the image of an archer shooting at the moon!' Amelie explained once the Oracle had softened the beating of the gong.

'An archer, you say?' Zara asked thoughtfully, her forefinger touching her chin.

'Aye, an archer!'

'An archer is one who shoots her arrow in the direction of the future. Oh my word, Amelie, this is the sign that we have been praying for!' Zara said, her eyes flashing.

The Oracle said nothing but looked sharply at Amelie as though she didn't fully trust what was going on. The beating of the gong continued in long echoing hits. Eliza's stomach quaked in unison with the beats.

'Winter daughters, I believe Ayla has spoken. I believe we have the answer we have been looking for. Amelie of Teragovia, our very own winter daughter, is the Midnight Daughter!'

Chapter Twenty Six

The calm before the storm

In the days that followed, the atmosphere in Teragovia livened up considerably. While the city of the free folk had been kind and respectful to each of the winter daughters, it was clear that Amelie would always be their favourite. Even when they weren't explicit about it, they were always rooting for her. There was much pomp and fanfare about Amelie's revelation, and she luxuriated in it. She didn't say much, she wasn't indelicate enough to toot her own horn, but her air of authority deepened. She was short with the other winter daughters and even more impatient with Eliza. Eliza, for one, had given up trying to reconnect with Amelie. It felt as though she was the only one still invested in their friendship, and if Amelie was too good for it, then why should she bother?

While Amelie began to take a seat at Council meetings, Eliza and the other winter daughters continued their lessons with the Oracle and the other teachers. Esther and Maud were openly upset about the revelations of Ayla's ritual.

'How do we know she was telling the truth?' Maud asked, crossing her arms and looking up at the sky as the girls walked back from the Oracle's home. 'I mean, she could've just made it up. There's no way of cross checking, is there!'

'Come on now,' Nala chided. 'She wouldn't tell such an endangering lie, would she? She wouldn't risk the fate of the entire realm just to receive undeserved adulation. If she's not the Midnight Daughter and someone else is, what will she do when her powers are unquestionably revealed? She's too smart not to have thought of that!'

Eliza kept silent in those conversations, but she didn't really doubt it. It had been clear to her from her first interaction with Amelie that this was someone who was destined for greatness. She wasn't thrilled at the idea of serving under Amelie if she was going to continue being so irritable, but what choice did she have about it really? Her own fate had been sealed when her parents had died in Earlford. The girls waited without much excitement for the Council to reveal whatever plan they were in the process of drawing up with Amelie.

In the meantime, Eliza continued to avoid the city folk, but this time for different reasons. She would race up the library stairs to avoid listening to the band that was now singing new ballads about the golden haired Midnight Daughter. She wasn't sure what her grudge was precisely - it wasn't as though she wanted to be the Midnight Daughter, so it wasn't jealousy per se. But it was something like it. Eliza ignored Tina's comments in praise of Amelie and was grateful that neither Lou nor Dion felt

231

the need to weigh in on the matter of saving Elatonia. Something about the way it had all gone down prickled her, and she wasn't quite sure why.

To get her mind off of it all, she devoured books at twice the normal speed. She read about myths and legends, great warriors of the past, the trifling battles that had been fought between cities of whisperers, and so on. Mysteriously, there never seemed to be any battle with the fey. She asked Miriam about it, for Miriam was the one who found her burning the midnight oil with a dusty copy of the book in her hands.

Miriam said, 'the fey are notoriously elusive. They have no desire to fight. The forest is their domain, and they care little about building cities and waging wars to defend them. They lead simpler lives in tune with the trees and the forest creatures. Even if you were to challenge a fey queen to battle, what would you gain upon conquest? A sack of carrots and some tapioca roots?'

'Is that why Grandalford hasn't attacked the fey yet?' Eliza asked, cupping her chin in her palm.

'Aye. In his plunderings, he desired wealth and magic that he could manipulate, so he saw no cause to waste time and the blood of his legions in attacking the fey. Now that he is stripping the woods bare, the fey will be brought into battle, whether they like it or not.'

Eliza thought it was strange that Grandalford didn't see that the fey held some of the most essential types of magic known to the realm - the knowledge of growing food, healing ailments, and nurturing the forest. How could these skills be seen as lesser than whatever it took to power mines, machines, and homes? Eliza wished desperately that she could take lessons from the fey too, that they could trade knowledge freely amongst them. Surely young fey folk were curious about whisperer skills; surely they would be happy to exchange that with them?

Instead, their lessons continued in the same fashion as before. Amelie sometimes showed up for it, and sometimes she was too busy with her Council duties to come by. She seemed particularly keen to avoid the lessons with the Oracle, which did not go unnoticed.

'What's she hiding? If she really did receive the image of the archer from Ayla herself, why can't she come down to the Oracle's home and repeat the feat with one of us? I'll send her the image of a duck, nothing complex, and all I ask is that she reports back with the information that the duck is upside down!' Maud said, rolling her eyes.

Again, Eliza said nothing but stuck her nose in a book and tried to stay out of the chaos that was ensuing in their lodging. Her own attempts at Ancient Magic were hit or miss. She'd make progress, take a step forward, and then it was five steps back. Her fainting spells continued, and the Oracle said nothing more to her about facing her fears.

She began to read a book about the Old World. The book outlined the story that Neil had told her the first time in great detail. It said that the night Ayla and Riaz were conceived, the Queen had had a dream about the sun and the moon chasing each other across the sky, desiring to dominate the heavens. Dreams were treated with utmost importance in the Old World, and what they revealed would always come to pass. This made Eliza worry about the things she saw in her own dreams - the blood, the gore, the brutality. The endless images of death and destruction. She also learned more about God Riaz, who was scarcely mentioned in whisperer lore. Apparently, he was a forest-dweller, much like the fey. Amongst his people, he was known for traveling on horseback to the furthest reaches of the realm where the sun had parched the land into desert. He used the Ancient Magic to plant food forests so that the first people could roam far and wide and never be in want of food. Riaz was hot-headed and bold, a contrast to the calm and poised Ayla, each of them embodying the opposite aspects of each other. As children, they were inseparable, and the King and Queen feared that they would never be able to rule with objectivity as they were far too immersed in their companionship. And then, something changed. Eliza kept reading as she chanced upon a part of the story that she had not heard from Neil. She closed the book and memorised the details, elated that she could recount something fresh and foreign to the children by the fireside tonight!

After a sumptuous dinner of honeyed figs, rye bread, and salty meat, Eliza surprised everyone by leaning close to the fire and saying, 'Neil, would you mind if I told the tale tonight? I've prepared something rather marvelous!' They all nodded, and Lou cheered her on.

'Now you all know the tale of how our world began. But there is something else about it that you do not know! Why the Old World started to fall apart!' Eliza repeated the early story to them, how the King and Queen and first people had been fashioned by the trees so that life could proliferate more freely and exist in the wilderness in a wider variety of forms. She included some additional details that she had only read a few hours before the telling of the tale. 'Back then, there were no cities. Much of the earth was made of forests and rivers, and seas. No one quite knows where the seat of the Old World was, but it is said to be in the southwest corner of the realm, beyond the Whispering Woods, beyond the Timeo Waterfall, just before the Cliffs of Nargis. Riaz and Ayla frolicked through the woods and bathed in the sea and seemed to need no one else in the first part of their life! And then something quite unexpected happened, something that was to change the course of their lives and the fate of the realm forevermore!'

'What happened, Eliza!' Both Lou and Dion cried out.

'The Queen began to have night terrors. In her dreams, she began to see the end of the world they had created. She saw something dark and demonic take over her beloved land, something cold and sickly that spread its dark blood through the mycelium so it could attack the trees from the inside and force them to rot to death with its damp and misty fingers. Before she knew it, the Queen bore a child in her belly again. She had every right to be terrified, for it was a monster that was growing in her womb. When he was born, he was deformed and pale; he looked more like an aged cripple than a robust infant, beaming with vigour and vitality! They named him Tenebris, or Bris, as he came to be known in the realm. The name meant darkness, and it was apt as every room he entered became devoid of light in an instant. Ayla and

Riaz were protective of their little brother, this helpless infant who was not to blame for his own condition. Even when the King and Queen found it hard to find empathy for their hapless child, Ayla and Riaz were magnanimous. They cared for him, taught him to speak, and carried him into the woods as he never learned to walk. These were the last moments of peace known to the Old World.' Lou and Dion were sitting up with their eyes wide as coins. That was all the encouragement that Eliza needed!

'For all his ailments, Bris could speak. He read poetry and had a fine appreciation for the arts and music. His soul was stunted though, for he craved the kind of love that his siblings received in the realm. People would stop what they were doing to kiss Ayla's hand or bow low to Riaz. They looked away when Bris was with them and tried to retch discreetly. Bris said little about this to his siblings but inside him burned a bright jealousy. He wanted not only what they had but more! When Ayla and Riaz grew older and began to fall in love with their suitors, Bris was angry. He did not want to share his siblings with anyone, and he wanted to be loved by a maiden too. As a God himself, he believed himself to be entitled to marriage. He beseeched the King and Queen, who put open an offer saying that they would offer a handsome reward of twenty bars of gold to any maiden who would wed Bris. Not a single woman came forward. Bris was rejected, pained and furious. His jealousy spilled over into the love he bore for his siblings. When the King and Queen announced that they were ready to ascend to the heavens and give up their earthly life, Bris saw an opportunity to settle the score. He began to whisper evil notions into the ears of Riaz and Ayla. He convinced each of them that the other one was plotting against them. He splintered the closest bond between siblings that has ever been seen in the realm, so much so that neither Ayla nor Riaz wanted to govern the realm together. They demanded an even split, and the world was cleaved into night and day.'

Lou gasped and wrapped her arms around Dion protectively. 'How awful of Bris! What became of him after that, Eliza?'

'No one is quite sure, little Lou. The story says that he disappeared into the shadows, cackling mirthlessly till the end of his days, and turned to frosty vapor upon his death. He lived amongst the shadows of evil and hate. Bris, the God of Darkness.'

'I'm scared, Eliza,' Dion said in a small voice.

'Don't be scared, Dion. You've got a big sister twice as strong as any Old World demon!'

'Mummy, can you make sure you and Papa don't make another baby? I don't want it to turn out like Bris!' Lou said.

The elders laughed, and Neil congratulated Eliza on telling her tale well. 'I'd not heard this version entirely, Eliza; thank you for the telling of it! Bris, Bris, Bris, that evil child. My Pa used to say to me whenever I played truant from school that he'd send me to Bris's lair for the summer holidays if I misbehaved once again!'

Proud of her first fireside story, Eliza walked home with a skip in her step. The moon overhead was waning and hung above the hills in a skinny curve. Ever since Ayla's ritual, Eliza felt more connected to the

237

moon's power. She noticed her energy receding as they crept closer to the dark moon. Her own inner cycle was one that ebbed and flowed in tandem with the many faces of the moon.

The lodging was obscured in darkness by the time Eliza got home. She opened the door to her room as quietly as she could, walking in on the tips of her toes, expecting Amelie to be asleep already. Instead, she walked in on an unexpected sight. Amelie sat at the foot of her bed, her arms on the bed and her face buried into the crook of her elbow. She was sobbing raspily, her breath quivering in jagged bursts as the intensity of her tears inhibited her from being able to take in gulps of air. She didn't notice Eliza entering the room. Unsure of what to do, Eliza cleared her throat. Amelie looked up, startled, her body stiffening in response to the intrusion. She wiped her tears with the back of her hand and tried desperately to regain control of the situation.

'I'm sorry, Amelie, I didn't mean to catch you unaware. I hope you don't mind me asking, but are you well? What is on your mind?' Eliza took a careful step towards Amelie, approaching her the same way as she had approached the foxes in the woods.

Amelie said nothing, her lips pursed closed, her shoulder still shaking, partly from the embarrassment of being caught in a vulnerable moment and partly from the sobs she was holding back. Eliza inched closer to her. She sat down on the cold stone floor next to her. She longed to reach out and embrace Amelie, but she knew that this would be too much for Amelie, who would retreat into her shell promptly. So she sat patiently and waited for her to weigh her options in her mind.

'You can tell me whatever you want. I won't tell anyone, of course,' Eliza said in a low voice. 'Go on, Amy, this is what friends are for.'

The use of Amelie's nickname did the trick. She looked at Eliza, her jaw wobbling from the concerted effort of not bursting into tears again. 'I...I...I just met up with Ravi in the woods. And he said that he wants to end things with me.' Upon saying these words out loud, the worst of Amelie's fears was realised and she started to cry again.

'Did he! What a fool! Does he know what he's missing out on?' Eliza exclaimed, shocked that anyone would want to break things off with Amelie. Despite her haughtiness to the other winter daughters, Eliza had seen Amelie display her soft side to Ravi, dancing and laughing with him. Who could resist that version of her?

'He doesn't want to be with the Midnight Daughter, he said,' Amelie said, her voice barely a whisper. 'He told me he doesn't even want to fight the war. He wants to stay at home and tend to his family's farm. He said he loves me, but he thinks my destiny is far greater than his. And that if he's honest with himself, all he really wants is to live a quiet life in Teragovia. He thinks it wouldn't be fair to either of us to stay together because we'd fall more and more in love and scar each other for life when I have to go into battle. How is this fair, Eliza? How is any of this fair!'

Eliza touched Amelie's forearm gingerly and stroked it. 'It's not fair; it's awful. Ravi is an idiot!'

'Is he, though? Or is he right? He'd be happier with someone like you, wouldn't he? Someone who wants a quiet life without war, someone who can muster up genuine excitement when her chicken lays its first egg! Where does that leave me, Eliza? Who would want to fall in love with a warrior? What kind of a home could anyone build with me?'

Amelie's tears flowed freely now, big fat drops falling onto the scratchy white bedsheet.

'It's not easy being the Midnight Daughter, is it?' Eliza said, holding Amelie's hand. Outside, the owls hooted in response as if to agree with Eliza's statement. 'You're asked to sacrifice so much for the realm. It's a lot for one person, is it not?'

'Aye, it is,' Amelie said, turning her head away from Eliza and looking outside the window. The darkness was thick and gluey, the shadows of trees barely visible as the meager moon was shrouded by a plumage of thick clouds in the sky. 'I wish I could want the life you want, Eliza. The farm and the children and the simplicity. But I don't. I'd be bored of it. The freedom fighters of Teragovia raised me to be a warrior. To be one of them. It's all I've ever known. Is that wrong? Am I wrong to want this life? Is it fair that I am kept at arm's length from love because of it? My duty is also my passion but does that mean that I do not get to experience the love of a man?'

Eliza shivered. Amelie's words reminded her of Bris, the God of Darkness, who had wanted nothing more than to be loved. The world's failure to provide him with that had poisoned his heart, and the poison had grown so strong and sticky that he had destroyed the only love he had ever been party to. She hoped that Amelie was not subjected to this, that her insides would not succumb to the cold devastation of a loveless landscape that would send her down the lonesome path of evil.

'Amelie, I am sure that the right person will want to build a life with you, regardless of your destiny. He will not make you feel that you are undesirable because you have a great destiny. He will revere your power and treat you like a blessing, because you are one! To him, to Elatonia, and also to me.' Eliza flushed, hesitating as she said the last part.

Amelie blinked. 'Thank you for saying that, Eliza. I'm sorry if I haven't been a very good friend to you of late. The weight of my future has been getting to me. Some days I feel like I could explode in an instant. I have this urge to run into the woods and never return. But it's what I was born to do, you know, there's no use contemplating any other version of my life. I was born at the brink of winter to lead Elatonia to victory. And that's what I shall do.'

Eliza nodded, knowing that it took a lot for Amelie to admit this even to herself, let alone out loud. 'I can imagine that it is difficult, Amy, but I don't think it'll do you any good to push away the love that you do have. Friendship is a much simpler and purer love than romance, surely. It's forgiving and does not care whether you are a warrior or farmer. Perhaps it is time that you let that love bring you closer to those that share the same fate as you!'

The owls hooted again, backing every word of Eliza's. Amelie tilted her head and scrutinised Eliza's face as though some part of it had been altered radically. 'When did you go and get so wise, little Eliza? Last I checked, you were fainting all over the place. And now you're delivering aphorisms like some Old World scholar herself!'

'Oh Amelie, I've always been a wise one. You just never thought to ask me!'

The two girls embraced and sat on the floor for hours, sharing stories of what they had been up to in the last few weeks. The distance between them had felt like a gaping hole all this time. It was surprisingly easy to build a bridge over that gap. Silence and hardness can make a person feel a million miles away even when they are right next to us. And warmth and openness can make a person a million miles away feel closer than ever. The two girls talked and talked until the wee hours of the morning when the sun came up, and the clouds blushed coyly with the first light of day. Eliza's resentment seemed to evaporate as if the seed of the issue all along had been that she missed her friend and nothing more. And as the two of them talked each other's ears off, trouble was brewing elsewhere. Trouble that neither of them would have expected, trouble that was marching at breakneck speed to their doorstep.

Chapter Twenty Seven

The plan of action

For the next couple of days, Eliza felt lighter than before. Having Amelie back in her life and being her friend brought more relief than she could have anticipated. Walking into her room at the end of the day was more pleasant, and Amelie did not keep up pretenses with Eliza. Behind closed doors, the two of them would talk for hours. Eliza finally told her about her conversation with Uncle Nano and what she had learned of her family.

'I can't believe you know who your Pa is! That's brilliant, Eliza,' Amelie said sincerely, patting Eliza's palm. It was a clear night, and a warm breeze blew in from the window. The sky was speckled with stars that glittered nonstop.

'I know! Josef from Earlford. It's a pity I'm nothing like him, you know? I wish I knew more about my Ma; maybe we might have more in common. But all Uncle Nano could tell me was that she was not from Earlford and that the marriage had been a complex affair. Perhaps she was wealthy, and her family disapproved of her marrying someone from a fishing clan? I don't know. I really don't know.' Eliza fanned herself, knowing that another night of tossing and turning in the heat was to follow.

'Or maybe your mother was one of the fey folk!' Amelie suggested, winking deviously.

'Oh Amelie! How wonderful that would be! Do whisperers wed fey folk often?'

Amelie shook her head. 'Almost never, but it has happened before. One of the warriors that was part of the freedom fighters of Teragovia when I was growing up ran away with a fey man. She returned a few years later. It's not easy to combine such opposite ways of life, she told us. The fey don't like it when whisperers use their magic in their territory. If we don't use the moon power that we imbibe, it builds up inside of us like rainwater in a dam. And sooner or later, the dam bursts, and the energy comes roaring out. So for Leah, that was her name; it was a choice between living without the man she loved or betraying her true nature.'

'I suppose no one can really betray their true nature. It'll always find its way out.'

'Precisely. Leah's magic exploded from her fingers during a fey ceremony. They had just harvested their barley and reckoned it would be an excellent year for beer. And Leah's magic burst from her at the worst moment possible and destroyed most of the yield. The village was not impressed, needless to say. Shortly after, Leah was back home. Rumour has it that she still meets up with her fey man whenever he is foraging close by. He never wed, and neither did she. Most whisperer-fey romance seems to end in tragedy.'

'Do whisperers interact with the fey at all? It seems so peculiar to me that we all dwell in the same forest and yet never see one another.' Eliza's brow had begun to sweat. Even in the thin fabric of her nightclothes, she felt too warm. Not for the first time, she cursed at the weather. In Bardoria, save for six weeks of long summer days, most of the year was a cold, windy, grey affair. Teragovian weather seemed not to care for the rhythm of the seasons and marched to the beat of its own drum.

'Well, we do have a monthly market. The third Sunday of every month. Whisperers, fey, and humans all trade in this market. There are precious stones and herbs and roots and various food from all over the realm. Garments, weaponry, teas, potions, elixirs. The finest entertainers performs for coin. Singers, artists, and theatre troupes all put on shows all day. It's quite the celebration!'

'It sounds marvelous! Where is it, and how does one get there?'

'It's in the outer reaches of the Whispering Woods. One of the entrances to Teragovia opens up close to the market. If you go on horseback, it only takes half a day to get there. We only just missed this one - it was the day after the Solstice Dance, so I suppose we wouldn't have made it anyway. But we can go next time if you'd like to.'

'Oh I'd love that, Amelie!'

'I'd love it too. Let's do it then.'

Eliza was thrilled to have something wonderful to look forward to rather than the plan of action that the Council was about to reveal. A meeting had been called for the late evening with the winter daughters where the next steps would be set in motion. The girls walked into the city together, their bellies full of warm pumpkin soup and cucumber sandwiches. The temperature had dropped close to freezing overnight, and frost clung to leaves. When Eliza exhaled, small spires of fog came out of her mouth.

'Almost makes you miss the consistent cold of Bardoria!' Maud grumbled, pulling her coat tightly around her.

The others nodded in agreement. If they had noticed that Eliza and Amelie had become close once again, the girls didn't let it on through any changes in their attitude towards Eliza. Nala still smiled at her kindly, and Aoife squeezed her hand when they stood next to one another. Maud whispered cheeky remarks in her ears when they walked side by side, and Seena splashed cold water on her face if she fainted during lessons. Without even realising it, Eliza had built a real life for herself in Teragovia. When she walked with the other winter daughters, she felt real and tangible, like she belonged with them. She didn't have to stand out or be exceptional, just walking with the girls helped her cement her identity. Eliza knew she was a good soldier; she thrived within the pack and was content to follow orders.

Amelie sat at the Council table with Zara and the other members. She had a seat close to the centre, to Zara's right, which revealed how enormously valuable the office of the Midnight Daughter was. Eliza wasn't sure what she had imagined the role to be, but sitting in meetings and skipping lessons didn't seem fitting somehow. She reasoned to herself that perhaps Amelie was so far ahead of all of them anyway that it mattered little whether or not she showed up for lessons. Just once, Amelie had asked her what the other girls thought of her being the Midnight Daughter. Eliza had picked her words carefully and said, 'nobody's surprised. They know you're the most skilled one of us!'

'Greetings, winter daughters, you have been summoned here today to become privy to the plan of action that the Council, along with the aid of the Midnight Daughter, has drawn up.' Zara's silver hair had been pulled into an elegant bun at the base of her neck. Next to her, Amelie stood with her own hair in a bun. It made her look like a younger version of Zara like she was being groomed for a future as a Council Mistress.

'I know I speak for all of Teragovia when I say that we are delighted that Ayla's ritual was a success. We knew that our Goddess would speak from above and give us the sign we needed. It is an honour to have the Midnight Daughter amongst us. Ever since the prophecy was declared, every whisperer in this city has waited. Each of us has lost someone to Bardorian hands. Many of us don't know if our friends and family have been slain or apprehended at camps. It is only by freeing those that are in captivity and alive that we can bring peace to the fettered hearts of the free folk.'

Although Uncle Nano had told her that there was no way Josef would have let himself be taken captive,

Eliza wondered if there was a chance her mother was still alive in the camps. But she knew better than to hope, for she had heard Hugo repeat this time and time - it's the hope that kills.

'Tonight is the night of the dark moon. Our powers are at their weakest but do not be fooled and think of this as a limitation. For each phase of the moon, we have an objective. When the moon is dark, we plant seeds. We set intentions. We build plans. Once the moon starts to reappear, we increase our efforts by the day. We take one step after another to make our plans come to life. The full moon is when we are at our strongest, and that is when we carry out the largest part of our plan. Every day after that, we take a step back. We evaluate, we assess, and we give thanks. We use what we have learned to build a new plan when the dark moon comes back around. This is the whisperers' way; this is how we have always functioned. This time is no different.'

Eliza looked up at the darkening sky overhead. The faint orange of the last light gave way to the purple glow of dusk. The moon was nowhere to be seen. She had hidden herself in the ether, but Eliza knew that she could always see them even if they couldn't see her.

'To honour the cycle of the moon, we have decided to present the plan to you on the dark moon, so together we can set our intentions and start to take action as the moon begins to bulge.' Zara looked each of them in the eye as she said these words. A chill went up Eliza's spine as she realised that she was running out of moments when the radius of her concern extended only to herself and those she cared for. As soon as Zara made her announcement, Eliza would be responsible for the entire realm.

'The city of the free folk has hidden itself from Bardorian eyes for so long that the last thing that Grandalford expects is for us to come out and attack him. He thinks that we will choose to defend, that we will let our city be besieged on all sides until our forces weaken and they can break through the enchantment. However, we will not bring the war home and endanger the children of Teragovia and let them lay waste to our city the way they did to Fionnos. We will not bring the war to the Whispering Woods and give the Bardorians an excuse to fell more trees and rip more mycelium. No, we will not invite more violence and bloodshed into the safe place that we call home. We will meet them in Bardoria, where they might have the advantage of home ground, but we have the advantage of surprise. They will not expect legions of whisperers and warriors to come to them. They will be unprepared. Their numbers are greater than ours, but their troops are scattered. If we let them come to us with the best of their battalions, I fear that we might not be able to sustain an attack of such horrific proportions. On the night of the full moon, two weeks from now, we intend to begin our march to Bardoria, to slay Grandalford and free the prisoners that still survive so we can restore peace to Elatonia!'

Eliza's jaw slacked. Two weeks? That was no time at all! They were not prepared; how could they defeat the Bardorians without at least six more months of training? The feeling left her face and hands, and she barely heard the rest of what Zara was saying. At some point, Amelie chimed in with a few words about how she believed this was the only way, to act fast and use the element of surprise. Eliza shook her head. Her stomach had crumpled into a ball of lead. Something about this plan didn't feel quite right. She wasn't letting her fears get the best of her; she knew in her heart that they were simply not prepared. From her window in the tower, she had seen Bardorian war horses run along the coast. Their sheer numbers were surreal; there was no way that the Teragovians could march straight into Bardoria on their own and defeat them. Something was missing and she knew what it was, but she didn't dare say it.

Zara said, 'even though it is the Midnight Daughter that sits at the table with us, we value the words and opinions of each and every one of you, for you have each experienced hardship in Bardoria and understand what we face. If there is something about this plan that does not seem wise to you, speak up. I assure you, this is a safe space!'

Eliza's mouth was open before she had even realized it, and the words were flowing haphazardly through her. 'I apologise if I am overstepping my position, Council Mistress, but I do not agree with this plan. I...we...I know the might of Bardorians, and they will recover from the surprise of our attack in a heartbeat. If we want to truly surprise them...what I'm saying is, we can't do it alone...the real surprise would not be us going to their city as much as....we need the fey to fight with us!'

Zara smiled at her politely as though she was duty-bound to humor Eliza but didn't actually have the patience for it. 'Thank you for your input, Eliza, but the fey are not skilled in warfare and have refused all of our attempts to speak on this matter. They will simply go underground and leave it to us to do the dirty work and emerge once the dust settles. That is their way, not ours.'

And thus, the matter was settled, but Eliza could not shake the feeling that Zara was wrong. That they had to try harder to form an allyship, that they had to come together to stand a chance against the evil that they were up against.

On the walk back home, Eliza could barely register the sounds around her. She did not participate in the nervous chatter of the others and walked with her head hanging low. They walked past the town square, and Eliza looked up, realising that she had only two weeks of this left before her life changed course yet again. The taste of warmth and music and family in Teragovia left her wanting more, like her life as it should have been had only just begun. She couldn't picture wading through the marshland again, her knapsack on her back, stopping only for a drink of water at icy pools, arriving at campsites with aching bones only to have to forage for heather and prepare her bedding for the night. No, she had grown accustomed to warm meals, the high ceiling library, fireside stories, and evenings of dance and chatter in the town square. She wasn't ready to give it all up again in two weeks.

'You're surprisingly plucky, Eliza, speaking your mind in front of the Council like that!' Maud said, nodding approvingly at her as they left the town square in their wake and hit the mud road. The sky was overcast. When the clouds covered the stars on a moonless night, it was hard to see where they were going. But Eliza had walked up and down this route so many times that her feet knew every twist and bump in the road. Was that what it meant to belong to a place, to be at home there?

'I don't know what came over me. It was as though my voice had a mind of its own. I do stand by what I said, however. I do not doubt the might of Teragovian warriors in the slightest, but I feel like the surprise of our attack will throw the Bardorians off for only a few seconds. Then they will reassemble and strike back. And then what? Even with the full moon on our side, we are not equipped. Our numbers do not compare. This is our one and only chance. I don't believe we will survive this attack.'

'And you think joining hands with the fey is the solution?' Amelie's voice piped up.

Eliza jumped; she hadn't noticed when Amelie had joined them. 'Well, it's something the Bardorians wouldn't expect, would they? The fey and whisperers fighting together, launching an attack from water and earth, stronger together than ever!'

Amelie's voice was steely and cold. She took Eliza's disagreement to the plan that she had helped build as a personal affront. 'Well, that might hold true in theory, Eliza, but the fey are farmers and foragers. What are they going to do, throw poisonous berries at Bardorians, hoping that they'll accidentally swallow them whole? The fey harness the sun's power to the extent that it helps them grow food and live in forests as though they are trees themselves. And as much as I revere their ancient wisdom, you don't enlist the support of trees in warfare!'

'But do we know the full extent of the sun channel, Amelie? Do we really know all the secrets of the fey? Do we know what they can do in warfare?'

'Oh yes, I'm sure you worked it all out while you were in the tower in Bardoria. I'm sure that traitor of a tutor made up myths about the fey in battle to entertain you. Take it from someone who has lived alongside the fey all her life, Eliza - they care little for the realm. As long as they can disappear into burrows and boughs, the fey will not be coaxed into acting for the realm!'

Before Eliza could respond, a loud wind blew in from the Woods. It shrieked like a banshee, carrying a haunted whisper from darker times. Her skin erupted in goosebumps and left her shivering. With the wind came a thick mist. Within seconds, the air around her turned opaque, a moving mass of white and grey that appeared to have long, curly fingers that caressed her neck and cradled her head. The air had a foul smell of rotten eggs, as though someone had forgotten to bury their rubbish in the ground and flung it out of the window instead. Eliza covered her mouth. Her head began to feel light from the stench as it wafted in through her nose and held her body hostage. She coughed and heard the sound of the other girls coughing too.

Eliza tried to wave the mist away using her fingers, but it was thick and dense, unlike the regular mist she was used to. She opened her mouth to comment on the peculiar nature of the mist when a loud bang ricocheted off the trees and pierced through the air. It was followed by a subsequent boom and multiple dull thumps as though a row of trees was hitting the ground slowly. And then a sound she had never heard before took over the night. Eliza and the winter daughters stood on the mud path, shrouded in the deathly mist, unaware of what was going on, when a loud foghorn was sounded, shriller and more piercing than any sound she had ever heard. And without knowing how she knew, Eliza was sure that the sound was a warning call for the entire city of the free folk: they were under attack. Someone had breached the walls of Teragovia!

Chapter Twenty Eight
The breach

Eliza's arms went limp at her sides. Amelie began to bark orders. The girls still couldn't see one another through the phlegmy texture of the mist, but the sound of Amelie's voice was louder than the wolfish whistle of the wind.

'Do not panic, winter daughters, and do as I say. We have not been trained for this, but we have always known that this was a possibility. We are under attack from Bardoria. We do not know if this is a breach by a rogue legion or if they have bypassed our scouts and informers and somehow managed to initiate a full-blown attack. Take the Igneous Orbs and use the Ancient Magic to light them up so we can see what we are up against.'

One by one, the girls lit up their Orbs. Eliza's hands shook as she fished around her pocket for the cool amber stone that stored light within it. Her Orb was the last to radiate light. The glow from the Orbs was powerful enough for them to see each other's faces through the fugue of the mist.

'Form a circle, winter daughters, and face outward to see any threat that might approach us.'

The girls obeyed and stood with slightly bent knees, poised to pounce on anyone that might apprehend them.

'Does anyone have any weapons?'

'Aye,' came a few voices.

'I've got my bow and arrow,' said Aoife.

'I've got a wooden hammer,' said Seena.

'I've got a spear,' said Nala.

'And I've got a sword,' said Amelie. 'The rest of you, stoop down quickly and see if you can find sharp stones. Fill your pockets with whatever you can get a hold of. Quick!'

Eliza bent low and patted the ground hastily for jagged stones. She found a few crystals with sharp edges and threw them in her pocket. Her breath was coming out in quick gasps. Around them, the wind howled with greater and greater ferocity. With their Orbs in one hand and weapons in the other, the girls were still comically underprepared for any assailant. What good were a few sharp stones and rudimentary weapons against an enemy on horseback with the finest metal shields and swords and spears that had been forged in a century? Eliza tried not to think of this as she kept her eyes peeled, trying to locate the tiniest movement in the dimly lit swatch of mist in front of her.

A raspy voice, barely above a whisper, sounded from the mist. It seemed to come from everywhere at once, as though the source of the voice stood behind every tree simultaneously or as if the mist formed a maze that made the sound bounce in every direction at once.

'You are no match for us, little whisperlings. Hand over the Midnight Daughter, and we will spare your city and her people. We are not here to wage war, but we shall not hesitate to shed blood if our demands are not met.'

Eliza's blood ran cold. This was not what any of them expected.

'You're not Grandalford's men! No human knows about the Midnight Daughter!' Amelie cried out, her voice steady and powerful, not betraying any fear she might feel. 'Reveal your identity to us!'

The voice responded with a whispery laugh that rose to a cackle. 'We take no orders from a whisperling. Your show of might is amusing, endearing even. It would be remiss of me not to humour you, however. Indeed, I am neither the foolish King Grandalford nor one of his power hungry men. Do not insult me by comparing me to a mere mortal such as that.'

Not Grandalford or one of his men? Who on earth could this be then? Who else could want to get their hands on the Midnight Daughter? Could it be the fey? It had been made clear to Eliza that the fey did not wage war in conventional ways - was this parade of mist and shadow a work of the fey? If so, why did they want Amelie? Was this how they intended to secure protection against the Bardorians? Did they want to trade Amelie and the news of the prophecy to the Bardorians in exchange for the protection of the Woods?

'Who are you then, if not a cheap trickster hired by Grandalford?' Amelie called out, matching his haughty boasting with her own. Perhaps this was what lay at the heart of admirable leadership - the cloak of bravado that obscured the fact that they were a bunch of whisperlings armed with scrawny weapons and little else.

'My name is no longer spoken with fondness in this lair, whisperling. I am the only knight in the realm that rides a hearse. I have surpassed the bounds known to the most powerful whisperers. I am a vassal to the greatest force known to the realm. I am Roran Storm!'

The name meant nothing to Eliza, but she could feel Amelie's body stiffen next to hers.

'Do not lie to me, dark one. Roran Storm has been dead for a decade!'

'If Roran Storm is dead, how do you explain the mercurial weather that hangs over your city? It is no coincidence, whisperling. Roran Storm now walks with the shadows. I am no longer what I once was. I have drunk the elixir of the truth and discovered the inverted world that is far greater than anything you will ever see. I am here to lay claim to the Midnight Daughter. My shadows will take her by force or by her own volition. The choice is yours - how many would you like to see perish before you hand her over to us?'

Who was Roran Storm? And why had he risen from the dead to claim the Midnight Daughter? Eliza was nonplussed. The foul stench had made the inside of her head feel like wet cotton. Her thoughts felt heavy and languid, and her body was a mass of lead.

'We do not fear the shadows or the walking dead,' Amelie sneered, raising her sword and looking intently from side to side. She nodded at Aoife and Nala, who tightened their grips on their weapons.

'I offer you one last chance, whisperling. Think carefully, for once we have slain every woman in your city; that is the end of Ayla's lineage. I wish no ill will for the city that raised and reared me, but the price for greatness has always been blood.'

Eliza's insides clenched as though they were making a fist inside her. She shook ever so slightly. Was it not enough to have the Bardorians after them that a new enemy, a rogue whisperer from the looks of it, was here to threaten to end them all?

Amelie signaled to Aoife. She lifted her bow, took aim, and shot an arrow into the mist where she believed the sound of the voice emerged from. She shot one arrow after another, changing the target by a little each time so as to widen her reach. The blood curdling sound of the cackle reached them once again.

'Ah, so you have made your choice then. You will not come quietly. It is as I expected. We will hit you with our full strength then. Be warned that you have openly provoked Roran Storm and his league of shadows.'

Suddenly, as though a sheet had been unclipped from the clothesline, the mist was lifted. Eliza blinked and slipped her Igneous Orb back into her pocket. The scant light that remained was just enough to recognise the silhouettes that hung in the thicket of trees in front of them. Lumpy shapes hovered over the ground without touching it. Aoife launched a series of arrows at them.

They passed right through the silhouettes and embedded themselves into the barks of trees behind the enemy.

'Arrows and swords count for nothing. Do you know nothing about this realm you call home? I am powered by the misty breath of the Ancient Magic; your toys cannot touch me. Behold my power!'

The silhouettes began to move towards them at an unsettling speed, gliding jerkily across the muddy plane. Eliza took a step back and then another one. She was about to take another when her foot sank into wet mud. Behind her, the purple river gurgled along, its sound hushed by the howling windy voice of Roran Storm.

The shadows crept towards them in their strange crawl, and the winter daughters had nowhere to go. One more step, and they would plunge to death in the icy, unforgiving waters of the river!

The closer they moved, the more clearly Eliza could see them. She whispered enchantments onto the rocks in her hands and threw them at the willowy bodies of the shadows, and watched as the rocks passed straight through them. They were hooded figures that glided shiftily, without feet to give them a clear direction, the slightest of wind altered their path, but they moved steadily towards the winter daughters.

'We need to use our collective power to draw upon the Ancient Magic,' said Aoife through gritted teeth. 'No individual among us is capable of calling the powers by themselves yet, but perhaps together we can!'

'Show yourself, Midnight Daughter,' came Roran Storm's voice through the mist that had started to snake in again. The ground had disappeared in the fog. Eliza's stomach began to churn like the sea on the stormiest day. 'I won't wait long before I set the shadows onto your little whisperling friends. And when my shadows are done with them, they will be rendered comatose, devoid of memory and identity and will. They will degenerate into the most muted forms of themselves. My voice will be their clarion call. When I say the word, they will emerge from the ground, fine as a mist, and do my bidding. Aye, there is always room for new recruits in Roran Storm's league of shadows!'

'Ground yourselves and clear your minds, winter daughters. Think beyond the province of fear and doubt. We must be entirely hollow for the Ancient Magic to find a passage within us.'

The winter daughters clasped their palms into each other's and held on tightly. Eliza attempted to calm herself and tried to do as Aoife said. But the hovering shadows were too close; their putrid stench made her want to retch. She clenched her jaw closed and tried harder than ever to drive the thoughts of panic and anxiety from her mind. But it seemed that the harder she tried, the more each thought held on. Her teeth chattered in a shaky death rattle, and she was sure her lips had turned blue from the haunting chill. If the Oracle's advice was to face her fears, meet them head-on and clear whatever blocked the path of the Ancient Magic within her, it seemed to Eliza that she was doing the exact opposite at this moment when she needed to get it right more than ever! One part of her had stiffened in shock, unable to wrap her head around the fact that mythical shadows were charging toward them, and the other part of her could only think the very worst thoughts. What if they lost Amelie? What if the shadows took them all? What if Teragovia fell?

For several long seconds, nothing happened, and Eliza was sure that the shadows would engulf them. Then something began to whir in the air around them, as though hundreds of butterflies were flapping their wings to create a gentle current. The motion generated heat, dispelling the chill slightly, and began to make a sound of its own. It was a hum, sweet and low, that seemed to emanate from the purple river that gushed behind them.

'Harder now! Visualise the light from the water exploding upwards and creating a shield around us!' Aoife called out, her voice was barely audible over the hum that had taken over the soundscape.

Roran Storm's morbid laughter sounded through the hum. 'You think fireworks and songs will stop the Lord of Darkness from taking what he wants? You have much to learn, whisperlings; you are so young, still young enough to believe you know everything! Ah, seasoned and toughened warriors do not falter like this.'

Eliza's throat had become parched. If she tried to utter a word, she was sure her voice would come out hoarse and scratchy. She looked up quickly and saw that a thin shield of light had begun to grow around them. She wasn't sure how long it would hold or what good it would do - they could buy time, but they were not strong enough to attack! The light repelled the shadows and they glided back towards the thicket. Amelie stood in the centre, next to Aoife. She whispered under her breath fiercely. A large golden bow had formed over her head. Arrows flew like

262

bolts of lightning from it. She rained them upon the shadows. Upon contact, they vanished into smoke.

From the corner of her eyes, Eliza saw that the purple river had turned incandescent, as though all that it sequestered beneath the icy current was stirring and shaking into awareness after a deep and long sleep. Was there the slightest chance that they could rouse the Ancient Creatures? She dared not dream; it was the hope that killed, after all!

Aoife's face had turned pale from the energy she was using to drive the flow of the Ancient Magic. The shield of light grew thicker and thicker around them, and Aoife's red curls quivered from the force. The winter daughters were working in unison, except Eliza, who found it impossible to keep her mind from panicking and concentrate. Her gaze drifted to the shadows, the thicket from which Roran Storm's disembodied voice radiated towards them. Amelie's arrows left the golden bow without stopping, appearing like streaks of vivid light, incandescent rains of fury. And yet, for every shadow that fell, another rose from the ground almost instantly. They continued their advance, edging toward the shield yet keeping out of its reach.

Finally, they crept close enough for Eliza to see what lay hidden under their hoods. The face of death itself, a grim skull with empty sockets where the eyes should have been, and an open mouth, round and angry, with two fangs like blades jutting out from the jaw. The shadows moved with their arms outstretched, reaching for the daughters. Eliza knew that they would not be able to touch the shadows, but the shadows would have no trouble touching them. She knew that nothing they did to thwart the shadows would suffice, save for the Ancient Magic. And who among them was skilled enough to do more than lift a feather or bend a twig? Who among them had whatever it took to call upon the dormant Ancient Magic that lay hidden in the very ground they stood on and the water that flowed a foot away from them?

Just as the shadows were inches from them, when they could feel the last dregs of heat getting sucked up from the air, Amelie's voice called out.

'Stop your hounds! I am the Midnight Daughter, and I voluntarily give myself up. Let my people walk free.'

Chapter Twenty Nine

Roran Storm and the league of shadows

This was the last thing Eliza expected to hear. Was this a ploy of some sort? It had to be! Amelie had no reservations about her own worth - surely she knew that the Midnight Daughter was more significant than all of the others combined. She strained her ears to listen for the sounds of Teragovian warriors coming their way. Now would be an excellent time for Tierza to swoop in and smash Roran Storm to bits! But there was no such sound to be heard; the evening was pregnant with the gasps of the winter daughters and their dismay.

'You can't do that, Amelie!' Eliza said, grabbing hold of Amelie's arm.

'She's right,' Aoife said. 'You are far too central to the mission to be lost before we even set foot outside Teragovia!'

'What other choice do we have?' Amelie snarled, the weight of the decision weighing heavily on her. 'It is a dark moon night; we are not strong enough to unleash the power of the moon channel!'

The shadowy figures had paused just inches from them. Their hooded garments blew like the flag on a pirate ship's mast. The whispery notes of Roran Storm's breath had chilled the girls to the bone. Eliza wasn't sure just what the shadows could do to them, but she was sure it wasn't pleasant!

'Let me say my goodbyes!' Amelie called out, her voice shaking now.

And then the shield began to vibrate precariously, and Eliza saw that Aoife's strength was depleting. Her face had turned a ghostly white, and a layer of sweat covered her body. Eliza tried desperately to repeat the feats that she had performed during their lessons, but it seemed that she was so blocked and heavy that the Ancient Magic simply bounced off her. She was the only other winter daughter familiar enough with the Ancient Magic to back Aoife and hold the fort, but her ability to summon it was lost. Eliza could do little but watch as the shield began to vibrate harder and harder. The shadows danced closer to the shield, and Roran Storm's icy breath licked the air around them. And then suddenly, the last reserves of Aoife's strength gave in, and the shield coiled itself tightly around the winter daughters in a chokehold before it exploded with a loud bang, the golden light rising through the mist in a projectile spire.

Now totally exposed, there was little the winter daughters could do to defend themselves. The luminescence of the purple river quickly faded into inky blackness, the Ancient Magic dormant once more. Aoife was on her knees, wrecked from the effort, holding her head in her hands. She held onto consciousness for a few tender seconds before dropping to the ground with glazed eyes. Amelie appeared to be frozen, her eyes darting from Aoife's limp body to the shadows and then back again. They couldn't run, they couldn't hide, they couldn't attack, and they couldn't defend. Without the shield to repel them, the shadows darted back onto their path and began to close in on the girls.

Roran Storm's mirthless whisper broke through the air and sang, 'what will you do next? Hand the Midnight Daughter over to me or watch as each of you is turned into a wraith!'

'Amelie! What do we do?' Eliza squealed. But Amelie was silent, her forehead furrowed in confusion as no solution presented itself. Was this it? Was this the end? Turned into wraiths by the Lord of Darkness, their mission over before it had even begun!

A loud cry rang through the night. Hope returned to the scene in the form of four warriors on horseback, a quartet the girls knew better than any other. Tierza, Lillian, Riani, and Kiani exploded onto the ravaged river bank and screeched to a halt in between the shadows and the winter daughters.

'Reveal yourself, intruder. You have no business breaching the city of the free folk!' Tierza's voice was confident. In her hand was a long sword that shone brightly despite the darkness of the night.

'Is that you, Tierza? Always the first to answer Teragovia's call, I have not forgotten this about you!' came Roran Storm's slithering tongue, detached from a visible, tangible form, seemed even more ominous now.

'Call your shadows off the whisperlings or face the wrath of the Teragovian army! The flare will bring the entire battalion to this spot in moments,' Tierza said, unfazed by Roran Storm's use of her name.

Roran Storm's response to Tierza's order was laughter. Through the echo of his laughter, more shadows rose from the thicket and poured out onto the riverbank like water gushing from an underground stream. They kept growing in number until the air around them was thick like smog with shadowy figures that did not touch the ground.

'Hand over the Midnight Daughter to me or watch as the Lord of Darkness brings Ayla's lineage to an end.'

As Eliza watched with her breath caught in her throat, a swift battle began. The four warriors charged through the mob of shadows with swords that burned bright and hot with flames of Ancient Magic. Their blades made contact with the shadows and obliterated them. As each shadowy figure fell to the ground, more were released by Roran Storm's creeping laughter.

'You can slash hundreds of them, even thousands, but they will rise again. You cannot kill what is already dead!'

Like a cat toying with a mouse in her paws, Eliza sensed that Roran Storm was simply playing with them. He enjoyed putting on a show, slowly revealing the full scope of his powers and breaking down the whisperers' morale brick by brick.

Riani and Kiani stood before the winter daughters, their swords blazing. Their horses neighed loudly, rearing their front limbs, uneasy in the company of the shadows, creatures unlike anything they had ever seen before. The purple glow of the river had returned, and Eliza could see fish and crabs swirling in circles, bearing witness to the whims of whisperers that fought their battles above the water's surface. Lillian and Tierza ran into the mob of shadows on horseback. They had laid an enchantment on the hooves of the horses. They glowed like embers and melted the shadows that drifted into their wake. From atop their mighty steeds, the two whisperers slashed their swords through the bodies of every shadow that stood in their path. Eliza watched; her stomach was leaden with fear, her eyes following the movements of the horses. The winter daughters, emboldened by the presence of the freedom fighters, took up their arms and reentered the fight with fervour. They held hands and threw the entirety of their being into the recreation of the shield. Without Aoife, it was much harder, but they pressed their hands tight into each other's and squeezed with all their might.

The golden dome reappeared, wafer-thin, but it held. Beads of sweat dripped down the foreheads of the daughters. In the centre, Amelie continued with the volley of arrows. The glow from her bow illuminated the riverbank, but the shadows remained dark and opaque. Though they were wispy and thin, they could not be touched by any light.

'Oh Tierza, you have not changed one bit! Still an obedient soldier, still a vassal strung to the destiny of a greater force than yours. You shouldn't be fighting on that side; the whisperer's cause will not serve you at all. Come

269

join me, Tierza; we could be great together!' Roran Storm's voice hissed from the thicket.

In response to this, Lillian and Tierza began to chant together in a low voice. With every word they uttered, the air around them started to sparkle and crackle. The static grew louder as their words in the ancient tongue sounded over battle cries. A column of light began to rise from the ground around them. It began to twist and swirl like a tornado, a tremendous gleaming tornado of light. It spun like a top on the spot and without warning, flew into the web of shadows with full force. It whizzed and cut through their bodies, a great, spitting orb of destruction.

'You have made your choice, the same choice you made ten years ago, Tierza. It gives me no pleasure to launch my beasts at you, but we both must abide by the path we have chosen. And so it is!'

'And so it is!' screamed Tierza, a crazed edge to her voice, as her spinning orb scattered the shadows.

Eliza saw Aoife's fallen bow next to her and picked it up. She knew that her powers were not contributing to the shield. She lifted the bow and launched herself into the battle, acting fast before she had the time to doubt herself. Amelie roared in encouragement, her bow of light flung arrow after arrow into the league of shadows at breakneck speed. Eliza's eyes barely registered the presence of each new one before it was strung and shot and a new one was in place.

Eliza grasped the bow tightly with sweaty palms and roared as she aimed at a shadowy figure. Without understanding what she was doing, energy that seemed to be welling up from her belly raced through her fingers and into the bow and arrows, the arrows head glowed brightly, and as she loosed the arrow, it plunged into where the shadow's heart should have been. The shadow evaporated, the vapour disappearing into the air to mark the end of its cursed afterlife. Behind her, the winter daughters formed a ring around Aoife's limp form to protect her from the shadows. Amelie fought with a fury unlike anything Eliza had ever seen before, felling shadows rapidly until the air around them was full of vanishing spires of pungent vapour.

For a few seconds, it appeared as though they had chanced upon a winning solution when Roran Storm's rage blew a gale into their midst. A cold wail erupted from the thicket, and the air grew freezing cold. A blanket of frost emerged from the trees, knitted by the invisible needles of Roran Storm's magic, each line appearing rapidly after the previous one. Hail began to fall from the sky before the frost had even touched the mud on which Eliza stood. The wind howled angrily as though someone had poked its open wound and cold hard stones of ice began to pelt down from the sky. Eliza looked behind her and saw that a layer of ice was forming on top of the river, thickening bit by bit. The hail grew heavier; each stone grew more jagged and dense until it began to cut through their tunics and then their skin, drawing rivulets of blood wherever it landed. Lillian and Tierza's faces were masked in concentration, but the wind was blowing furiously, and soon their strength would give away.

'You might have the moon channel at your disposal, but I am a master of all of the elements! You might store your magic in the water and think yourself invincible, but what will you do when the rivers freeze over? You rely on a certain order, the waxing and waning of your Goddess, to apply your powers. I bring about chaos. I dance with the unpredictable; I harness that which cannot be known, that which is invisible to the naked eye. I am Roran Storm, and there is nothing you can do to defeat me! Give me the Midnight Daughter, or watch as I drain your rivers and empty your groundwater! Give me the Midnight Daughter, and I will do you no harm. You have one minute to decide, and then my shadows will take her!'

Chapter Thirty

The Master of the Elements

E ven as the wind bit down harder and the ghoulish laughter of Roran Storm echoed through the woods, Tierza and Lillian showed no signs of stopping. The hailstones grew sharper and sharper and made deep cuts on their skin. A few fat drops of freezing water landed on Eliza's lips, and she realised that it was brackish. Roran Storm had engineered salty rain just to exacerbate the pain the whisperers would feel when their blood made contact with the hail. Her entire body was shaking from the cold and the sharp pain from her cuts, but Eliza did not stop shooting her glowing arrows at incoming shadows. All around her, the winter daughters cried out, 'for Elatonia!' or 'For Teragovia!' Even though they were fighting with all their might, Eliza could see that they could not sustain the effort for a long time. Her muscles burned with the pain of shooting the bow continuously, and her eyes stung from the salty rain and sharp hail that she could not deflect with her hands. At some point, the cold and the wind and the hail would weather them down and they would succumb. Then the shadows would feast on their souls and drain them of all the lift they had within them. And then what? Would they join the league of shadows and turn on their own people? The thought spurred Eliza to push past the fear and exhaustion even as every bone in her body quaked and shook in the cold.

'Where are the battalions?' Amelie screamed, her arrows vanquishing a mob of shadows, even as twenty more emerged from the woods on the other side.

'They saw your flare, I'm certain. These wretched shadows have leaked into the city through multiple breaches. I am certain the battalions will make their way over as soon as they can!' said Riani, who had now taken up a sword in each hand.

A loud crashing sound made Eliza turn her head. Behind her, the ice was cracking on the water's surface as it began to whirlpool animatedly. It roiled and heaved as though purging its chest of a nasty cough. Small waves had started to form and break in the otherwise seamless flow of the river. Each wave rose sharply, reared its foamy head, and crashed back into the water with a blood-curdling scream. As she fought the shadows, Eliza sneaked glances at the river only to see the waves rising taller and crashing harder. One of them grew twice her height and bucked violently before crashing hard on the bank, its foamy maw reaching her boots. The water hit Aoife with a splash and roused her from her unconscious state. She looked up at the scene unfolding in front of her with wide bleary eyes. Her tunic was soaked, and her face and arms were covered with thousands of tiny nicks from the jagged hailstones. She joined Amelie at the forefront, and with some unknown source of strength, she entered the fight.

Aoife's return to the fight gave the winter daughters a fresh boost of hope, and even though Roran Storm had turned their river into a malicious sea, the girls persisted in their fight. Each wave grew taller and taller and smacked the river bank aggressively. One of them landed hard on the back of Eliza's knees, knocking her to the ground. She had to hold onto a rock embedded in the earth to stop the current from dragging her into the icy water. She sucked air into her lungs in thick gulps, pushed the damp strings of hair away from her face, and willed her arms to continue their fight until the battalions of Teragovia could make their way to the river bank.

'How long will you keep this up for? I could fight you for a hundred years without ever running out of strength, but you are only minutes away from dropping to the ground. That was the biggest failure of the realm - when Ayla and Riaz split the day and the night and thereby halved the potential of power available to the strongest in Elatonia. I do not abide by this division, I do not crave the powers of the sun or the moon, and that is why you cannot beat me, no matter how hard you try! He who has mastered death has nothing to fear!'

The tidal waves made the ground tremor as they took over the river bank. They made the fighting whisperers inch closer and closer to the woods until the strip of land on which the battle ensued was narrow and crowded. The shadows were wispy and squeezed past one another to surround the whisperers. Their cold presence engulfed the whisperers breathlessly. It was like a snake coiling itself around the branch of a tree. Round and round it went before fanning its hood angrily, its forked tongue hissing viciously as it threatened to devour the enemy with the tiniest vial of its venom.

Eliza had never been taught to pray, but in that moment, she put the energy of her whole being into opening her heart to Ayla, beseeching her for assistance; even the smallest display of miracles and strength would protect her lineage from the crooked whisperer named Roran Storm.

At that very moment, a small band of whisperers ran down the muddy path with blazing swords and threw themselves into the fight. Some help, finally!

'Where are the others?' Tierza called out to them.

'The whole city is swarming with these nefarious shadows! The warriors are fighting all along the city walls! We saw your flare and fought our way here to provide assistance! We brought some more weapons if you need them!'

One of them tossed a burlap sack of swords onto the ground. The winter daughters that held the shield broke away instantly and joined the fight. This was not a time to defend; it was a time to attack!

There were about six new warriors, and they were all skilled blades. With each of them on the offense, there were a few fleeting moments in which it seemed like the whisperers had regained the upper hand. They roared and charged at the shadows, dropping one after the other with their blades of light. The two glowing bows held up. It was a glorious sight, a mythical scene in which it seemed confident that the brightly lit beams of the whisperers would prevail.

And then, Roran Storm revealed himself. At first, a snarl of rage echoed from the thicket. And then a thick dark mass began to gather. The dark sky overhead began to thicken with clouds. As though attracted by a magnet, heaving grey masses drifted towards a point in the centre. The clouds hung lower than Eliza had ever seen them, making the forest appear ethereal and eerie. A roar of thunder erupted like a battle cry from the sky, and a lightning bolt flashed a sinister glow. Two gleaming red eyes appeared against the dark sky, followed by a crooked grin. Disembodied and enormous, Roran Storm was projected onto the cloudy sky as though he owned it and had claimed the entire dark expanse for himself. His sinister laugh rang through the night as lightning bolts flew down upon the earth.

The sight of Roran Storm high in the sky sent a wave of terror through the whisperers. What type of magic was this! For a couple of horrific seconds, Eliza saw the ashen faces of her comrades, streaked with blood and tears, and dirt. Their bright shining eyes fighting the strain of weariness. Their flushed cheeks and torn clothing revealed the tenuousness of their strength.

And then the lightning grew wicked and fast, bolt after bolt launching itself from various points in the sky. Every treetop it hit caught on fire. Every piece of empty land turned into a crater. Sleeping birds cried shrilly as they flapped their wings away from their ravaged nests, forced to leave their flightless younglings behind. Underground creatures scampered out of their burrows as the craters caved in their lairs and crumbled them to dust. Eliza stopped short, almost letting the cloaked arms of a shadow figure grab her as she took in the tumultuous world around her. Only an hour ago, the peace and harmony of Teragovia was something they had been able to take for granted. Their impenetrable fortress had protected them without allowing the slightest bit of concern to enter their minds. Now, here they were, every creature in the city of free folk lamenting their complacency as their world went up in flames and ice.

Shooting at the shadows repeatedly with her rapidly depleting arrows, Eliza cried out to Amelie, 'Amelie! Do something!'

'I'm doing my best!' came Amelie's strangled voice.

The thunder snarled testily in the sky and roused all the animals so that the air was filled with howls and croaks and hisses and neighs. The cacophony spelled turmoil for everyone. Eliza could even hear the distant cries of the city folk and see burning blips of light that she assessed to be torches. She heard a scream of pain from one of the warriors that had just arrived. He had been struck by a bolt of lightning and was now rolling on the ground, trying to put out the fire that blazed on his back. Eliza's voice was stuck in her throat. She wanted to drop her weapon and help him, but if she stopped fighting for a split second, the shadows would seize her. They had grown colder and bolder. The air around her was thick with the preying arms of the shadows, reaching for the warriors. Roran Storm had changed his command. They were no longer meant to be puppets of fear but to attack viciously now.

'Is this enough, or will you have me turn this whole city into a wasteland before I take what I want?', came Roran Storm's voice, a hiss so sharp that it cut through the thunder and the cries of the forest creatures. 'Must another city of whisperers crumble to oblivion before you learn to lay down your arms in time? Was the fall of Fionnos not enough for you?' The face in the clouds darted across the sky, blood red and glowing. Roran Storm could manipulate even the wind so that his voice appeared to come from everywhere at once. Eliza looked behind her shoulder every time he spoke, afraid that he would suddenly appear behind her back.

'Don't humiliate us with your false show of concern, Roran,' Tierza cried out, her voice laced with disdain. 'You were born and raised in these woods; you scouted the land to bring refugees in from the fallen cities; you cared for lost children as though they were your own. And then you disappeared, leaving us all thinking you were dead. You come back now to throw your own city into destruction - how dare you, traitor, how dare you pretend to care for us now!'

These words shocked Eliza. How could someone who had served this city with all their heart betray its people so cruelly? She looked at the forest, catching flames around her, and shuddered. A ring of fire now surrounded them; every tree encircling them had bright orange flames licking its trunk. And yet, despite the heat, there was a thickening layer of frost on the ground beneath her feet. The hail continued to blast from the sky, even as the lightning bore holes into the bare earth. The destruction around them was so total and complete that Eliza was surprised that she hadn't laid down her sword and shed tears in agony. Each blow that Roran Storm dealt to her beloved city felt like an attack on her physical body, every fibre of her being was in pain. She had never felt so helpless and small before, a mere speck of dust swirling in a tumultuous gale caused by forces greater than she could ever be. She wished desperately that Amelie would wring out her hidden powers from somewhere and prove to them just what the Midnight Daughter could do.

But as Eliza watched whole trees splinter into halves and fall to the ground from the force of the lightning, she began to doubt what the powers of the Midnight Daughter could do. After all, what singular being could match up against the imminent destruction around them? What could Amelie ever hope to produce - even as the most skilled whisperling amongst them - that could send Roran Storm and his league of shadows reeling?

'Give her to me!' cried Roran Storm, his voice rising an octave as he unleashed horror after horror upon them.

Eliza wasn't sure if she imagined it, but she felt certain she could hear the chilling screams of trees as they swayed against the wind before crashing to the ground with rumbling thuds.

Riani and Kiani had dropped their swords. They stood back, their palms joined, regrowing the shield around the whisperers. But before the golden layer of protection could be fully formed, lightning struck the ground to their side, tossing them to the side with a sickening thud. Riani tried to raise herself, but the shadows immediately surrounded the two as they lay on the ground.

'Never!' cried Tierza, even as her voice shook. She and Lillian stood in the epicentre, fighting bravely. This feat, formerly brave, now looked pitiful as the numbers of the black shadows grew and closed in around the whisperers. It seemed that Roran Storm had become bored of toying with his food and was ready to finally claim it. Something hot and heavy began to boil in Eliza's blood as she witnessed the shadows floating above the ground, creating ring after ring of defense around the blood-streaked whisperers. The winter daughters fought tooth and nail against them, but their efforts were barely enough to stop the shadows from penetrating. So far, Roran Storm had made his shadows do little except reach for the whisperers with their clammy hands. Now, he was about to reveal their true power.

The shadows began to wail as they encircled the whisperers tighter and tighter. Eliza felt the air from her lungs disappear as the shadows sapped away her life force with their presence. She began to dry heave, gasping for air even as her body tried to expunge the dark energy that radiated from the shadows. Her vision began to cloud as they drew closer. It seemed pointless to continue to fight now. She tipped her head to one side and saw Nala and Maud stupified in terror too, their actions inhibited by the dense vibrations of the shadows. On her other side, Aoife and Seena had turned colourless, their skin flushed and bloodied and their eyes betraying a dissipation of life force as a deathly glaze took over.

The shadows wailed louder and louder, screeching out a morbid lament that escalated into a ballad of hunger and greed. They appeared ravenous, ready to feast on the souls of the whisperlings before them. Eliza felt a sensation that was beyond fear, beyond everything she had ever known. She looked down at her hands, and the bow slipped from her fingers and fell to the ground, causing a crack in the blanket of frost. Her hands were long and white and empty, the hands she had inherited from a mother and father she had never known, a mother and father who had perished in a battle much like this one, a mother and father that she might be reunited with in the afterlife if there was such a thing. Oh, to be Josef's daughter in some mysterious universe! Perhaps death would not be so bad after all. The world around her was too unpredictable; it offered no rest or respite for her frail heart. It gave her things only to wrench them away soon after. What was the point really? What was the point of anything at all?

Eliza's mind felt impossibly calm as the wails of the shadows commanded all her senses. Her skin flared up in goosebumps, and her ears rang from the tinny clamour of her surroundings. It was as though she had been seized and taken away from the present moment, as though her body was tethered to it, but her soul had started to drift away, further and further away from reach, off to some blessed eternity of peace and quiet, where neither friend nor foe could reach her, where she would be alone in a deep sleep, the deepest sleep she had ever known.

And just as the drowsiness had begun to make her knees go weak, Eliza saw Amelie being lifted by the shadows, her long and lithe frame like a ragdoll held in the embrace of the hungry shadows that raised her horizontal frame up and floated her away from the ring of whisperers. With the last bit of wakefulness that Eliza had left, she saw her very first friend in the world being taken away from her and jolted back into consciousness with a start.

Chapter Thirty One
The revelation

Suddenly, Eliza wasn't in the dizzying stupor that had laid its vice grip on her seconds ago. All of a sudden, she was wide awake, every sense in her body on high alert. The same could not be said for the other winter daughters. Entranced, their bodies were slack, suspended like marionettes in thin air. They appeared totally powerless, completely erased from their own reality. Their life force was draining from them, their faces overcast with the grim premonition of death. Snowflakes fell from the sky in swirls of powder. The hail had ceased, and the roar of the river had subsided. Roran Storm had taken away the fanfare and fuss - once his shadows stole the conscious minds of his victims, the display of his powers had no audience and was therefore worthless. The shadows hung close to them, and Eliza tried not to move a muscle, not even to blink in case they realised that she had bounced back into awareness. Roran Storm's face had disappeared from the clouds. Instead, a tall and dark figure appeared at the edge of the woods. His features were sharp, his expression impossibly calm as he wreaked havoc all around him. It seemed that chaos was Roran Storm's home turf; he seemed to thrive with horror and destruction unraveling all around him.

Eliza breathed in deeply as she saw Amelie's limp body cradled by wispy beasts of terror, gliding slowly through the streams of snowflakes; she couldn't help but tear up. At that moment, every single one of the losses that Eliza had ever known stacked up tall in front of her. First, her parents in a city that she would never see because it had perished along with them. Second, Hugo and with him, the chance to have a normal human life in Bardoria. Third, Amelie and the fall of Teragovia, the city she had believed would shield her from all further harm.

And suddenly, the sorrow welled up inside her so enormously that it felt like a glass shattered within her. A dam broke, and all of the pain she had tried to take into her stride seemed to come down on her at once. Although Eliza did tend to feel sorry for herself every now and then, she never saw herself as abjectly miserable. But there she was, this tragic creature who seemed to repel all kinds of love. Even as an infant, her parents had not been able to hold onto her. Something about her squirmed right out of the grip of family. It was as though she wasn't intended to belong anywhere or with anyone, as though a curse hung over her head that forced her to tread on the path of the lone wolf. But this was not the life she wanted. Eliza did not want to be someone that stood there and watched silently while swords and shadows took away everyone she loved.

'You need to grieve now, little whisperling; grief is the only way you will release those blockages!' The

Oracle's disembodied voice came to her from nowhere, that silken, perennially amused tone that made it seem like the wizened old woman was in on a joke that no one else was allowed to know.

And so, Eliza grieved. Instead of trying to fight the pain, she marched right into it. She let herself freefall into the pitch-black abyss, where the images of all the families she'd come so close to having and then lost haunted her. She had tried and failed several times to bring her parents' faces to mind, but this time, something was different. A long-forgotten memory from her childhood swam back to her. Beyond the veil of grief lay two faces, clear as day, smiling down upon her. A tall, sturdy man, his arms encircling a vivacious woman, her dark hair fluttering in the breeze as she smiled in contentment. Eliza could almost smell the salt that clung to the man's tunic and taste the wild sorrel and chives heaped in the basket that the woman carried. Their aura exuded a sense of steadiness and comfort, a shared familiarity and strength. In their faces, Eliza began to see bits of her own. Her mother's dark hair and wide eyes, her father's dark complexion and prominent nose. There they were, her flesh and blood, the people whose love had created her. She was a creature that had been wrought from love, not fury or warfare, but love.

Eliza's desire to deny her own sorrow had kept these faces away from her for so long. She had never let herself ruminate too long on what could have been - what was the use when what could have been never was?

A montage seemed to be building in her mind. Her parents were joined by the jovial Hugo, shaking breadcrumbs out of his fluffy beard as he looked contently upon her. Hugo, with the impossible choice between his beloved nation and the strange whisperling he had grown to love as his own. Eliza didn't fault him for not knowing how to pick one side; he had done right by her eventually. Although he could never bring her into his home and give her the life he had always promised her, he had sacrificed his life to make sure that she could roam free instead of living in a dungeon at an internment camp. He had been her sole companion for ten years - Eliza could not doubt that he had loved her and loved her with all his heart. And she had loved him just as much. And now he was gone, and he would never ever return.

The tears fell faster, forming rivulets down her cheeks. Time seemed to have screeched to a halt. The images and memories flashed through her mind at a tremendous speed for what felt like minutes, although it all happened in an instant. Through wet eyes, she looked up and saw that Amelie and the shadows had almost reached the thicket where Roran Storm hid, waiting to claim the life of the Midnight Daughter. The horror engulfed her then. As the prettiest snow she had ever seen descended upon them like a song, Eliza felt utterly helpless and stricken with grief as she looked on at the scene before her eyes. She was losing yet another person she loved, this girl who had saved her life, confided in her, opened her heart to Eliza, and showed her what it was like to have a friend, to not be lonely in the world. What could she do about it but watch? She was no match, no match at all for these loathsome shadows or Roran Storm.

What next? Without Amelie, they would not stand a chance against the Bardorians. They would crush Teragovia with all their might. And that was without even contemplating the horrors that Roran Storm intended to make commonplace with his shadows. Was this it? Was this the end of the brief era of peace and joy that she had known?

And then the faces of Dion and Lou swam to her mind and jerked her out of her misery. The two of them, bickering and tickling each other, chasing butterflies along the riverbank, oohing and aahing at stories around the fire, looking to Eliza with dewey eyes to settle the score between them. These two children were her family, as were Tina and Neil. Her insides, which had turned into a gluey mess, began to solidify. Her dissipating sense of self began to coalesce once more as she pictured their sweet faces looking up at her while she mediated their conflicts. How could she stand and watch helplessly while the last glimmer of hope that represented their shot at a safe and happy future was being carried away in front of her?

The sorrow turned into fear which quickly turned into anguish as Eliza's yearning to protect the last remaining loved ones grew more and more desperate. Without even realising it, a pained shriek escaped her lips. It was loud and jarring against the sweet song of the snowflakes, but it did little to rouse the other winter daughters from their dreamlike sleep. The shadows paid her no mind; they were crossing into the thicket, Amelie's body tight in their hold; they cared little for the woeful, embittered screams of a whisperling.

'Clear your mind and open yourself to the Ancient Magic,' came the Oracle's voice once more. It felt as though the voice was coming from Eliza's own head rather than an external source.

Eliza clenched her fists and did as she was told. She took a deep breath and drowned her surroundings out of her mind. She let the air travel to every part of her body, her fingers, toes, belly, shins, and neck. She exhaled the frustration she felt, the longing, the fear, and the grief. She visualised a stream of golden light engulfing her, the source of the Ancient Magic, the invisible strings that held the world together. Something unusual was happening within her, something she had not quite experienced before. Her thoughts stopped bumping into each other haphazardly but dutifully exited her mind. A point in the centre of her head drew in all her focus, and her sensory awareness became subservient to it. Eliza pictured a clean open pathway that began at the centre of her forehead and coursed through her entire body in a network of tributaries. The sticky grief that had created roadblocks seemed to disappear upon confrontation. It seemed that all she ever had to do was let it pass through her. If she turned her being into a sieve, everything that was trapped within could find its way out, and all that served her well could remain.

For the first time, Eliza experienced what it was like to have an open and clear mind. She murmured the incantations that the Oracle had taught them and called in the Ancient Magic and its guiding light. She visualised the outcome - the release of Amelie, the destruction of the shadows, the vanquishment of Roran Storm, and the liberation of Teragovia. She activated her heart-space, the soft singe of urgency as she held her manifestations with love and grace. She kept her eyes closed, but around her, she could feel a ray of warmth ribboning out of the ground and encircling her. It wound itself around her and seeped into her skin. It amalgamated with her particles, her essence, and ballooned around her heart and head, unifying the two strongest forces in the body. Her skin grew warm, and light, and its temperature continued to rise till she was sure that she was burning up. The snowflakes around her started to melt and turn into fat water drops. Her stomach roiled and crashed at first and then began to become light too. Her entire body imbibed the heat until she could barely feel her limbs or her nose as separate parts of her. Eliza was one ball of flaming heat; the Ancient Magic had created a dome around her that gave her a sense of oneness in her being like never before.

The river, which had quietened down after the taking of Amelie, began to whirlpool again. Eliza opened her eyes and sank to her knees. She pressed her fingers into the earth, melted the layer of frost with the heat from her knuckles, and roared a guttural scream. The Ancient Magic was intoxicating; it made her head spin. She grounded down and sought the stability of the earth as she kept her mind honed on the outcome she desired.

The river began to grunt and heave as though a vat of milk was being churned into butter against its will. And suddenly, from the frothy purple river, something broke out of the surface. A creature made of golden white light, tossing its mane as it jumped out of the water with its front legs in the air and charged into the mass of shadows. Behind the first creature was another, and another. They sprang from the river as though they had been standing in line the whole time, waiting for someone to call to them. They neighed fiercely as they bounded towards the thicket, radiant creatures of light and magic, rising from a deep slumber to do Eliza's bidding. She could scarcely believe her eyes - these were the water horses from Neil's tales! They had woken from the river at her call!

The shadows wailed when the water horses ran into them. Their light was suffocating to them; they shook and disappeared into smoke. And the horses kept coming, running up with their glorious manes aflame and plunged right into the heart of darkness. In seconds, the horses were everywhere; they outnumbered the shadows and cast a light so bright that it appeared to be midday. Their sleek, translucent coats shimmered and shone as they seemed to dance amongst the shadows. Having been underwater for so long, there was a joy to their movements as they tasted the crisp night's air for the first time in thousands of years! Eliza's forehead seared from the weight of the magic she was harnessing; she was on all fours now, her body heaving and whirring as the magic passed through the open pathways within her.

Roran Storm's raging hiss said, 'who dares double-cross me like this! This has been a ruse! The Midnight Daughter is clearly still at large. I have no use for this whisperling!'

Amelie was dropped to the ground by the shadows that held onto her despite the charging water horses circling the mob. The shock of the drop woke her, and she looked up to see the wispy shadows retreat into the thicket behind her.

Roran Storm's voice rang out again. 'You have angered me with your games, whisperers. You led me to believe that I had taken the Midnight Daughter when it was nothing but a farce. Whether its tonight or many moons from now, mark my words, I will take the real Midnight Daughter with me!'

Amelie looked aghast as she placed what was going on around them. She looked at Eliza, clutching the ground, her body lit up and shimmering with the Ancient Magic. Her skin looked similar to that of the water horses; it contained the same glow of magic, the same heat, and the same ethereal quality.

The sight of Amelie, alive and shaking, gave Eliza a fresh burst of energy. From deep in her heart, she called in one final bout of strength. The horses neighed, buoyed by her command as they charged at Roran Storm. A look of panic appeared on his face, and he raised his cloak and disappeared in a flash.

The water horses drove the shadows deeper and deeper into the thicket until the shadows were long gone. Roran Storm's voice did not pierce the night again; he seemed to have accepted his momentary defeat and retreated. Eliza's vision had begun to blur; she did not know how much longer she could channel magic of this scale. She saw Amelie crawl towards her through the corner of her eye, blood and dirt staining her face. Relief surged through her as she saw that her friend was safe from the shadows and whatever evil lay in wait with them. Although Roran Storm and his shadows had merely been driven away, not defeated, and the threat of Bardoria was ever-present, Eliza didn't care about anything else at that moment except that Amelie was safe and sound.

The water horses returned from the thicket and walked towards Eliza. Each of them dipped its head to her before plunging back into the icy water and returning to its slumber. Eliza let go of the ground and reached her arms out to embrace Amelie. But Amelie's face was stricken.

Jumping to her feet, she cried, 'you're the Midnight Daughter! You knew all along and didn't tell me. I trusted you...I thought we were friends...oh, how am I to face anyone after this! You've betrayed me, Eliza; you've well and truly betrayed me!'

The last reserves of Eliza's energy had faded, and she could barely string together a response. Her vision began to cloud. The horses kept bowing to her before departing. Eliza's head started to spin in circles. She reached out once again to hold onto Amelie, to let her touch say all the things that her voice was unable to, but she was so depleted that her arms could barely go more than a couple of inches off the ground. The last thing she saw before her vision turned black was Amelie turning on her heel and running into the woods, leaving Eliza and the winter daughters behind in a haze of bright light.

Chapter Thirty Two

Eliza's secret

When Eliza opened her eyes, she could barely tell objects apart from each other in front of her. Hazy shapes blurred into each other. Everything was too bright for her to bear, and so she closed her eyes again and let out a weak sigh. Her throat was parched. As the physical sensations returned to her body, she became aware of how much pain she was in. Every part of her was sore, stiff, and achy. It was as though she had scaled several hills without any prior preparation, and now her whole body was protesting to teach her a lesson. She lifted her hand to her face. It was stone cold, marble-like even. She had pushed past her ability to generate heat. The aftermath had left her limp, pained, and woozy.

'Oh look, she's stirring!' came a voice from somewhere far away. A set of footsteps clattered on a wooden floor as they made their way to her.

A warm hand touched her forehead, and someone blew softly on her face. The relief was enormous. Eliza fluttered her eyes open again and saw Lillian and Tierza standing on either side of her.

'What - where am I? Did Roran Storm come back? I tried to hold out longer, I swear I did, but I just collapsed!'

'Shhhh. There, there, now. You've single-handedly saved Teragovia; there's nothing to be sorry for,' said Lillian in a soothing voice.

'Where am I?'

'You're in the sanatorium. You've been comatose for a full two days. You exerted yourself a great deal; your body needed the rest.' The stone walls looked unfamiliar, as did the row of beds on her left side. To her right was a big window. Her vision was still too weak to see what lay on the outside.

'Is the battle over?' Eliza croaked.

'For now it is.'

'Is everyone safe?'

'Aye, most of them even awoke in time to see the last of the water horses jump back into the water. That was some fine magic you pulled out of your hat, Eliza!' Lillian said, squeezing Eliza's palm. Tierza had remained quiet so far. Her expression was wounded, as though each breath she took was a great source of pain.

'Is Amelie okay?'

Neither of them said a word. Tierza swiftly turned on her heel and slammed her forearm into the stone wall behind her. She buried her head in the crook of her elbow.

'There was nothing any of us could have done, Eliza. She was taken by the shadows. Roran Storm will find out soon that she is not the Midnight Daughter. Whether he releases her after that or uses her as a bargaining chip is anyone's guess.'

Eliza blinked. Lillian continued to speak, reassuring her that it was not her fault and that they had already sent scouts to look for her. But the words rolled off her like water off a duck's back. She could not muster the strength to reveal that Amelie had not been taken by the shadows. Eliza had succeeded in driving the shadows away before they could take her. Amelie had run away; she had made that choice because she believed that Eliza had betrayed her in some unforgivable fashion. She hadn't been able to stop her. She hadn't had the energy.

She sat up a little and groaned. Lillian handed her a glass of water, and she accepted it. She drained its contents and shook her head at the bowl of soup that was put on a tray next to her. She was too exhausted and far too riddled with guilt to eat just yet.

'I need to go back to sleep,' she murmured, hoping that Amelie would return by the time she was awake again.

The next time Eliza opened her eyes, there was no one else around. She sat up in her bed and gazed out of the big window to her right. It overlooked a small alley. The sun shone brightly on the cobblestones. There was a house on the other side of the alley, with bright red and yellow pansies hanging out of a basket by the window. She got out of bed and pressed her nose against the glass to get a wider look. There were stumps instead of trees on either end of the street. They had probably been struck by Roran Storm's lightning and collapsed to the ground.

Eliza gulped. She wondered how much destruction the city had seen. She was terrified to find out. Perhaps she didn't have to. Perhaps she could stay in bed and take her time to recover so that by the time she left, the city would have been restored to its former glory. That would have been her usual instinct. But could she still do that? Another voice piped up in her head. Surely not, surely she had to go and face all events head-on now that it had become abundantly clear that she was the Midnight Daughter.

This was the first time she had articulated the thought to herself. It sounded like a myth, a fiction. Surely someone would saunter up to her any moment now and tell her there had been a mistake, and actually, she had only been able to channel the Ancient Magic because Aoife was too sick to do it on her own. A thought struck her then - what if the winter daughters hated her for being the Midnight Daughter? She, who had displayed barely passable skills in each of their lessons. They had accepted their fate when Amelie declared herself the Midnight Daughter, but they hadn't been thrilled about it. In fact, they always seemed on the brink of mutiny. What if it was the same with her? What if her leadership was so weak that they realised they could not count on her in the slightest? Or, what if they too thought that she had betrayed Amelie, her first friend, and took that as proof of how she wasn't to be trusted? What if they ran from her too?

Before she could process any of the implications of what it would mean if she was in fact, the Midnight Daughter, there was a knock at the door. There was no time to respond, the door was flung wide open, and all of the winter daughters stormed in from the narrow frame.

'Eliza! You legend!'

'You absolute genius!'

'I can't believe you saved us from the shadows all by yourself. The way the water horses bowed to you!'

'Midnight Daughter! And you didn't think to mention it to any of us!'

'Go on, tell us how you summoned those water horses!'

'Can you summon them now? Will they come to you pretty much whenever you call them?'

And then finally, Nala's voice cut in through the excited babble. 'Stop it, all of you, can't you see she's overwhelmed? Get back into bed, Eliza, and don't you worry, we'll be behaving ourselves now!'

The winter daughters all perched at the edge of her bed or stood around it and gazed at her with smiling eyes. In their faces, Eliza saw no scorn or derision but only acceptance. They seemed not to be too shocked that it was the hapless underdog who had revealed herself to be the Midnight Daughter. They didn't even seem to mind that she hadn't given any indication of this before. Not that she had known, but it was easily something they could have held against her if they believed that she had knowingly kept them all in the dark.

'Everyone has questions, Eliza, but the first thing we'd like to know is how you're feeling,' said Aoife, reaching over and squeezing Eliza's hand.

Eliza nodded weakly, trying not to let the tears fall from her eyes. 'I've never been better,' she said cheerily, and they all laughed.

'And the second thing we'd like to say is congratulations on being the Midnight Daughter!'

The others echoed Aoife's sentiment and congratulated her, squeezing her hand, patting her shoulder, and offering such a great deal of warmth and encouragement to Eliza that she felt as though she might disappear into the ground.

'Now tell us, did you know all along?' Maud interjected, the devious twinkle in her eyes ever-present.

'I don't even know now, to be perfectly honest!' Eliza said, covering her reddened face with her palms.

'Did you receive a sign at the full moon ritual?' asked Seena.

'I didn't realise it at the time, but I suppose I did. I felt the Ancient Magic welling up inside me. All the creatures in the forest came out to dance and sway with me. I've always had an affinity for woodland creatures, so I thought nothing of it, but now I think they were the ones bearing the sign from Ayla!'

'That makes perfect sense, does it not! Do you remember how the prophecy went? *At the very brink of winter, the daughter of the earth is born. Her power simmers underneath until the shadows rise from above and below. She is the Midnight Daughter. She, who holds both keys. Bringer of peace, holder of unity. This is the winter daughter's realm.* Eliza is the daughter of the earth; that's why the forest creatures dancing with her was the sign we asked for!'

'And the shadows were Roran Storm's shadow army! Eliza's powers practically exploded out of her when the shadows rose.'

'That's the thing about signs - you can't know if you're interpreting them the right way except in hindsight,' said Nala, shaking her head sagely.

'Poor Amelie! It's no fault of her own that she thought she had received a sign from Ayla. Everyone treated her as though she was the Midnight Daughter all her life. Surely it would take the smallest hint of a sign to have you thinking it was the final piece of the puzzle!'

The winter daughters all tut-tutted sympathetically. In her absence, Amelie had regained the compassion of her cohorts.

'No sign of her then?' Eliza asked through pursed lips.

'No, Eliza, none at all.'

After hearing the kindness with which they all spoke of Amelie, Eliza didn't have the heart to reveal that Amelie had turned her back on them and chosen to run away of her own accord. No, she would keep Amelie's secret for another day and tell them tomorrow. And then one day became one more day which eventually became a week. By the time Eliza left the sanatorium and returned to the lodging, she still hadn't uttered a word about Amelie's disappearance. Those days were quiet and short. She drifted in and out of sleep, sat up in her bed whenever she had visitors, and pondered absent-mindedly the rest of the time. It was a time reminiscent of her life in the tower when a single window was her only outlet to the world. By the time Eliza left, she dreadfully missed the feeling of fresh air and warm sunshine on her skin. She had lived most of her life in a tower, but she was no longer that girl anymore. Everything had changed now.

Eliza took a deep breath and marched into the street. The city was not intact, but it wasn't as bad as she had feared. She walked gingerly from the quiet of the sanatorium and into the bustle of the town square. The taller trees that lined the paths had disappeared. Only the stumps remained alongside the smaller trees that had missed the brunt of the lightning. There were craters here and there, some as small as a plate and others the size of her bed. But the people of Teragovia were resilient. They had already begun to fill up the craters with soil. She waved to a young boy who told her that he was going to plant bulbs in them that would yield sweet-smelling flowers in the spring. The atmosphere was lively to the naked eye, but Amelie's disappearance had added a sense of heaviness to the atmosphere. At every corner, young men and women chattered about the shadows and what they could use to ward them off. No one walked the streets unarmed anymore. Even the children carried small daggers in their belts. Teragovia had bounced back, but it would not fall back into a restful slumber; that much was clear.

Eliza walked by two young whisperers sitting by the stumps with their carving knives. Two older men were carving a scene onto the stump of the tree. She squatted down next to one of them and saw that they were almost as old as she was. They were etching the battle scene against the shadows onto the stump. They paid her no mind. She was unrecognisable with her hood up. Their illustrations were impeccable. Horses with their feet in the air driving away cloaked figures and a young girl at the centre, her hands touching the earth.

'It's not every day you get to see ancient creatures rising from rivers, you know!' one of the men said, without turning away from the stump.

'A fine story to tell future generations one day!' said the other.

'All we have is our stories,' said the first one. 'And this story deserves to be remembered. It was the day that an ordinary whisperling saved her city all on her own! This is history being made!'

'I wish I could have been there!' one of the younger girls said.

'I want to be a warrior like her when I grow up!' said the other one.

Eliza flushed, got up again, and kept walking. She didn't know what she had expected from the city folk, but it was certainly not this. The dim light of the overcast sky offered a hazy glow above the rolling hills. Somewhere up in the sky, a new future was being written. It was hard to imagine that she was at the centre of the story being told. She was a reader, a storyteller even; what business did she have being in the story?

Eliza kept walking, relishing the feeling of freedom and drinking in everything in her field of vision. This was Teragovia, her home, her city. The clusters of stone houses disappeared and gave way to the open road. She walked along the familiar path with its brambles and burrs, past the point where the battle had taken place.

She didn't stop there - she wasn't ready yet. No, today was a day reserved only for joy.

She had intentionally kept her hood up to avoid recognition. But Lou and Dion would have known her from the sound of her footsteps alone. She gently opened the gate to their yard and walked down the muddy path. A sense of ease pervaded the second she laid her eyes on them. The strength she had drawn from wanting to protect them had helped her summon the water horses. This was the important thing, the most important thing. They ran up the path and hugged her tightly.

'Mum said you've been ill; is that why you haven't come around?' Dion asked.

'Yes, but I'm better now, which means you'll have to bring some extra heather for me by the fireside!'

Lou and Dion marched Eliza to the backyard, hand in hand as they caught her up on all that she had missed. All the beavers they'd seen, the herbs they'd planted in craters with their dad, the new songs that were being sung in the town square, and so on. One last day of peace, Eliza told herself, one last day of being just Eliza, and tomorrow she would go and meet the Council to accept her fate as the Midnight Daughter.

Chapter Thirty Three

A visit from the Oracle

The next morning, Eliza woke up in an empty room. She had overslept without Amelie there to rouse her. A restless itch was gnawing at her. She pocketed Hugo's blue button and slunk out of the lodging unnoticed. The morning was bright and still. The sun drifted in and out of the clouds lazily. She walked down the forest road, where the trees that still had their tops stood like statues in the unmoving air. Her feet hit the river bank. The flow of the purple waters was gentle without the wind raising whitecaps in it. She walked to the site of the battle. It betrayed no signs of there ever having been a conflict. The trees were singed and scarred, but ivy had already begun to creep up the burned streaks. The ground had been levelled, and seeds had been planted into each crater. The river, which had shapeshifted menacingly before her eyes, was now calmer than ever, without any indication of its ability to rise into colossal waves.

Eliza sank to her knees and began to cry. It wasn't an urgent sort of crying but a wretched, slow one. The floodgates to her grief had been opened right here a week ago, and upon returning to the spot, she was washed anew with sadness. Amelie was gone, Hugo was gone, and her parents had always been gone. She was supposed to meet the Council at dusk and accept her fate all on her own. The evening would mark a turning point in her life, yet she would have to embrace it all on her own. She put her hand in her pocket and felt the weight of the blue button.

'Are you searching for laurels too?' came a crackly voice behind her.

Eliza wiped her tears with the back of her hand and turned around. The Oracle was crouched by a smattering of ankle-high greens growing from the ground. She ripped a fistful of leaves and bit into them. Her eyes closed, and she smacked her lips. 'So sweet and so sour at the same time, a fine leaf indeed!'

'Uh no, I'm not looking for anything in particular,' said Eliza, rearranging her features to look more cheerful.

'Ah, but everyone is always looking for something, are they not? If not a herb, then an antidote to their misery. A clue, an answer, a poem, a sunset. What weighs you down, Midnight Daughter?' the Oracle asked, sitting on the grass next to Eliza. She carried a staff in one hand and a wicker basket in the other. Placing them on either side of her, she fixed her eyes on the flowing river, seeing things that Eliza never could.

'It feels peculiar to hear you say that, Oracle Moonfall,' Eliza said, her cheeks turning red.

'But I have always called you that in my mind, little whisperling,' the Oracle said, chuckling to herself.

'You knew it was me?'

'But of course. I knew from the moment you were born!'

'With all due respect, why didn't you say anything when I arrived? Or when Amelie was declared the Midnight Daughter?' Knots began to form in Eliza's stomach.

'It was not my place, dearie. A hero's journey is theirs alone. It is not for me to create a straight road between you and your destiny. My only duty is to prepare you for each of the perils and pitfalls along the crooked, snaking path.'

Eliza nodded uncertainly. She was not convinced.

'You'll see for yourself one day, sure you will. The pieces of the puzzle are being laid out in a confusing manner, but one day, you'll gaze upon it from the highest plain and know that it always had to happen this way.'

'I thought that we make our own fate, write our own destiny. That's what Hugo always told me.'

'Ah yes, that is the Bardorian ethos. The humans of the north have grown too accustomed to manipulating other creatures and even nature. They cast themselves as creators in the story. And they are not totally wrong in claiming agency. Where they err is in forgetting that our environment shapes us as much as we shape it.'

'I don't quite understand.'

'The circumstances are predetermined, but the choices we make within them are up to us. It was never your choice to be the Midnight Daughter; that was always your fate. But how you choose to lead is your choice alone. Do you see what I mean?'

'So we have power over some things but not everything? Our lives are moulded a certain way but not set in stone?'

'Aye, little whisperling,' said the Oracle, picking up her staff, dipping it into the water, and drawing little circles with it. From the circle, an image began to form in the foam. It was Eliza's own face, her eyes shining bright with joy, victory blazing across her features. 'This could be you if you manage to pull off this enormous feat.' The Oracle dragged the staff across the surface of the water and began to stir it in another spot. Eliza's face reappeared in the foam, streaked with blood and tears. She reeked of defeat and loss. 'However, the choices you make could also lead you here. The stakes have never been higher. But you have every chance of getting it right, dearie.'

Eliza gulped. The face vanished, and the water resumed its regular course. 'I-I-I just can't shake the feeling that there has been a mistake! How could it be me? I can think of thousands of reasons why Aoife or Nala or Amelie would be better suited for this role.'

'And yet, you were the one destined for it. If the Ancient Magic sought you out, it must mean that you are perfectly suited, in fact. You were not chosen because you can do it. You can do it because you were chosen. Do you see what I mean?'

'I suppose so,' said Eliza, turning her gaze away, where the still trees stood silently in the distance, calling her name. 'I can hear the trees talk sometimes, you know.'

'In your waking state or in your dreams?' the Oracle asked. 'Not that it makes a difference. We are as awake in our dreams as we are outside of them.'

'All the time, if I'm to be perfectly honest. Sometimes I can block them out, but I think that is what makes me weary. The effort of resisting whatever it is that they are trying to say. My dreams...they've been a constant source of worry since my moon cycle commenced. Each month, as we creep closer and closer to the full moon, my mind conjures the most horrific images. The world is fractured, the trees are dead, and the darkness prevails everywhere. Now that I think of it, I feel like it might have been a premonition for Roran Storm's shadows and the havoc they can wreak!'

'Aye, little whisperling. By letting the grief pass through you, you took the first big step. You opened yourself up to the Ancient Magic. Now you must keep treading along that path. The next thing you must do is let yourself See. The gift of the Sight has been bestowed upon you. Whether you are awake or dreaming, Ayla is sending you signs and messages. You must receive them even when they frighten you. They are being sent to you for a reason!' The Oracle cast a sidelong glance at Eliza and then lifted her basket onto her lap. From it, she gathered a mixture of berries and herbs and gave them to Eliza. 'Everything you need is already within and around you. Here, eat these. The finest fennel grows along this river in particular, I find.'

Eliza graciously accepted the leaves and munched on them. Her eyes widened at the delightful freshness of each skinny leaf in her mouth. The most modest of leaves could contain so much flavour! She continued, 'it was easier when I lived in the tower with Hugo. He used to bring me parchment and charcoal to sketch my dreams. When they were mere playthings that carried no weight, it was easier to hold them with ease,' Eliza said wistfully.

'Who says you can't continue to hold them with ease? If parchment and charcoal are what helps you distill the messages without strain, then you must continue to do so. Each person must adapt to themselves, no one else, little whisperling!'

'What do you mean, Oracle Moonfall?' Eliza asked, her eyebrows furrowed.

The Oracle used her staff to gesture at the wider world around them and all that it held. 'There are scores of ways to do a thing, and none of those ways are right or wrong. We're not here to find one single way to do things that trumps all others. Each person must find a way that is their way, theirs and theirs alone. Only then can they hope to succeed in their endeavours.'

'How will I know what my way is?' Eliza asked, looking around at the wild ferns and bushes, the fish swimming beneath the water's surface, the clouds that blocked the sun's light as it shimmered down upon the glade. It was as if she expected the answer to suddenly jump out from somewhere there. The vista remained dormant, attending to its own business without a care for Eliza's idle questioning.

'You already know what your way is. You have always known, as a matter of fact,' the Oracle said, winking at her.

'Have I?'

'Most certainly. Think back to questions in our lessons. Who are you? What defines you? What makes you who you are? Ponder upon those, and you will see what has been in front of you all along.' The Oracle rose to her feet. Eliza looked up at her frail frame, draped in colourful shawls. Today she wore no beads, only a crown of flowers and feathers. She looked and dressed, unlike anyone Eliza had ever seen. She had the features of a whisperer but the garb of the fey. It was as if she dressed herself to blend right into nature.

'Oh, and I nearly forgot. I was on my way to the Council to inform them of something. I found you first, and so I will reveal it to you first,' the Oracle said, leaning on her staff as the basket dangled daintily from her other arm. 'Ever since the battle, I have been communing with Ayla. And in no uncertain terms, she has conveyed a matter of great importance to me! A matter that changes the course of everything.'

As the Oracle spoke, Eliza felt chills travel down her spine. It seemed that Ayla had kept a few cards close to her chest all this time. There were things that had not been revealed to anyone else, anyone at all. Now that Eliza's powers had been awakened, she had deemed it to be the right time to present the message to the Oracle. The information unveiled forced Eliza to reconsider everything. She was glad to have obtained it before her meeting with the Council, as it gave her time to think. Eliza bid the Oracle goodbye and stayed in her spot by the river bank, listening to the murmur of the river as it flowed by. She pondered on the questions that the Oracle had posed to her.

Who am I?
What defines me?
What makes me who I am?

Eliza watched the hares sprint across the grassy patches of the bank. She held her hand out and a couple of them jumped to her and nuzzled her palm. She looked with interest at the tiny sprouts rising from the wet earth where the lightning had hit. So delicate and fragile was the dance of life. Things that broke cleared the way for other things to burgeon. There was an intent to all movements and motions. The path revealed itself with each step you took. Was there a way to preserve this way of life? This harmony that bound people to one another and to the natural world? Did they have to see themselves as separate from it? Could there be a way to learn the secrets of the natural world so that they could be stored in living memory across the realm, each living being a keeper of the balance, the dance? Eliza didn't know much about herself, but she knew that she had no desire to be the sort of leader who could allow the trees and rivers and birds and forest creatures to pay the price for a war waged by people against people. No, that would simply not do. Perhaps the answer, whatever it was, could be discovered by choosing the opposite thing to war. What was the opposite of war though? The opposite of blood and battle and savagery? The opposite of death and ego and evil?

Surely, the answer was love, compassion, and togetherness: harmony and sorority. Reverence and devotion to life itself, all of life, whether it swam, flew, fluttered, or crawled.

All of a sudden, Eliza knew what she had to do. She jumped to her feet and began to make her way to the library as fast as possible.

Chapter Thirty Four

The Midnight Daughter and the Council of Elders

Standing in front of the Council of Elders, Eliza's confidence began to falter. She had spent the last few hours in the library, trying to find answers lost in the lore that would back up the bold plan that she was about to propose. Walking to the Council House, through the corridor with vivid paintings of the Council Mistresses, she had felt a surge of bravery. The shoe fit, and she intended to wear it with pride. And then the keen gaze on their wise old faces in front of her shook her out of her reverie. These were immensely powerful women who had mastered their craft, stewarded over Elatonia for years and years, and performed magic of the highest order. And she, a mere whisperling, was about to ask that they turn a blind eye to centuries of conduct and trust her intuition not to lead them astray as they marched in the opposite direction? She swallowed nervously.

'Welcome to the Council of the Elders, Eliza. On behalf of the entire city of Teragovia and the realm of Elatonia, we thank you and welcome you into our fold,' said Zara, lifting her sword in the air so it glinted in the moonlight. 'Your performance in the battle was stellar; there has not been such a fine display of magic by a whisperling in all living memory. The Midnight Daughter - it is apparent that your powers are not diminished by the dark moon. The word of the prophecy rings true now. You protected the winter daughters, our city, and our people. We owe you tremendously. We honour you and offer you a seat on our Council, Midnight Daughter! Henceforth, you will have a vote in all matters concerning the salvation of the realm. If you desire a role in governance in the future, after the battle, we will begin to train you so you may one day succeed as Council Mistress. That is something to mull over. For now, do you accept a seat at our table?'

Eliza nodded, keeping her head low. Her skin prickled with goosebumps and her tongue felt heavy in her mouth as she searched for the right words. 'Thank you, Council. I am humbled and honoured to accept a seat at your table. I hope that I will not let you down and succeed in protecting the realm, the whole of the realm.'

'With our help and the help of our most skilled warriors, we do not doubt that you'll succeed, daughter,' said Zara, sitting down.

Eliza bit her lip and turned her gaze skyward. The dusk had turned the sky a creamy orange. There was a warm haze in the air that meant that even when the sun surrendered in totality, the night would not be as dark as it usually was. An owl hooted as it used the airspace above her as a thoroughfare, and Eliza took it as a sign of encouragement.

'The Oracle has told us that she has already conveyed Ayla's message to you,' Zara said.

'Aye, Council Mistress, the Oracle paid me a visit this morning and we spoke for a long time. Her advice was invaluable and helped me see a great many things regarding my destiny, my choices, and how I can align those things with the vision for the realm,' Eliza said, her voice shaking as she spoke.

'Marvellous. The Council was admittedly shocked to learn that there is a second part to the prophecy that remains hidden in the ruins of Fionnos. But I suppose it had to be that way in order to ensure that the Midnight Daughter would have some kind of an advantage over her enemies. Roran Storm was the most skilled whisperer in our fold; he knew all our secrets, including the prophecy, and look where that got us. He disappeared on a quest several years ago, after the fall of Fionnos, never to return. We all believed him to be dead and mourned him, for we had lost a good man and a great warrior. It is painful to learn that he voluntarily left us to side with the darkness. But it is what it is. And now we must count him amongst our enemies rather than our well-wishers. However, we must be careful with how we proceed. The shadows do not seem to be hindered by the enchantments that hide Teragovia. They are able to breach our walls with ease. Roran Storm has dredged up dark magic from who knows where! And we are in no position to anticipate his next move, for we do not know what he wants. We do not know what he wishes to do with the Midnight Daughter. We must act fast and strong and move forward before they have a chance to regroup, regain numbers and attack us again.'

Eliza's mouth went dry. 'Council Mistress, I'd like to say something. I do not know much about Roran Storm's motives, but I have every reason to believe that he is not acting alone. That he is not the worst of the threat but is, in fact, doing the bidding for another.'

The Council Mistress raised her eyebrow. Eliza got the feeling that if she had not been the Midnight Daughter, the Council Mistress would have loved to dismiss whatever she was about to say next. She felt Hugo's button in her pocket and derived some strength from it. All those losses had brought her here; she could not let her fear get the best of her and let those losses be in vain.

'Do go on, Eliza!'

'I believe that the shadows that he released are not phantoms of his own making. No whisperer magic could create such vile creatures that feed off the life force of another. That is not our way, which makes me believe he must have released those shadows from elsewhere. I know that what I am about to say, in all seriousness, has only ever been regarded as lore within our culture. However, I do believe that we must regard our lore, our stories, with utmost importance. I believe that they're here to remind us of the simple truth.' She paused for a second to look at the bemused faces of the Council looking at her expectantly. She had gone to the library and read and reread everything she could find about the topic, but it did not feel like enough. She tried to keep the shrillness out of her voice as she continued. 'I believe that

Roran Storm has been communing with Bris, the Lord of Darkness. I am not sure how he has opened this channel or to what end, but our lore tells us that Bris was never happy about dividing the world between Ayla and Riaz. His disappearance is not clear either. It is said that he vanished into the smog one day. But everything we know about his days in the Old World was that he was darkness incarnate, and he lusted for power. We can only speculate as to the full extent of his power, but it seems to me that he is the only creature in the realm powerful enough to raise the dead to do his bidding and to tempt someone as powerful as Roran Storm to join his mission.'

Zara took a few moments before she responded to Eliza. Her face betrayed no emotion, but there was an air to her movements that implied that she was in no mood to deal with conspiracy theories. 'It is plausible, Eliza; thank you for sharing your...theory with the Council. We will be on the lookout for any signs that further your claim. Now for the matter at hand!'

Eliza nodded bleakly. She had known that her claim would not be treated with the significance she felt it deserved. But what more could she do at this stage?

'We need to think about what we are going to do next. The prophecy is somewhere in the ruins of Fionnos. In order to get there, we will need to send a team of scouts all the way through the Whispering Woods, past the last human outcrops, and all the way to the southwestern coast where the fallen city remains. We will need to be stealthy, for the Bardorians must not catch a whiff of our scent or know that we are venturing in the opposite direction to them, or they will think us to be weakened and attack us post haste!' Zara said, flattening her palms on the cool marble table in front of her.

'Council Mistress, I believe that it is not a team of scouts that should go on to Fionnos to retrieve the prophecy alone. I believe that it is vital that I accompany them.'

'This is bound to be a dangerous mission, Eliza. There are informants and spies and search parties and bloodthirsty hounds all along the way. Wouldn't you rather wait in Teragovia and continue your lessons? It is not my intention to belittle you, but your skills in warfare could use some polishing. The battles ahead will greatly benefit from you wielding a sword and bow well!'

Eliza sucked in a deep breath. This was it; this was the moment that the Oracle had been hinting at. This was where she had to display real courage and make the biggest claim so far. The blue button was warm in her palm. She blew hot air from her mouth and began to speak.

'Council Mistress, with all due respect, it is not for me to lead in warfare the way Amelie would have. I have not been picked by the Ancient Magic as the Midnight Daughter because it is my destiny to plunge swords into the bellies of our enemies. The mere thought is enough to bring a tear to my eye. As per the Oracle's counsel, it is for me to find my own path as a leader, and I can do so only by identifying what sets me apart. And what sets me apart is that I do not believe that we must fight this fight alone!'

'Whatever do you mean?' Zara asked, a suspicious weariness entering her face.

'I mean that no amount of battle expertise is going to be enough to help us win a war against the Bardorians. I've said so before, and I'll say it again. We are no match for them in strength and numbers. Even if we are able to retrieve the second part of the prophecy in time and it contains the key to Bardorian defeat, I do not think that the answer lies in us fighting this war all alone. We need the fey on our side, Council Mistress, and we need to ensure that the protection of the realm involves the protection of the fey too. They are the keepers of the balance in the natural world; they are the ones who till the land, make medicine, and nurse wounded trees. The sun channel is open to them, and because of their dealings with the trees, they live closer to the Ancient Magic than any of us. The fey are full of secrets, and they might not have shared them with us willingly all of these years, but everything is different now. The peaceful existence of the fey is under threat too. Grandalford will stop at nothing in order to weaken both the sun and moon channel so that his powers can dominate the realm. That leaves us with little to do but unite in our quest to topple him. I truly believe that this is the way forward!'

'Eliza, what you are proposing is unheard of! The fey are a reticent lot; they have never before accepted counsel from whisperers nor allowed any of ours to live in harmony in their lairs. How can we work together without there being trust between us?'

'That is what I hope to correct on this journey, Council Mistress. In the final reaches of the woods, the Fey Queen, Azalea, has her lair. I hope to pass through there and speak with her. I want to discuss with her what it would take for us to work together and what the fey could bring to our shared cause. If the Queen herself is convinced, the rest of the fey will follow suit. I am confident in my ability to get her to work with us, Council Mistress. I may not be skilled in warfare or building, but I am a daughter of the Earth, that is my principal skill. I can hear the messages of the trees, feel the presence of Ancient Creatures in the woods, and commune with every forest creature there is. I know what is most dear to the fey, for it is the same that is most dear to me. It is my heart's greatest delight to feed a fawn from the palm of my hand. I am enamoured by the mysteries of farming. I wish to be a medicine woman when all of this is over. The fey can trust me because I am like them too.'

The evening was alive with the sound of crickets chirping in the bushes. The moon had peeked out from the cloud clover, a skinny sickle gazing down at them. Eliza prayed for Ayla's blessing to help her convince the Council that this was the best course of action. From where she stood, it was so obvious and so clear. The last few months had brought Eliza surprise after surprise, and as a result, it had become evident to her how little she knew about the world. But she had never been more sure of anything in her life than this!

The Council members looked at each other, helpless and aghast. There was no hiding that they disapproved of Eliza's contentious proposal. 'Eliza, what you are suggesting is, quite frankly, preposterous!'

'This was the sign I received at the full moon ritual. The forest creatures began to dance with me; they told me to revel with them. I believe this was Goddess

Ayla's will - that my path would lead me to uncover the ways of the forest and thereby, to the fey!'

And there it was - Ayla's word. The Council knew that they could not veto a proposal when it bore a direct sign from the moon goddess herself, no matter how hard it was for them, no matter how foolhardy it seemed at first glance. This little whisperling who knew nothing about war or governance had hatched a plan to unify the realm, and she gazed at them with wide, innocent eyes believing that she had it in her to accomplish this small task. And there was nothing that the wise and experienced Council could do but grudgingly approve of it.

'The Council harks caution but votes favour your proposal, Midnight Daughter. Let us make arrangements for your journey to the other end of the realm!'

Chapter Thirty Five
The winter daughters make a declaration

Eliza found herself at the bank of the purple river more and more often these days. Ever since she had seen those glorious water horses rise from the crystalline waters, she was transfixed by the beauty of this spot. It never ceased to amaze her that the miracles of nature were so many. Nothing was ever what it seemed. Whether it was the mightiest of the candied rivers or the smallest snail hiding underneath a toadstool in the rain, there was always more that happened that met the eye.

'I am the daughter of the earth,' she said softly, her voice barely a whisper. Picking up a clump of chocolatey brown silt, she turned it over and over in her hands until it was a softball. Her skin still zinged whenever she touched the bare ground, but she had stopped resisting it. The electricity passed through her and left her more alert, more present in her surroundings. She repeated, more loudly this time, 'I am a daughter of the earth!'

That was it. Finally, a name she could wear with pride, a name that felt like her own. Being a human had never been her destiny; being a whisperer had felt too surreal. Accepting her fate as the Midnight Daughter had an element of farce to it. But being the daughter of the earth - that was who she had been all along. A moonblood who could commune with all of life. Her gaze drifted past the moss-riddled rocks along the riverbank, the fat ants crawling on their glistening surfaces, the blades of dewy green grass that shot up tall all around her. She stretched her fingers out and called an image to her mind. Seconds later, a sparrow chirped loudly as it landed on her palm. It looked up at her with its calm brown eyes. She held its gaze and smiled adoringly at this little creature, much like all of the other creatures that had always known who she was—a daughter of the earth.

Eliza almost couldn't believe that the Council had agreed to let her go on this journey and make a stop in Azalea's lair to conscript her support. Ultimately, she knew that the Council would have to yield to her will, but it surprised her how easy it had been. She was still getting used to the powers of the Midnight Daughter, and having others adhere to her views was highly unnatural for her. Would she ever get used to it? Only time would tell.

She watched a stick insect move its leaf-like body gracefully to a tune she could hear and wondered whom the Council would assign to her as scouts. Who would accompany her across the length of the Whispering Woods, the last human outcrops, Azalea's lair, and all the way to the fallen city of Fionnos? They would only begin their journey at the onset of the full moon, which was still two weeks away. And then who knew what would happen! It was official now: these were her last two weeks of peace in a city she had come to love and accept as her own home. She was determined to make the most of this time, to spend as much time as she could with Lou and Dion, the other winter daughters, and on this very spot, this battle-scarred river bank. She had told Neil and Tina of her upcoming journey in strict confidence, on the condition that they would not tell a soul. They had both strongly approved of her plan, especially Neil, who had never believed that the realm should be divided in this fashion.

'We'll miss you, lovey; you know we will. But who are we to complain when the fate of Elatonia hangs in the balance?' Tina had said, stroking Eliza's hair.

She hadn't said anything to Lou or Dion yet. The time would come when she would have to bid them goodbye, not knowing if she would see them again. But she knew that her love for them would fuel her strength even from a distance! And if she succeeded, it would be because of her desire to make this realm a place where children like them could thrive, even if she didn't live long enough to enjoy it herself. She looked up at the fruit trees that lined the bank. Whoever had planted them had probably done so without expecting to bask in its shade or eat its fruit. They had done so with the intention of gifting both those things to the people of the future. That was the way of the world; that was the larger cycle that held everyone and everything in place. Eliza knew that if she looked long and hard at the world around her, she would be able to glean endless metaphors from her surroundings. Nature had plenty of wisdom to offer - all you had to do was look! The Oracle's advice had set Eliza on a path, her very own path, and for the first time in her life, she felt brave enough to tread it, even though she wished she didn't have to do it on her own!

'We knew we'd find you here!' came an impatient voice and then a stomping of boots through the mucky glade. Eliza turned around to see Maud walking up to her, followed by Nala and Aoife. She waved at them, squinting in the bright light of the sun that shone high in the sky behind them.

'Where's Seena?' Eliza asked.

'Oh, she and Esther found some driftwood thrown up on the banks of the orange river, and they're busy crafting it into bows,' Maud offered as she plonked down on the patch of grass next to her. Aoife and Nala claimed the spots on the other side of her.

'You were looking for me for a reason, I imagine,' Eliza said, looking at the sparkling eyes of the others.

'I mean, we haven't seen you in a couple of days, so we wondered what had become of you. That's what friends do you know,' Aoife said in her casual lilting voice.

'Is that right?' said Eliza, not convinced. She picked up a stone from the mud, a flat round one, and flung it on the water's surface. It cut through the air with a whoosh before jumping from two spots on the water and whizzing to an end in the deep belly of the river.

'We were wondering how you were getting on without Amelie,' said Nala gently, casting Eliza a sidelong glance.

The sun warmed the back of Eliza's neck, but hearing Amelie's name made her skin prickle nonetheless. 'I'm fine. I'm worried half to death about her, obviously, but fine otherwise.' She hadn't admitted this to anyone, least of all herself, but a large part of what she intended to do in her journey through the Whispering Woods was to find Amelie. She was the only one who knew that Amelie was hiding out in the Woods rather than being tortured by Roran Storm somewhere. The time for revealing her secret had come and gone. If she spoke up now, she would reveal herself as a weak and confused character who could not be trusted. No, all she could do now was to find Amelie on her own and then reveal her secret.

'That's good to hear. I hope that the scouts will bring word soon.'

From their expressions and the way they kept glancing at one another, Eliza knew that this wasn't what they'd come to talk to her about. She knew there was something more, but for whatever reason, they weren't coming outright to say it.

'Sooooo,' began Maud, with her usual directness. She had business to attend to with Eliza, and she saw no point in deflecting from it, unlike the others, who were trying to beat around the bush. 'We hear that you're going off on this wild journey through the woods.'

'Aye,' said Eliza, trying to sound carefree. 'It's the only way to do this that allows us to have a shot at reversing the wrongs committed in the realm. I intend to seek help from the fey and join forces.'

'You're going to rock up to the Fey Queen's lair and assume that you'll be the first whisperer in centuries to be allowed to see her?' Maud asked, raising her eyebrows.

Eliza nodded with that same free-falling feeling in the pit of her stomach that she'd had when she'd spoken to the Council a couple of days ago. No one seemed to think that her plan was viable; they were humouring her because they had to - she was the Midnight Daughter, after all!

'Marvellous! I mean it's absolutely mental, but kind of marvelous too. You've got real pluck, Eliza, I'll tell you that much. I don't know if you're a mad genius or just mad, but I absolutely support where you're going with this!' said Maud, jovially punching Eliza just below her shoulder.

Eliza smiled at her, confused. From the other side of her, Aoife and Nala began to speak at once, then stopped and gestured for the other to continue. Eliza looked at the three of them and knew something was up. 'Goodness me! Just spit it out, girls. You've clearly got something you'd like to say so please say it!'

'It's just that...this journey of yours...do you know who's going to come with you?' Nala asked, licking the inside of her teeth and not meeting Eliza's gaze.

'That's for the Council to decide, but I reckon it'll be a handful of scouts and warriors. The very best ones, I imagine, since this is an important quest,' said Eliza.

'The quest of all quests, some would say,' added Aoife.

'Aye,' said Eliza, raising her eyebrows. What was going on!

'And do you feel happy about going on this quest with the most skilled scouts and warriors of Teragovia?'

Nala said, continuing the line of questions in an exasperating fashion.

'I don't know if happy is the word I would use to describe how I feel about leaving all of my friends and loved ones behind to go on a high-risk quest, funnily enough,' answered Eliza, her patience on the brink of running out. The mystery made her feel anxious, which made her defensive, and the result was bouts of unexpected sarcasm.

'Ah, but what if you didn't have to?' asked Aoife softly. She crossed and then uncrossed her arms and finally let them fall to the ground, where they fidgeted with the grass.

'I'm not sure what you mean to say, Aoife.'

'Oh gosh, enough with this,' said Maud, lifting her palm to her face. 'Eliza, what these two muppets are trying to say is that we'd like to go with you. All of us, Esther and Seena too!'

Eliza's jaw dropped. 'Go with me all the way through the woods and the human cities and Azalea's lair and Fionnos?'

'Aye,' chimed the others in unison.

'You know that this journey is far more perilous than anything we have done so far, right?' Eliza said, not wanting to believe what they were saying until she could be sure that they had considered it in the truest sense.

'Oh no, I figured it'd be a walk in the park compared to last time!' Maud said, rolling her eyes again.

'Eliza, we don't want to intrude upon your journey or impose ourselves in any way. But since we are all winter daughters and have had our fates entwined through this fate, it feels peculiar to think of you going away without us. It is your destiny to lead, but who are you leading if not us?' Nala said, a thoughtful look spreading over her features. Ever the voice of wisdom, Nala made everything around her glow with ease and warmth.

'Impose! Intrude! Those are the last things on my mind. I would be utterly delighted to have all of you with me on this journey. I only hark at the notion of endangering you so gravely!' Eliza said, the words tumbling out of her mouth.

'There's danger awaiting us in every corner from here on out,' said Aoife, shrugging. 'We can't do much to change that. But protecting you on this mission, marching towards a purpose, a goal, that'd make all the danger feel worthwhile. I'd rather be fighting off Bardorian soldiers in the woods than be sitting here, waiting for them to descend upon us!'

'I didn't even dare to think you'd want to accompany me!' Eliza said. 'You can't possibly imagine how much strength I will derive from your presence!' Tears had welled up in her eyes.

'So it's a yes, then?' Nala asked tentatively.

'Of course!' cried Eliza, embracing them.

'The winter daughters on another quest. Who knew we'd be off again so soon?' said Aoife, her voice muffled as they held each other long and tight. Overhead, the sun continued to burn brightly, and the girls hugged and whispered joyously in its glow.

'Is it just me, or is the name "winter daughters" a bit mundane? It makes me feel like a sickly maiden rather than a warrior,' Maud said, pulling away from the girls.

'What would you rather have us called?' asked Nala.

'I dunno - something subtle but fierce!'

'Like the freedom fighters of Teragovia?' asked Aoife.

'Not quite, because we fight for all of Elatonia, don't we?'

'How about...the Daughters of Elatonia?' asked Eliza.

'That's it!' said Maud. 'The Daughters of Elatonia pledge themselves to the Midnight Daughter.'

Something that felt dangerously like happiness bloomed in Eliza's belly. She looked at the smiling faces around her, felt the love in their embrace, and felt immeasurable gratitude in knowing that she would not be doing this alone but with them. She had no desire to seek out the fame and glory that came with solitary heroes and warriors.

No, Eliza was a pack animal; she knew her strength lay in working together with those around her. And who better to do this with than the girls that were like sisters to her, the only ones in the realm who could understand what it was like to have an inevitable destiny, an unprecedented fate?

Yes, their cause was infinitely strengthened by the Daughters of Elatonia pledging themselves to the quest. She closed her eyes, and in the heat of the tepid winter sun, Eliza surrendered herself to something she had not allowed herself to feel in a long, long time: hope!

THE DARK MOON SERIES BOOK II

THE PROPHECY UNVEILED

ANDREA WILSON